AXEVIATHON - SON OF DRAGONS

A PANTHEON OF DRAGONS NOVEL

TESSA DAWN

Published by Ghost Pines Publishing, LLC
Volume II in the Pantheon of Dragons Series by Tessa Dawn
First Edition Trade Paperback Published April 22, 2019
10 9 8 7 6 5 4 3 2
First Edition eBook Published April 22, 2019

Author may be contacted at: http://www.tessadawn.com

This is a work of fiction. All characters and events portrayed in this novel are either
fictitious or are used fictitiously. Any resemblance to actual persons, living or dead,
business establishments, events, or locales is entirely coincidental.

Ghost Pines Publishing, LLC

CREDITS AND ACKNOWLEDGMENTS

Ghost Pines Publishing, LLC., *Publishing*
   Damonza, *Cover Art*
   Reba Hilbert, *Editing*

The Wonderful Wizard of Oz, written by L. Frank Baum in 1900.

The enemy of my enemy is my friend is an ancient proverb which *appears* to have originated with the Indian philosopher Chanakya (also referenced, Kautilya) Arthashastra around the fourth century BCE. It was also spoken by Winston Churchill during WWII.

PANTHEON OF DRAGONS

Before time was a recognized paradigm, seven dragon lords created a parallel primordial world for their glory...and their future offspring. They harnessed seven preternatural powers from seven sacred stones and erected the *Temple of Seven* beyond the hidden passage of a mystical portal that would lead back and forth between Earth and the Dragons Domain. And finally, they set about creating a race of beings—the Dragyr—that would exist on blood and fire, and they gifted their progeny with unimaginable powers, unearthly beauty, and immortal life.

For all of this, the dragon lords required only one thing: *absolute and unwavering obedience* to the *Four Principal Laws*...

1. Thou shalt pledge thy eternal fealty to the sacred Dragons Pantheon.
2. Thou shalt serve as a mercenary for the house of thy birth by seeking out and destroying all *pagan* enemies: whether demons, shadows, or humans.

3. Thou shalt *feed* on the blood and heat of human prey in order to reanimate your fire.
4. Thou shalt propagate the species by siring *dragyri* sons and providing the Pantheon with future warriors. In so doing, thou shalt capture, claim, and render unto thy lords whatsoever human female the gods have selected to become *dragyra*. And she shall be taken to the sacred *Temple of Seven*—on the tenth day, following discovery—to die as a mortal being, to be reborn as a dragon's consort, and to forever serve the sacred pantheon.

And so it came to pass that seven sacred lairs were erected in the archaic domain of the dragons in order to house the powerful race begotten of the ancient gods, each lair in honor of its ruling dragon lord:

Lord Dragos, Keeper of the Diamond
Lord Ethyron, Keeper of the Emerald
Lord Saphyrius, Keeper of the Sapphire
Lord Amarkyus, Keeper of the Amethyst
Lord Onyhanzian, Keeper of the Onyx
Lord Cytarius, Keeper of the Citrine
& Lord Topenzi, Keeper of the Topaz

While a *dragyri* may appear to be human, *he is not*.

While a *dragyra* may appear to belong to her mate, *she does not*.

While the Dragyr may be fierce, invincible, and strong, they are *never* truly free...

PROLOGUE

Axeviathon Saphyrius, better known as Axe, strolled into the lobby of the King's Castle Credit Union around ten o'clock, Monday morning. A well-dressed brunette, who looked equal parts eager and insecure, greeted him at the front entrance with a smile and a nod.

"Good morning. How can we help you today?"

Axe spared her a sidelong glance and kept right on walking.

One, he didn't have the time, nor the desire, to deal with extraneous humans today; and two, he knew exactly where he was going: through the lobby, past the tellers, and down the long, narrow hall on the right—straight to the opulent office of the bank's newest manager, Warren Simmons.

Warren was a card-carrying member of the Cult of Hades, a faction of clueless humans who dabbled in the occult—or so they thought. In reality, they served a dangerous, supernatural god, and they didn't even know it.

Drakkar Hades.

King of the underworld and ruler of demons and shades.

Father of the Pagan Horde.

The ancient pagan had messed with the Temple of Seven. He had ticked off the dragon lords by trying to destroy an original dragyri son, Zane Saphyrius—Axe's lair mate. And in doing so, the dark king had provoked the Seven's wrath. Not only had Drak sent Salem Thorne, a despicable, caustic demon, to try to slay Zane's new mate, but he had manipulated the female's best friend, Macy, by using her surgeon to take advantage of her vulnerable heart. In short, he had planned to use the women's friendship to one day get to Zane, and the doctor had just been a pawn: an accessible, pliant, easy-to-manipulate tool, due to a weakness in his character...

And a fissure in his soul.

Pagans were bottom-feeders at best.

No better than carp or vultures.

They fed on the souls—and the sins—of humans.

If the pagan was a shadow-walker (or a "shade"), he simply fed on the human's essence; he reanimated his immortal, skeletal carcass by devouring the person's spirit. But if he was a demon—and especially if he was ancient—then he fed on the human's sins: He encouraged them, milked them, caught them in the act, and grew stronger by association...

And proxy.

Salem had taken advantage of the surgeon's pride, his never-ending ambition to rise in the eyes of others, no matter the stakes or the costs, and Lord Drakkar Hades had hoped to use the not-so-fine doctor sometime in the future, in a manner as old as time. As Zane grew closer to his new dragyra, as her burgeoning role in the Pantheon was cemented, Drakkar had hoped to draw on her enduring friendship with Macy to sneak a wolf in sheep's clothing into Dragons Domain. Whether on Christmas, Valentine's Day, or some other uniquely human holiday, the pagan king was gambling on the certainty that a time would surely come when Macy would want to send her BFF a box of chocolates, or a bag stuffed with gifts—hell, a simple housewarming present would do.

And then Drakkar could use the doctor, and the doctor could use Macy...

The pretty wrapped gifts would not contain delectable chocolates. They would not contain a snow globe or a bottle of fine wine. They would be the pagan substitute of a Trojan horse: ten, fifteen, maybe twenty ancient demons, all in beetle form, nestled snugly inside the packages, waiting to invade, shift, and attack. Drakkar was gambling on the fact that the doctor could get Drak's pagans through the portal—and into that foreign realm —that they could one day slip in, undetected, posing as harmless gifts. And then they could strike swiftly—and definitively—at The Pantheon of Dragons.

And that's why Axe was at the bank.

That's why he was carrying a large box of chocolates, stuffed with Dr. Kyle Parker's right hand, and wrapped in pretty gold paper, secured by a blood-red bow (truly, the bow had been dipped in blood), and the accompanying card was simple, elegant, and to the point: *For Drak; the best-laid plans of mice and pagans often go astray.*

The king would get the message.

A young African-American security guard rounded the corner in a rush and called out to Axe—the greeter must have tipped him off. Axeviathon spun around, lowered his shades, and gave the youngster a clear, up-close-and-personal view of his sapphire irises and his jet-black pupils, his otherworldly dragon eyes, and he smiled. "Go back to your post, son, and stay there." His words were laced with an implicit compulsion, and the human stopped dead in his tracks. He blinked three times, scanned the hallway in confusion, and immediately turned on his heels.

Good human, Axe thought.

3

He continued to saunter down the hallway to the last door on the right. Then he reached for the handle, turned it clockwise, and strolled into the room. Warren Simmons bolted upright, stepped back from his desk, and immediately reached for the fly on his pants. A skinny female *companion*, who didn't look a day over seventeen years old, reached for the sides of her skirt, yanked it into place, and shimmied off Warren's desk.

Both of them looked ashamed.

Axe snorted and shook his head.

Well, it didn't take a rocket scientist to figure out Warren's *sin of entry*, how he had exposed himself to the pagans.

So the man was a pedophile...

Disgusting, but whatever.

The Dragyr did not get involved in human affairs, at least not beyond any direct or interlocking business with the Pantheon.

They did their masters' bidding.

It wasn't an optional clause.

And that, as they say, was that.

As the short blonde female scurried around Axe and headed for the manager's door, Axe tapped her on the shoulder. "Sweetheart," he said in a husky voice, laced with lethal intention. "You never saw me, okay?"

Her light-green eyes grew cloudy, and she slowly nodded her head. "Yeah," she whispered, "okay."

"Oh, and one other thing."

She shifted back and forth, nervously, as she waited.

"This old piece of shit—the one you were about to get it on with, on the desk. That's finished. Find someone your own age."

She drew back in surprise, but she nodded. Then she hurried out of the room.

Warren's face flushed red. "Who the hell are you? And what makes you think you can just walk into my office without an appointment?" He reached for the intercom on his phone and grunted into the speaker: "Jackson? Jackson! Get in here."

Jackson must have been the African-American security guard, and if so, he wasn't coming. Axe's compulsion would hold —probably for the rest of the day. But just to be safe—and to make sure Warren didn't reach out to anyone else—he flicked his pinky in the direction of the intercom, sent a slender electrical flame through the air, and blew out the internal wiring. "Sit down," he barked.

Now, there was no point in going into Pantheon business with this pitiful Cult of Hades' sycophant. Truth be told, the low-level human had probably never even met Lord Drakkar, and he likely never would. He was just a pawn on a chessboard—a naïve, corruptible mind that the pagans could use until they were finished with him—until they had sucked all the anima out of him or left him on the sidewalk for dead. The leeching could take a day, a year, or a lifetime, depending on how much sin they consumed from Mr. Simmons—and at what rate they consumed it.

"You got a tattoo on the back of your neck?" Axe asked.

The human's eyes narrowed. He looked instantly guilty, and he reached up to scratch his nape. Yep, he was sporting a medieval sword with a witch's pentacle etched into the pommel, on the back of his neck. Sure as shit, he was. And that meant that somewhere in the underworld, a demon was watching, listening, and tuning in to Warren Simmons several times a day. They would read his distress, catch the disruption in his sin, and even-tually come to investigate. Hopefully, the hand wouldn't stink too badly before they found the box of chocolates.

Axe figured he'd better speed things up.

He dropped the "gift" on Warren's desk, planted his fore-finger in the center of the bow, and seared his gaze into Warren's. "You leave this right here until someone...important...comes to get it. You don't open it; you don't talk about it; you don't mention it until then. We copacetic on that?"

The man looked decidedly pissed off, like he wanted to rip Axe's head off—good luck with that one—but somewhere deep inside, where predators recognized prey and quarry hid from hunters, his common sense kicked in. "Yeah," he mumbled in a surly tone, "we're copacetic."

"Good," Axe said.

He was about to pull a disappearing act, simply vanish from the bank, when he thought better of it: He should make one last pass through the lobby, make sure nothing had gone wrong— make sure no humans had been tipped off—before he made his way back through the portal. His muscles bunched and contracted in the lithe, smooth gait of a hunter—it was the animal nature of a dragyri—as he sauntered out of the office, headed back down the hall, into the lobby, and quickly checked all human eyes for signs of awareness.

Convinced that everything was A-Okay, he passed by the last female teller—and his amulet heated up.

What the hell...

The timeless, heavy sapphire stone hanging around his neck —the one that linked his soul to the Pantheon and his life to Lord Saphyrius—suddenly singed his flesh, leaving a trail of smoke in the lobby.

His inner dragon drew to immediate attention.

He angled his body toward the nice-looking teller and regarded her *much more* closely.

Her beautiful dark amber eyes, which matched the color of her hair almost perfectly, began to glow inside her irises, and then, just for an instant, her pupils turned deep dark blue.

Sapphire.

Just like Axe's stone.

The precious gem seared a scar into his flesh, and in that moment, he knew...

Oh yeah, he knew...

And, holy hell, the realization was stunning.

He was staring at his *fated* dragyra.

His beast began to snarl as he took a step in her direction—just what the hell was she doing in King's Castle Credit Union?

CHAPTER ONE

A mber Carpenter's fingers froze on the ten-key unit of her keyboard, which was all well and good because she suddenly forgot what she was doing: Was she logging out with her passcode in order to go on break, or was she pulling a report so she could reconcile her drawer?

It didn't really matter, she reasoned—the cash wouldn't add up anyway.

It never did.

It wasn't supposed to.

And Warren would handle it later...

In the meantime, *holy shit!*

The tall, muscular menace, the guy with dirty-blond hair— the one who had strolled into the lobby about thirty minutes earlier with the swagger of a jungle cat and the aura of a Viking— he was stalking toward Amber's station, staring at her in earnest, prowling...slinking...marauding, whether he meant to be over-bearing or not. And his cocky, masculine presence, that powerful, tangible aura, radiated off him in waves—it was enough to make Amber go weak at the knees, her palms begin to sweat, and her fingers freeze in mid-stroke. "Just a moment, sir," she muttered, trying desperately not to stutter. "There'll be another teller here to assist you in a minute." She took an unwitting step back and gestured toward the stanchion rope in the lobby. "In fact, could you please wait behind that line?"

Damn, that was rude, but he was making her so nervous...

The Viking thumbed his dark sunglasses, took a step *toward* the counter, and swiped the underside of his thick upper lip with his tongue in a rapid, almost feline gesture. *Yeah,* Amber thought, *definitely a jungle cat, maybe a jaguar or a cougar.*

"What's your name, pretty lady?" he rasped, leaning far too possessively against the counter.

So much for waiting behind the rope.

Amber gulped. "My...my name? Um..." She fidgeted with a charm on her bracelet, and the corner of his mouth quirked up in a smile.

"Your name is *Um*?"

She shook her head in annoyance and maybe a little fear. "No...*no!* Of course not. My name is...it's, um...it."

"Your name is *It*?" His tone was more playful this time, at least in a lion-about-to-eat-a-mouse kind of way.

She sighed, feeling both flustered and irritated. "Yes, my name is *it*," she snapped in a snarky tone. To hell with it—he didn't need to know her name. And besides, if he thought she was bat-shit crazy, he might be inclined to stop asking questions.

He chuckled, unfazed, and then he raised his glasses, forcing her gaze with his intense scrutiny, and for the space of two heart-beats, Amber was wholly transfixed by the oddest, most mesmer-izing eyes she had ever seen. *What in the world?* His pupils were ringed in pure sapphire irises, and they flickered like there were flames in their depths.

"Amber girl..." He spoke softly this time, tasting her name on his tongue. "Ambrosia Carpenter, but you go by Amber on account of the color of your eyes...and your hair." He narrowed that strange otherworldly gaze on her dark curly lashes and murmured, "Spectacular."

Amber wanted to turn on her heel and run—her first name was on her name tag, but the rest? How did he know? She forced a congenial smile instead. "Can I help you, sir?" The sooner she could find out what he needed and refer him to someone else, the better.

"What time do you get off work?" he asked, the flames in his eyes beginning to smolder.

She gulped. "Excuse me?"

"What time do you get off work?"

None of your business, she thought with indignance. "Four thirty," she said aloud.

He smiled a roguish grin, and her heart must have skipped three beats. "Where do you live, Amber girl?"

"Where do I live?" she echoed, sounding as incredulous as she felt. *How arrogant. How presumptuous. How completely inappropriate!* Yet just like before, she felt compelled to answer: "I live at 318 Syracuse Lane. It's in Upper Midtown, behind the mall."

She couldn't believe she had said that. She may as well have drawn him a map. And if, God forbid, he followed up—*Tony was going to kill her*.

His flawless features tightened, and he leaned further across the cabinet. "Who's Tony?"

That was it!

Amber had seen and heard enough.

How the heck did this man know the origins of her name, and how the heck did he know about Tony?

Was he reading her freakin' thoughts?

Impossible!

Fight-or-flight finally kicked in, along with her common

11

sense, and she returned to the task at hand—getting the hell away from her station: Her mind shifted into overdrive; her fingers remembered what they were doing; and she keyed in the remaining digits of her passcode with speed, determination, and purpose. Then she snatched a report from the printer and backed away from the counter. "Marissa!" she called, scanning the back of the lobby for the tall, skinny blonde who was due to take over her station. "Could you please help this gentleman? I need to go on break." Without awaiting a reply, she retrieved the key to her drawer, unlocked her cash, and slid it out of the panel, sighing in relief as Marissa cut a path straight toward her.

"What's up, Amber?" Marissa called amiably. "Is everything okay?" She shimmied into the partition and stepped up to the counter.

"Everything's fine," Amber said brusquely. "I just need you to help this gentleman. As I said, I'm going on break." She snatched her purse from beneath the counter, shuffled backward like she was fleeing a fire, and made a beeline for the bank's vault, where she swiftly unloaded her register. "There's a discrepancy in the drawer," she told the vault cashier. "The forms and tape are at the bottom, but Warren will look at it later."

The short brunette didn't ask any questions.

No one at the credit union ever did.

And why would they?

The bank's employees were paid double the industry standard; the tellers received three times the perks; and the benefit package was outrageous. Beyond the employee benefits and pay, the credit union's patrons enjoyed high returns on their savings, lower-than-average rates on their debt, and the bank had never defaulted on anything. If the government was aware of the obvious shady dealings, then a whole lot of people were looking the other way.

No matter.

Amber had stopped thinking about it years ago.

She had much more pressing matters to contend with—like the guy who had stepped up to her counter.

Having unloaded her drawer, she headed out of the vault and into the break room, where she crumpled like a wadded piece of paper into a hard plastic chair and let out a slow, deep breath.

What—the—actual—hell—was—that?

She stared blankly ahead at the break-room wall, placing both hands, palms down, on the cheap industrial table, and fought through a wave of nausea.

Who—the—actual—hell—was—that?

And why had he come into the credit union?

Like an oscillating fan whirling in circles, her mind continued to churn and spin as she replayed the unsettling encounter: "Ambrosia Carpenter, but you go by Amber on account of the color of your eyes and your hair." He *knew who she was!* "What time do you get off...where do you live...who is Tony?" He had *read her thoughts—but how?*

Her stomach tightened as another wave of vertigo assailed her—was the guy a detective, maybe a bounty hunter? Were Zeik and Grunge ticked off at Amber? Had Tony finally turned her in? She felt like she was going to vomit.

And then, just like a thousand times before, a sweltering summer's day emerged from the vault of her memory and began to replay on her temporal lobe like a blasted defective video stuck on auto-play:

It was suddenly ten years earlier.

August 28th.

And Amber was fifteen years old...

Broke, tired, and desperate, she had lost count of which foster home she lived in, the names of her so-called parents, or where she attended school, but she vividly recalled the precocious eighteen-month-old girl who kept her up most nights: *Yeah, Amber remembered her foster sister, Tina.*

She remembered the little girl's hunger and her high-pitched wailing.

She remembered the smell of Tina's dirty diapers and how the flesh on the child's bottom would often turn red with blisters. She remembered the telltale signs of dehydration—dry skin, rapid breathing, sunken eyes, and an ashen complexion—that accompanied Tina's crying. And Amber Carpenter remembered finally having had enough, feeling like she would explode if the wailing didn't stop—*if Tina's suffering didn't cease*—and deciding, once and for all, to do something drastic about it...

* * *

It was a sweltering hot August afternoon when fifteen-year-old Amber walked into the cramped convenience store on the corner of Ninth and Vine. She had a shabby diaper bag draped over one shoulder and an empty stroller in tow...

She stopped in the doorway to cover the vacant carriage with a bright green-and-blue blanket—pale lime green, like the color of mint ice cream, and cornflower blue, like the color of Tina's bottle, the one that was usually filled with water instead of milk—and then she meandered beyond the doorway and headed toward the nearest aisle.

The heat that assailed her was beyond description—it felt like a gust of desert wind or the rush of a blazing backdraft escaping a roaring fire—and she had to stop to catch her breath.

Her brow beaded with sweat.

Her T-shirt clung to her rib cage.

And her palms turned so slick and clammy she wasn't sure she was going to be able to maintain her grip on the stroller, let alone the three or four cans of formula she intended to stuff inside the carriage...to hide from watchful eyes.

She managed to pilfer four cans, after all, as well as two packs of diapers, a container of Pedialyte, and a small rectangular carton containing a tube of Neosporin. Granted, the gel wouldn't work as well as diaper-rash cream, but it was only a neighborhood convenience store—the antibiotic ointment would have to do.

And as for the fact that Amber was shoplifting?

She no longer cared.

Someone had to take care of Tina...

Besides, it was only this one time.

Amber had no intentions of ever stealing again—she just had to stage a dramatic intervention before the little girl got really, really sick.

Acutely aware of an uneven stack of potato chips, empty boxes, and several stale packs of doughnuts, Amber slowed the stroller to a crawl in order to maneuver it—*carefully*—around the unstable display case. If she bumped into the stack, if the wheel got caught on a box, or if she jarred the display even a smidgeon, the handsome teenage cashier who was already watching her too closely would probably come running over, and the jig would definitely be up.

Amber had no intentions of getting caught.

And maybe that was why she didn't immediately react to the three menacing thugs who strolled into the store wearing dark matching hoodies, black leather gloves, and grungy, tattered blue jeans in the stifling August heat.

"Don't move! Don't speak! Don't even breathe!" the tallest of the three had barked at the startled teenager behind the register, and then the goon had cleared the narrow counter in one nimble leap, brandished a gun from beneath his hoodie, and shoved it against the cashier's temple. "Open the fucking drawer!"

Now, that got Amber's attention.

The reckless behavior, the inappropriate clothes, and the crazed, wild look in the gunman's eyes: These thugs weren't just hell-bent on robbing a store—they *wanted* to get into trouble. Their pupils were stamped with lust and greed—some savage hunger for power—and their bodies were practically twitching with a craven thirst for violence.

"Please don't hurt me," the cashier pleaded as he flung open the drawer, held up both hands, and took a wary step backward, painfully aware of the gun at his temple. "Just take the money and go."

The gunman whispered something in the cashier's ear— Amber couldn't make it out—and the poor, terrified teenager instantly wet his pants.

"Damn, Zeik..." the second thug cackled, stroking his flame-red beard. "You forgot to tell the little bitch not to piss on himself —I suggest you warn him not to shit himself, too." The red-bearded thug climbed on the counter, made a beeline for the security camera, and started to remove the videotape from the player beneath it.

Amber ducked down behind the stroller and pressed her hand over her mouth—

What the hell was she going to do?

If she ran for the door, she'd get shot.

If she stayed where she was, they would find her.

But if she tried to sneak down the aisle and hide—well, she wasn't sure she could do it...

Her legs were trembling; her stomach was roiling; and her heart was thundering in her chest. She was as likely to pass out as escape. "*Shit*," she whispered beneath her breath, and then her eyes swept back to the gun.

Six shots, she thought. *At least it's not a semiautomatic.*

Hell, the old-fashioned revolver looked like a Wild West relic —like Zeik had somehow traveled through time, stormed into a saloon, and robbed the nearest outlaw of his six-shooter: antiquated grip; long, thin barrel; discolored, ragged hammer. Maybe it wouldn't even fire. One way or another, the bastard would have to cock the hammer at least six times before he could unload the ammo.

"Yo, Grunge!" Zeik's dark, raspy voice was profane in the silence. "Don't forget to check the lockbox—it's right there, behind the camera and the video player."

So the redhead's name was Grunge, and they had cased the joint ahead of time—but that's not what gave Amber pause: As Grunge declined his head in a nod and began to fish behind the security camera, Amber couldn't help but notice the idiots were using each other's names too freely. They weren't worried about being identified. And that meant they had no intentions of letting any witnesses live.

The terrified teenager must have come to the same conclusion because he pressed one hand to his stomach, appeared to heave in his mouth, and then quickly covered his lips with the palm of his hand to stop the vomit from spewing out.

"You nasty motherfucker," Zeik growled, pressing the barrel even tighter against the cashier's temple. "Do that shit again, and I'll blow your brains out." He cocked the hammer slowly for emphasis.

Amber winced, but she didn't scream.

She laid her forehead on the handle of the stroller, panted beneath her breath, and tried to collect her thoughts. Unfortunately, the carriage rolled forward and bumped one of the cardboard boxes.

Amber gasped, then held her breath, watching the display like a hawk: *Please don't tip over; please don't tip over.* She repeated the prayer like a mantra.

Nothing moved, and nothing fell.

The unsteady display did not topple over.

Thank God!

And then—*clomp, clomp, clomp*—the heavy sound of footfalls, moving in and out of aisles, coming ever closer to the stack and the stroller.

Had the third assailant heard her?

Her throat grew scratchy; her vision turned blurry; and she wanted to close her eyes, hide from whatever was about to happen, but she couldn't because the third assailant was standing right there, less than five feet away and one aisle over, staring straight through her.

His glassy green gaze was void of recognition.

Had he seen her?

She wasn't sure.

She couldn't tell.

But if he had, then he was a first-rate bastard because he continued to stroll through the parallel aisle, stalking closer and closer toward her, almost like a lazy lion who didn't have a care in the world.

He stopped in mid-stride to sample a candy bar, and then he opened a pack of chips. He stuffed two or three chips in his mouth, spit them out, and tossed the package on the floor. He meandered to the refrigerator next, paused to crack open a beer, then stood there drinking—taking long, greedy sips—before crumpling the can in his fist.

The seconds felt like minutes, and the minutes felt like days, as Amber perched behind the stroller, waiting for the bastard to round the bend—or for Zeik to turn the gun in her direction.

Terrified, trapped, and certain she was about to get caught, Amber did the only thing she could: She began to memorize details, record information, store facts away like an impartial robot. If she made it through the robbery—if she got shot, but somehow survived—she would have a treasure trove of information to give the police.

Besides, it wasn't like Amber was an innocent bystander—she had been robbing the store herself. The more she knew, the more she remembered, the more she could trade for a lighter sentence.

Her pulse slowed down.

Her senses grew alert.

And she composed her mental report:

Zeik is the leader. He's six-feet-two. Dark, narrow eyes with a pencil-straight nose. His hairline is concealed beneath his hoodie, but the section near his temple—the fade above his ears—is visible. His hair is jet black, and it's shaved so tight it looks more like a shadow than a skull-trim.

The one they call Grunge, he's maybe six feet even.

Average build, except for his thighs—the muscles in his hamstrings are the size of watermelons—and he has light-blue eyes; wide, flared nostrils; and a flame-red beard, maybe three inches long. His sideburns are scraggly, his mustache is curvy, and his lips are really, *really* pale...unnaturally thin, like a gash was carved where his mouth should have been.

As for the bastard prowling up and down the aisles—she would never forget that face: glassy green eyes; flawless, stunning features; and full, pouty lips that belonged on a model. His hair was blond, and he kept it cropped short—he was possibly five-feet-eleven.

She was just about to "record" the details of the third man's physique when a crumpled beer can plopped into the stroller, and the bastard rounded the corner. "What the hell's in the baby carriage?" he barked before tossing back his head and laughing. And then he did something as provocative as it was telling: He peeled back the hood of his jacket, exposing a terrifying tattoo on the nape of his neck, and squatted down in front of Amber. "What the hell's in the stroller?" he repeated, this time speaking in a menacing urban drawl.

Zeik leaned over the counter and snorted. "Well, looky here—I think Tony found a new playmate."

Amber winced in dread.

She now knew all three of their names—and so did the poor cashier.

Tony pulled back the blanket and looked inside the carriage, rifling through the items one by one. "Hey, Zeik, looks like we're not the only hoodlums casing the joint." He palmed a can of formula, then tossed it in the air; twisted the lid off the Pedialyte and gave it a couple of sniffs; and then he withdrew a pack of diapers and slowly shook his head. "Damn, somebody's got a baby at home that she can't afford to feed."

"Maybe she needs a job," Grunge chimed in, crawling out from behind the security camera with a wad of cash in his hand.

Zeik cackled like a cartoon villain, training his gaze on the trembling cashier. "I think I just had a lightbulb moment—is our little mother wearing gloves? Did she even bother to hide her fingerprints?"

"Good question," Tony said. And then he snatched her by the arm, dragged her to her feet, and examined Amber up and down, from the roots of her hair to the tips of her toes. "Nope," he finally conceded, "but damn, this girl is fine." He ogled her breasts, scrutinized her ass, then pressed the tip of his forefinger to his lower lip. "I think I just might have to keep her."

Grunge snorted. "Looks like we may have just found a teller for King's Castle Credit Union." He eyed Zeik sideways before turning his attention back to Tony and Amber, then raised both eyebrows in question.

"Yeah," Tony said, "two birds with one stone. I say go for it, Zeik."

The bastard didn't even hesitate.

He didn't flinch; he didn't talk shit; and he didn't give the cashier a warning.

He just pulled the trigger and fired the gun, dropping the kid where he stood.

Stunned by the deafening retort of the bullet—and propelled by the spatter of blood—Amber shoved the stroller between herself and Tony and practically dove for the door.

Grunge was there in an instant.

She hadn't even seen him move.

He snatched her from behind with one arm, shoved a gloved hand over her mouth, and snarled in her ear like some bestial monster. "Shut the fuck up! You wanna die next?"

Amber sucked in air, tucked her lips around her teeth, and shook her head in a frantic nod. Her teeth chattered as she mumbled through the glove. "No...I'm sorry...please don't hurt me."

"That's right, baby," Tony drawled, sauntering toward the two of them. "There's no need for all that drama when we'd rather be your friends. What do you say? Can we start over?" He brushed the backs of his fingers over her cheek, and she had to fight the urge to gag. "Zeik!" he barked before she could reply. "Let's do the damn thing and get the hell outta Dodge before we have a handful of cops to deal with."

Amber's eyes grew wide as saucers.

Do the damn thing?

What was he talking about?

Once again, Zeik was cool as a cucumber as he playfully tossed the revolver to Tony, like it was nothing more than a harmless toy pistol.

Tony caught it by the barrel, took Amber by the wrist, and placed the palm of her hand against the back of the grip, her finger around the trigger. "Squeeze a little, baby," he whispered, turning the barrel away from his chest. "Don't worry, it's not cocked at the moment."

Trembling like a leaf, Amber pulled back on the trigger.

"That's it," Tony crooned in her ear. "Just like that—good girl." His hands still encased in gloves, he removed the pistol from Amber's grasp, pressed a tender kiss to her forehead, and tossed the revolver back to Zeik.

Grunge snorted with indifference. "You sure about this, Rossi?" he said to Tony. "You absolutely sure you want the girl... her baby...and her baby's daddy?" He shrugged a shoulder and cocked both brows. "It's not too late to forget about the credit union...we can still plant the gun and make her disappear."

Tony's placid features contorted into fury as he narrowed his gaze on Amber. "Where's your baby's father?" he demanded, snatching her by the jaw. "Where the fuck does your boyfriend live?"

Amber's eyes bulged in their sockets, and her mind started racing: *What in the heck was he talking about now?* And then she eyed the stroller and the strewn-about contents, and it all came crystal clear. "I don't have a baby!" She rushed the words, terrified by their implications, but wanting to survive at least five minutes longer... "The formula...the diapers...it's for my foster sister. *I swear.* There's no boyfriend, and there's no baby's daddy."

As quick as he'd angered, Tony cooled. He released her jaw and nodded at Grunge. "Yeah, I'm sure." Then he raised his arm and gave Zeik a thumbs-up.

Zeik replied with a wink, and just like that, all three criminals worked quickly in tandem: Tony upended the stroller and scattered the contents about the floor, each and every item containing Amber's fingerprints, while Zeik placed the gun *just so* behind the counter, making it look like Amber had dropped it in a panic—he even plucked a hair from her head and draped it over the barrel. Meanwhile, Grunge rifled through the diaper bag, retrieved Amber's wallet, and checked to make sure she carried an ID—he tossed it on the sidewalk, about two feet outside the door, so it would look like she had dropped it as she fled.

Without pity or remorse, Tony slid the hood of his jacket back over his head, encircled Amber's waist with his arm, and bent to whisper in her ear as the three of them left the convenience store. "I'm going to treat you like a queen—just wait and see—you're gonna love your new life, I promise." His hand slid down her waist to her hip. "And all this shit—it'll never catch up to you, just so long as you do as you're told. The police won't find you; no judge will ever sentence you—you'll be free as a bird as long as you never fly south...as long as you stick close to home."

As Amber's past disappeared, and her future loomed dark, Tony's sadistic words drifted into the ether—and two haunting thoughts settled in her mind...

They hadn't even asked Amber her name.

And what would become of Tina...

* * *

"Amber. *Amber!*" Marissa's voice drew Amber away from the fog, jolting her out of her trance. "Girl, what the hell is going on? You're a million miles away."

"Oh," Amber muttered, "sorry, Marissa. I guess I was just... remembering something...something I shouldn't remember." She immediately turned her attention to the present before Marissa could start asking questions. "Thanks for taking over my station— how did it go with that strange guy, anyway?"

Marissa took two strides forward, plopped down in an adjacent chair, and braced both elbows on the table. "You mean that *gorgeous* guy, the one at your counter? Not much to tell—he left the moment you headed for the vault. In fact, I don't think he was here for a transaction. I think he was here for you."

Amber bit her lip and cringed.

Damn...

Just damn.

She sat up straight and tried to play it off—after all, what could she say? *He scared the shit out of me? I thought he might be a detective or a bounty hunter—maybe an enemy to the Cult of Hades, someone after Grunge, Zeik, or Tony?*

"Yeah, he was kind of freaky," she murmured. "Oh well, at least he left quietly."

A shiver, colder than the ice in Zeik's voice, thinner than the wiry strands in Grunge's beard, and stonier than the glass in Tony's green eyes ran down the length of Amber's spine: *Where do you live, Amber girl?*

No, the man hadn't left quietly.

That stare...

That voice...

The possession in his eyes...

She had seen that once before...in Tony's.

And she didn't have a doubt in her mind—the man with the sapphire irises and the predatory smile would be back—she was sure of it.

CHAPTER TWO

D
eep in the bowels of the Pagan Underworld, in a firelit cavern situated toward the rear of Drakkar Hades' gothic castle, Trader Vice, a notorious sin-eater, swept his long, wavy golden hair behind his shoulders and sat to attention on one of three blood-red leather sofas. Sinners' Cave, as the pagans often referred to it, was a low-key lounge of sorts: a dark, circular chamber furnished with three crimson sofas, the trinity set in a semicircle; a floor-to-ceiling fireplace adorned with black, pitch-covered stones; and numerous liquid screens shaped almost like television sets, yet bearing the appearance of aquariums, each framed in medieval swords with witch's pentacles etched into the pommels...all for pagan viewing.

And the sin-show had just gotten interesting.

Trader licked his full bottom lip, leaned forward, and stared more intently at an upper right screen. The likeness of Warren Simmons, the depraved manager of King's Castle Credit Union, had flashed onto the fluid canopy, and the image was bisected by a thin green line—which meant that Warren's most recent sin had been interrupted. And of course, that mattered to Trader because he fed regularly off Warren's iniquities. Closing his luminous copper-colored eyes, he tapped into the anima of Requiem Pyre, chief sorcerer to King Drakkar, in order to borrow some extra divining, and then he slowly reopened his mystical peepers. *Ah yes, the screen was clearer now*: Warren's dalliance with a seventeen-year-old girl had been broken up by a visitor, a visitor who had delivered—a box of chocolates?—to the credit union.

Trader stretched out his arm, angled his hand toward the screen, and rotated his wrist 180 degrees, turning the chocolates around to study them, and that's when the liquid pool began to undulate, a stream of words slowly scrolling across the monitor in a snake-like missive: *For Drak; the best-laid plans of mice and pagans often go astray.*

Trader gasped aloud, and then he shuddered.

So, someone was provoking King Drakkar, and quite directly —someone had sent the pagan leader a message. The thought of incurring Drak's wrath was so terrifying, Trader had to catch his breath and recompose himself. He couldn't tell what the missive was scribed upon, nor could he see inside the container, the box concealing the chocolates, but if the sonic pulses emanating from the screen were any indication of the contents, there was something other than candy in that package.

He stood to his full six-feet-five-inch height and strolled languidly toward the cavern entrance—it was time to alert his pagan brothers, to take a handful of demons and possibly some shades with him as he traveled to Denver...to Earth...to investigate.

No need to alert Drak's chief counselor quite yet, nor would he involve the congress. The commission of sins and the interplay of sinners was Trader's domain, all the demons' domain, quite frankly, and their masters would require a full report: evidence, details, descriptions—not *I saw something funky on the cavern screen.*

The delicate nature of the mission acknowledged, the bottom line remained the same: Someone was confronting the lord of the underworld; the vision was vitally important; and time was of the essence. Trader couldn't screw around with this one. No, he would make a beeline to the credit union, collect the box of chocolates, and then he would seek out his two demon brothers— Zeik Craven and Grunge Ahab—pagans who dwelled upon Earth disguised as humans, living ordinary lives with two unsuspecting companions: Antonio "Tony" Rossi, a card-carrying member in the Cult of Hades who had no idea he was living with literal, real-life demons, and Amber Carpenter, a worthless, innocent human girl who, one decade earlier, just happened to be in the wrong place at the wrong time.

CHAPTER THREE

Axeviathon Saphyrius sauntered outside the King's
Castle Credit Union, strolled around the corner, and
braced his palms on his thighs, leaning into the warm
summer breeze.

Holy lords of the Pantheon, he had just met his dragyra.

Amber Carpenter.

And the female was a teller at King's Castle Credit Union.

What. The. Devil.

She was beautiful, subtly exotic, with her long, slender neck;
elegant, graceful hands; and dark amber coloring—*those gorgeous
eyes; that luxurious hair*—and hell, that heart-shaped ass didn't
hurt one bit. But there was something else going on with Amber:
The taint of demons was all around her, like a perfume she wore
over her clothes, and maybe—just maybe—it was no big deal. She
couldn't possibly work at that bank and remain untainted...
survive unblemished.

Still, all the Dragyr knew the deal: King's Castle was a front
for Drakkar Hades, pure and simple. The dark lord used the
establishment to embezzle mortal funds, to make international

loans to Earth's most notorious sinners, and to manipulate the human realm to the pagans' own ends. Needless to say, all the crimes went undetected—human law enforcement agencies were no match for supernatural pagans: evidence versus magic; a well-crafted sting versus the craft of divination; human courts versus Drakkar's congress...

His chief sorcerer, Requiem Pyre...

His chief counselor, Killian Kross...

His omniscient powers of distortion and manipulation.

No, the pagans used—and typically staffed—the credit union to their own evil ends, and the Dragyr allowed the establishment to remain standing, not because they could not have destroyed it, but because it saved them a lot of time and effort. They could find their enemy quickly if needed, and they could also keep an eye on the pagans' comings and goings, at least to some extent. They could keep track of relationships, the ebb and flow of money, new criminal dealings, and emerging, lucrative partnerships.

At the end of the day, it was better than being blind, better than being uninformed or kept in the dark. Besides, if the Dragyr wanted a war with their soulless pagan cousins—which, ultimately, they did not—they knew precisely where to fire the first shot.

Axe blinked his sapphire orbs and pinched the bridge of his nose, bringing his attention back to the present situation: Amber Carpenter.

His fated...

His dragyra...

The woman he had to not only claim, but convince to enter the temple in ten days' time...for conversion.

Rebirth by dragons' fire.

Holy.

Hell.

Axe hadn't seen this coming.

Standing up straight, he stretched his back and popped his neck—he would let his lair mates know what had happened later. For right now, he needed to do a little reconnaissance, get the lay of the land, so to speak.

Glancing at the path of the sun, he made careful note of the time—it was 10:45 in the morning; Amber got off work at 4:30 PM; and Axe still had to meet Ghostaniaz Dragos later that evening, around 8 PM. The Genesis offspring—*Ghost*—was the progeny of Lord Dragos, the harshest and most unforgiving of the seven dragon gods, and as one of the original hatchlings, Ghost was temporarily restricted from traveling beyond the portal alone.

Following a recent pagan attack on Zanaikeyros, Axe's own pantheon lair mate—who also happened to be the Genesis offspring of Lord Saphyrius—the Seven had banned their original progeny from traveling to Earth without escort. It wasn't that the badass males couldn't handle their own or make waste of any enemy they ran into—far from it; they were lethal, one and all. It was just too damn dangerous, plain and simple. The risk wasn't worth the potential cost. In short, the gods were not willing to risk one of their firstborn sons, and the pagans were growing bold... restless...decidedly defiant. They were taking risks they had never taken before; they were gunning for a Genesis offspring, just to land a blow to the Seven; and the gods were reacting with uncommon caution. Plus—all that aside—Ghost needed to *feed*.

The dark, brutal—*broken*—dragyri needed to reanimate his fire.

And that required human essence and blood...

Since Axe was already earthside, on the mortal half of the portal, he had agreed to meet Ghost the moment the dragyri emerged from the gateway—to accompany the ruthless, haunted dragon while he hunted—and that meant Axe couldn't take

Amber with him. He couldn't remove her from the human-realm...just yet.

But what he could do, he would.

He would make use of this downtime to check out her residence: 3 1 8 *Syracuse Lane.* He would see how she was living; find out if she stayed with family or a roommate; and if—gods forbid—she had a lover, a fiancé, or a boyfriend.

Who the hell was Tony, anyway?

He would learn who she hung out with and why.

He would investigate her employment, at least as much as he could, and then he would meet up with Ghost and play it by ear.

Would his actions constitute snooping—an unseemly invasion of Amber's privacy?

Yeah—*shit yeah*—they would.

But what-the-hell-ever...

Axeviathon Saphyrius wasn't made of hearts, unicorns, and flowers, although he considered himself a fairly decent, honorable male. Yet and still, he had no intentions of ending up in the Garden of Grace as a sapphire pillar—an eternal statue—having had his amulet removed by the gods and his immortal flame extinguished, simply because he had failed at one compulsory task: to claim his chosen dragyra.

Amber Carpenter worked at King's Castle Credit Union.

And that was one helluva coincidence.

This wasn't going to be an ordinary claiming...

As if there was any such thing.

CHAPTER FOUR

Trader Vice entered King's Castle Credit Union with an entourage of shades behind him. As it was eleven o'clock in the morning, the sun was at its full zenith, and demons were not so easily disguised, he had changed his mind about bringing both species of pagans and chosen his shadowy kin, instead.

After all, the shades were also called *shadow-walkers* for a reason.

Skeletal and translucent in the light of day, gaunt and wispy if they hadn't fed, they were barely detectable by the human eye; and their dark, inky forms—their dull, blotchy shadows—dotted the tile floors and clung to the walls like an invisible army of roaches. They crawled, they scampered, and they spread out like vermin, and all the while, the humans were none the wiser.

They had no idea that their lobby had just been infested by supernatural parasites.

Trader, on the other hand, was wearing his demon form, simply trying to blend in with the Homo sapiens, while greatly diluting his otherworldly power. There was little he could do to mask his wavy golden hair or to conceal his luminous copper eyes —and being six-foot-five-inches tall didn't help him camouflage his powerful body—but he was more than capable of compelling witless humans.

Keep walking.

Look away.

Nothing to see here, you inferior, noxious peasants.

Now, as he made his way across the lobby, down the hall, and around the corner to Warren's workspace—the shadows scampering eerily behind him—he ducked into the air-conditioned office and cut a path to Warren's desk.

The human wasn't sitting in his chair; in fact, the entire room was empty, which was all well and good: one less nuisance for Trader to contend with, one less mind to deceive and control.

As expected, the box of supposed chocolates was sitting atop the manager's desk, and the elegant gold paper, secured by a bow that had clearly been dipped in blood, jumped out like it had been wrapped in neon—it may as well have been bearing a sign that said: *Hey, demon! Come and get us; we're right here, asshole.* Such was the taint of the Dragyr's power emanating from the container.

Trader slinked behind the desk, dropped into Warren's plush leather chair, and slid the base of the seat beneath the desktop, eager to explore the box and its contents. He had already read the missive on an upper right-hand scrying screen in the Sinner's Cave. "Just what do we have here?" he hissed beneath his breath as he reached for the container, slowly unwrapped the blood-red bow, and carefully opened the lid. A shade, in the distance, scurried up the wall, scampered along the ceiling, and hovered directly above Trader, his muted, glassy eyes gleaming as he watched with equal curiosity and anticipation.

Trader gagged, drew back, and pinched the bridge of his nose as the noxious odor assailed him. A hand. A rotten, decaying, decapitated hand. He raised it by the tip of the pinky, dangled it at eye level, and studied what was left of the palm and the telltale lifelines.

Yes.

Yes...

He recognized the sinner by the demon-taint on the hand, the markings in the lifeline, and the distinctive golden class ring wrapped about the rigid fourth finger.

The limb belonged to Dr. Kyle Parker, a surgeon at Denver Exploratory Medical Center—correction, an *ex-surgeon*—who had been *feeding* a fellow demon by the name of Salem Thorne for months. Alas, the blasted Dragyr were too cute by half: Salem had used the doctor's susceptibility to get at a newfound dragyra, the mate of Zanaikeyros Saphyrius, by seducing her best friend Macy. Needless to say, it was a long-ass story, but the moral to the tale was succinct.

The entire plan had failed.

The Dragyr obviously knew what the pagans had been up to —*exactly* what Dr. Kyle Parker had been up to—and they had sent the surgeon's hand, along with the missive, as a clear, unmistakable message to both Salem and Lord Drakkar: *Fuck off*.

Trader shook his head, shut his eyes, and lowered the hand back into the box by feel, using telekinesis to reattach the lid and re-affix the wrapping.

No one told Lord Drakkar Hades to fuck off.

And Trader was going to have to deliver the message...

The shade on the ceiling scampered away, ostensibly afraid that he might be recruited for the perilous duty. They all knew Lord Drakkar was known to shoot the messenger—*correction, the dark lord of the underworld was known, on occasion, to disembowel the messenger*—it all just depended on his mood.

Trader's nostrils flared as he sniffed fresh air, opened his eyes, and rose from the chair. He stuffed the box and its gory contents into a conjured satchel to carry back to the castle...later.

First, he needed to do some investigating.

Where was Warren Simmons?

He sent his psychic feelers outward...searching...homing in upon the energy and the imprint he had stored in his memory from feeding off the human's sins for so many years...

Ah yes, the male was in the employee's restroom, getting carnally acquainted with the vault cashier. Well, that at least explained why he wasn't in his office, and Trader didn't need divination to figure out why Warren hadn't touched, reported, or opened the package, even as it sat rotting on his desk—the Dragyr had undoubtedly compelled him to leave it be. They had known the demons would be watching both Warren and the credit union, that whoever fed from the manager would eventually check in. The Dragyr must have seen the manager's tattoo, and they knew he belonged to the Cult of Hades.

No matter.

The Dragyr would never screw with the bank.

They had known about the credit union forever, just as the pagans were aware of all the Dragyr's earthly holdings. To try to stop the pagan species from manipulating human events, economies, and undertakings would be like playing a perpetual game of whack-a-mole: pointless, trivial, and it wouldn't serve the Seven. Not when spying on one's enemies was far more lucrative.

Trader turned his attention back to the matter at hand—back to the disaster waiting to happen—the box and the missive the Dragyr had left for Drak.

He closed his eyes once again; only this time, he reached for a familiar telepathic bandwidth, the line that connected the demons from the underworld, and he sought his fellow earth-bound cohorts: Zeik Craven and Grunge Ahab: *Yo, asshats*, he snarled psychically, pushing forcefully into both minds at once.

Have you been keeping track of what goes on at the credit union lately?

True to form, Zeik answered first. *Who's this?*

Trader rolled his eyes beneath his lids. *Figure it out.*

That you, Trader? Grunge cut in.

No, it's your mother, Trader snapped.

Grunge chuckled like he didn't have a care in the world. *I ain't got a mama, Trader. And neither do you.* His psychic voice grew ever-more playful. *My king is my only mother...and father... and his bosom is my only true home.*

Yeah, well, Trader snarled, *you might not have a demon lord— or a Pagan Horde—to go home to, if you don't have a good explanation for the shit I just found.* Hopefully, Trader's no-nonsense voice would nip the misguided humor in the bud.

What the fuck are you talkin' about? Zeik's raspy growl.

I'm at the credit union right now, Trader explained, *sitting in Warren's office, and I just took possession of a gruesome little gift —courtesy of the Dragyr and the Seven. They chopped off Dr. Kyle Parker's hand, stuffed it in a box of chocolates, and delivered it to Warren's office with a smart-ass note...meant for Lord Drakkar.*

Shit, Grunge grumbled.

Yeah, Trader agreed. They were finally beginning to get the picture.

How do you know it's Dr. Kyle Parker's? Zeik asked, always the analytical, strategic thinker.

Trader sighed. *First of all, because I know what's going on in the Pagan Underworld at all times—who else's could it be? Second, Salem's taint is all over the digits. Does anyone else feed from Kyle Parker, assuming the male is still alive? And third, the lifeline was unmistakable, and he was wearing his familiar class ring.* The rejoinder was met with silence, as it probably should have been, and then Trader shifted directions. *Is that human—*

your roommate, Tony—still screwing that hot little teller? What the hell is her name, anyway? Ah yes…Amber.

She lives with us, Trader, Zeik answered brusquely. *Nothing has changed in the whole arrangement—Tony still owns the girl's soul.*

Yeah, Trader sniffed. *And you guys still own Tony, right?*

He's sitting right here, none the wiser, and yes, we own every evil, sinful inch. Grunge was clearly getting annoyed. *What the hell has that got to do with Dr. Kyle Parker, the box of chocolates, or the Dragyr's note?*

Trader shook his head and put a little extra vitriol into his psychic voice. *Not a damn thing, Grunge. Just making sure the ship is still tight. When a dragyri warrior strolls through the lobby, down the hall, and into one of our back offices—and when he drops off a severed limb, all in broad daylight—I'm just asking the same damn question Drak is gonna ask: Who the hell left their post?*

Once again…silence.

Tick tock…

Tick tock…

Several pregnant moments lingered before Zeik, at last, spoke up. *What's the plan, Trader?*

Trader opened his eyes, snatched the satchel, and strolled purposefully out of Warren's office, heading straight for the employee restroom. As his shadowy entourage trailed behind him, leaping from one panel of the wall to another, he reconnected to the telepathic bandwidth. *I'm on my way to view Warren's memories right now. Assuming the sycophant was at his desk when the box was delivered, I want to hear through his ears and see through his eyes, record the face of the bastard—or bastards —that delivered the package and the missive. I want my king to know who had the balls to provoke him.*

A tall, skinny brunette, clearly an employee, passed Trader in the hall, and he looked the other way. He had no intentions of making eye contact with *any* of the bank's employees right now. Not that a member of such an inferior species would have the courage to stop Trader Vice—to interrupt an immortal demon—but he didn't have time for any unnecessary nonsense: Prey could always sense a predator—a sheep could always sense a wolf—and that innate survival mechanism could sometime wreak havoc on a human's better judgment. The men were known to freak out, to either become confrontational or dive out the nearest window; whereas, human women were known to take one look at Trader, get a bad-boy rush a hundred times stronger than injecting liquid sugar, and practically shimmy out of their skirts, offer the demon their goods right then and there. It could be as annoying as it could be pleasing, depending upon the demon's mood.

But today—and in this moment?

Trader didn't have time for the drama...

When I'm done with Warren, I will return to the underworld, he told his silent cohorts. *Like it or not, I need to get this shit to Drak, posthaste—the king has a right to know that his enemy is fucking with him, and he will not be forgiving of an unnecessary delay.* He paused to consider his next words more carefully—who knew how Lord Drakkar would react? *Assuming I'm still breathing, I will follow up with the two of you later; meet me at the Upper Midtown house at 9 PM. And Zeik...Grunge? Make sure Amber is home when I get there. Warren's memories are one thing, but he rarely leaves his office—and no one has time to go through days...perhaps weeks...of security footage. I plan to scan the girl's memories, in addition to Warren's, but I don't want to do it here at the bank. I'd like to take my time and see, firsthand, who has entered—and exited—the lobby...find out if there's more to this gory, insolent tale than meets the eye.*

He didn't wait for the demons to reply.

Having arrived at the door to the employee's restroom, he disconnected the telepathic bandwidth and tuned in to Warren's grunts: Trader would either have to kill the woman or scrub her memories—maybe he'd share in the use of her body, first—allow each of the shades to take a turn.

Who knew...

But first, he would have to deal with his unwitting servant, as humans who dabbled in the occult were so strange: They prayed, they conjured, they recited incantations, but at the end of the day, they didn't really believe...

They were as likely to shit their pants as rejoice, the moment a true entity showed up.

No matter.

Trader could handle Warren.

And he would decide what to do with the woman...later... once he had retrieved what he came for.

As for Zeik, Grunge, Tony, and Amber—well, the demons had been caught sleeping at their posts; the humans might still be of value; and either way, Trader was going to have to clean up this mess...and pray that Lord Drakkar was feeling merciful.

CHAPTER FIVE

A xe showed up at Amber's residence just as a dark Cadillac Escalade backed out of the carport, turned down the street, and headed in the direction of the mall. One glance, and he had his first batch of data: three large males; a redhead, a blond, and a guy who was either bald or sporting a really tight skull trim. The latter had a dark, creepy aura, and he was definitely driving—but Axe didn't have a chance to listen in or scan the back of their necks; he was too busy taking a mental picture of the license plate and committing it to memory. If the house didn't give him the necessary information— or if his fated dragyra was less than forthcoming—his lair mate, Jace, could always run the plates later. Besides, who knew if these were roommates, family, or visitors. At this juncture, Axe was just collecting puzzle pieces, building the edges of a mysterious picture...

He turned his attention to the equivalent of a corner piece: the sleek gray house looming before him—*just what did this section of the puzzle reveal?*

The tall, architectural lines were clean, and the aesthetic

details were immaculate and high-end. Coupled with a profes-sionally manicured lawn, the entire structure screamed *affluence*. No one lived here on a teller's salary—perhaps Amber had a boyfriend after all, maybe one of the males in the Cadillac. A low, insidious growl rumbled in Axe's chest, and he rolled his head on his shoulders to release some tension. Now was not the time for his dragon to rear its feral head; he needed to keep his wits about him.

Flashing out of view, he reappeared just outside a double-paned bay window that ostensibly gave view to the living room. Peering through the squeaky clean glass, he caught a glimpse of a weathered leather jacket—definitely belonged to a male—strewn over the end of a large sectional sofa. Just behind it, on a chrome end table, were a series of intimate pictures, placed tastefully inside a sequence of modern frames. The third one, in the back, displayed a picture of Amber, leaning back against a guy who had his arms wrapped around her, and the glass was embossed with custom gold lettering that read *Amber and Tony* at the top of the rectangle.

"Son of a bitch," Axe mumbled, realizing his intuition had been right. Amber was involved with a human male—he could smell his dragyra's scent all over the leather jacket, even through the thick double-pane glass. *Doesn't matter,* he told himself. *Just a minor glitch.*

That was then.

This was now.

Whatever—and whoever—had come before was inconse-quential.

It might make the claiming a bit more complicated, but Axe would work with what the Seven had given him, what the gods of the Pantheon had decreed.

From this point forward, Amber was his.

Scattering his molecules into a thin, diffused mist, he transported through the front door of the structure and reappeared in a large domed-ceiling foyer that stretched forward into a wide, deep hall, the floors adorned in marble. Glancing to the right, he saw the whole of the primary living space: a huge, open concept living room and gourmet kitchen, complete with a large center island dissecting the opulent rooms, and both professionally decorated.

What the heck did Tony do for a living?

He sauntered down the hall, past a closet, a bathroom, and a main-floor laundry, then rounded the corner toward the bedrooms, hoping to find Amber's private quarters. First room on the left: king-sized bed with an expensive headboard, a dark brown chest of drawers, and a huge flat-screen TV. The linens smelled disgusting, like they hadn't been laundered in a month, and the floor was littered with piles of dirty gym clothes, flanked by a heavy set of free-weights, clearly well-used.

Probably not Amber's room.

Next door down, same side of the hall, the opposite of the previous grungy quarters, but it still belonged to a male: Everything was either black or gray, from the posh-yet-elegant king-sized bed to the sleek, satin sheets tucked around it; from the wide-planked, horizontal wood floors to the metallic desk—and the Xbox—beside it. This room belonged to a neat freak, and after a little more scrutiny, opening a few drawers, peeking inside the adjoining en suite bathroom, it was clear there was nothing feminine present.

Axe continued to the end of the hall, where he passed through a set of framed, double doors and entered an obvious master bedroom...

And there it was.

At least one thousand square feet of custom décor, both male and female in its composition. The first thing that struck him was Amber's scent, the same soft cologne she had been wearing at the credit union—it was all over the black-and-gold duvet and wafting out from one of two walk-in closets. The second thing that struck him was Tony's footprint: from the open, velvet-lined watch collection, sporting half a dozen extravagant timepieces, to the section of the closet filled with sportswear, T-shirts, and jeans. So the guy liked to walk both sides of the fence: casual, yet flashy; rich, but simple. If Axe had to guess, Tony came up in the streets—he had probably hustled before he made his cash. And now, he had to constantly remind himself that he was rich, even as his modest roots felt more comfortable.

Axe sauntered over to the foot of the bed, sat down on the edge of the duvet, braced his elbows on his knees, and hung his head—he could no longer ignore the big, fat elephant squatting in the middle of the bedroom.

Hell, lounging in the kitchen and the living room.

Trampling the entire damn house.

The residence reeked of darkness and malevolence, and not just the average, run-of-the-mill bad intentions. The place reeked of pagans and the Cult of Hades. It practically screamed debauchery, malignance, and sin.

It was time to alert his lair mates, if only telepathically, let Zane, Levi, Jace, and Nakai know what was going down: that Axe had found his dragyra in King's Castle Credit Union; that he was waiting to bring her home—later, tonight—after he met Ghost at eight; that he was at her residence, checking shit out, and the place wasn't any more copacetic than the bank.

It was time to get down and dirty with the reconnaissance, use the next seven and a half hours wisely.

Axe needed to investigate Amber's background—where she grew up, where she attended school, every job she had ever had—hell, what kind of car did she drive? What was her freakin' credit score? Who did she hang out with...when...where...and why? Sure, he could take it all from her memories, but that would require a hell of a lot of time, and he had already invaded her most intimate space—if he could leave the deepest recesses of her gray matter untouched, he would only be half as much of an ass...

And no, he did not want one of his sapphire brothers to fill in for him with Ghost. He needed to exercise some patience, wait the evening out, and return to 318 Syracuse Lane later that night so he could watch his dragyra interact with her roommates, check Amber out in her native environs...*see what he could see*, so to speak.

That said, he wanted his brothers on high alert.

Ready to stream through the portal at a moment's notice, if needed.

His temples began to throb.

This was way too convoluted for his liking.

Zane, he called out, opening the Sapphire Lair's telepathic bandwidth. *Brother, you there?*

A couple of seconds, then: *Axeviathon, what's up?*

Where's Jordan? Where's Nakai? Are Levi and Jace around?

The line went silent for a few. *Jordan's right here, working on a brief. I think Levi and Jace are in the kitchen, and Nakai is on some errand for Lord Saphyrius. Why, what do you need?*

Axe swept his hand through his hair and sighed. *No need to involve your dragyra—let her work—but I need to talk to all four of you.*

I can hear you just fine, Nakai cut in. *I can walk and chew gum at the same time. Besides, I've got a few minutes, so go ahead.*

Levi and I are right here with Zane, heading to the living room right now, Jace added.

Good, Axe replied. *Because you need to be sitting down for this shit. Oh, and Jace, when time permits, I need you to run a license plate for me...*

CHAPTER SIX

Lord Drakkar Hades sniffed the decaying human hand, crushed it in his palm, and tossed the pulp across the throne room, even as smoke began to waft from his demon-shade nostrils. "Who the hell do these dragyri think they are!" he lamented. "I will peel the skin back from their bones, remove their muscles from their tendons, and watch as the blood seeps out of their veins! I will send their remains in pint-sized storage containers, one by one, to each of their insidious masters— their arrogant, crafty dragon fathers—but not before I squat and take a shit on their corpses."

Trader Vice blanched and looked askance at Killian Kross, Lord Drakkar's venerable chief counselor. *All right,* Trader reasoned, *so Drak was good and pissed.* This was nothing he hadn't expected.

Killian opened his reedy lips to speak, but the lord of the underworld cut him off—

"*For Drak,*" he spat, "*the best-laid plans of mice and pagans often go astray.* How clever. How witty. How moronic and trite! I wonder if the Seven will feel half as self-satisfied when their offspring arrive, FedEx...in parts."

Killian bowed his head and swept one hand in a graceful arc, showing his king the respect he had due, while acknowledging that he had heard his sire's lament. "If I might, my liege..."

Drakkar rolled his eyes. "Spit it out, Killian. I'm not in the mood."

"Very well." The counselor folded his hands behind his back. "I couldn't agree more—the act was bold and infantile; the missive was pedestrian and childish at best; but at the end of the day, what do we care if Kyle Parker lost his money-making digits, if the sinner is no longer a surgeon?" He sniffed and brushed some invisible dust off his shoulder. "Nay, the human was only a pawn on a board, and to that end—and as I am your principal counselor—I might gently remind you that you have a castle full of demons and shades eagerly waiting to do your bidding. Surely, you don't intend to go after a dragyri...on Earth...and in person?"

Trader slithered several paces away from the red velvet throne, just in case the shit hit the fan before it could land on the corpse of a dragyri.

"While it might feel quite satisfying," Killian continued, "to at last extinguish several Dragyr with your own immaculate hands, the war that would ensue would be disastrous for all concerned: epic in its scope and consequence. Surely, you understand, the moment one supreme being reaches out beyond the netherworlds, strikes at his enemy from Earth's humble realm, or makes a move to enact retribution, all supreme beings will soon be involved. The dragon lords would leave their thrones faster than you could recite their gemstones—they would meet you earthside and all hell would break loose. You would have to engage in combat with all seven primordial beings. And this is to say nothing of what would happen to the human planet, what would happen to our lives as we know them...and live them, now...what would happen to the cosmic order we've achieved."

Lord Drakkar snatched Killian by his long, white, baby-fine hair, tugged his head beneath the glow of the torchlight, and glared into his eyes with menace. "Lord Dragos, Lord Ethyron, Lord Saphyrius, and Lord Amarkyus." He spat each name with derision. "Lord Onyhanzian, the loser; Lord Cytarius, the wimp; or Lord Topenzi, the piteous peacemaker—I'd like to see them try."

Trader bit his lip, relaxed his face muscles, and strained not to roll his eyes. *Really?* he thought. *All seven dragon lords? You'd like to see them strike at the pagans? You'd like to take on all seven at once?* Apparently, Lord Hades was eager to die, but again, Trader said nothing aloud.

"True, so true," Killian genuflected, "however, I would counsel my liege to choose caution over impulse. Let your servants be your eyes, your hand, and your sword—let your armies strike your enemies for you."

At this, the king flicked his wrist and snapped Killian's head out of the firelight and away from the throne. He pinched the bridge of his nose. "It's hyperbole, Killian. Musical language. I don't really intend to battle the Seven...on my own." He pointed at the pulverized, severed hand, littered on the floor, brushed up against the edge of an obsidian pillar, and growled. "However, *that*—such blatant insult—cannot go unanswered. What are your intentions, Trader—what are your plans? How do you intend to punish the male who delivered it? How do you intend to avenge your lord's honor?"

Trader grimaced.

How did he intend to avenge his lord's honor?

Shit.

And what the hell?

Axeviathon Saphyrius—the male he had discovered in

Warren Simmons' memories—was an immortal Dragyr, the servant of Lord Saphyrius. If Trader, or any other sin-eater, could just walk up to a dragyri, slice his throat, and bring his blood back in a bowl to serve to Lord Drakkar, they would have already done it. Granted, the male was not a Genesis hatchling, but still, he was one of Lord Saphyrius' beloved children. "I, um, I was hoping—"

"Shut up, Trader," Lord Drakkar snarled. "And give me one of your hands."

Trader gulped. "Excuse me, my liege?"

Lord Drakkar's voice grew dark and menacing. "Did I stutter?"

Trader shook his head. "No, my king; it's just—*it's just*—I am not the demon who messed this plan up; I believe it was Salem Thorne who was supposed to wield Kyle Parker as a weapon." He dropped to his knees and bowed his head.

"Yes...yessss," Lord Drak hissed, sounding more like a snake than a king, "and I believe Salem already paid with his penis. I believe Zanaikeyros, another of Lord Saphyrius' progeny, ripped the organ from Salem's pelvis in the magical cove, inside the Pantheon, where the sea fills with dragon's fire. You do recall that Salem managed to slip through the portal, to follow my enemy and wage war with two dragyris. I was able to pull him out through a rift before he was slaughtered, but there was just something about that water—he wasn't able to regenerate the organ." He leaned in closer and snarled. "Now, I ask you: Is it fair that Salem has lost so much, when you have lost so little?"

Trader blanched.

Fuck!

The king's reasoning was ass-backwards, as usual.

Trader had nothing to do with Salem, Dr. Parker, the missive, the credit union, or even the box of chocolates—he just saw it on the screen in the Sinner's Cave—he was just the unfortunate messenger.

"Are. You. Not. The Demon. Who feeds on Warren Simmons?" Drak asked, his tone growing perilously sinister.

"Yes, my liege," Trader said, fixing his eyes on the ground.

"Well, then; would you rather lose your hand or your penis? Which...appendage...would cause you the greatest loss of pleasure going forward?" He angled his head to the side and cackled. "Actually, don't answer that question—in your case, it could go either way." He turned toward Killian and nodded. "Counselor, remove whatever is closest. Do it now."

Killian reached inside his cloak and withdrew a sharpened, curved sickle, bending over toward Trader's bent legs.

Trader held out his left arm. "The hand. *The hand!* Just take my blasted—*shittttt!*" he cried, as the limb fell to the floor and landed in a bloody heap.

"Don't regenerate that, boy," the king snarled. "Oh, and clean up the mess, return to the earth, and give Zeik and Grunge an unmistakable warning: If they sleep on the job again, they'll lose both a hand and an organ. And as for Tony and Amber, the humans involved"—he shrugged one shoulder with indifference —"I suppose it isn't either one's fault, but it will make me feel better if you punish them both. Take Tony aside and beat the unholy crap out of him—do to him what you would like to do to me. Let him know that the lord of the cult he worships is terribly displeased with his laziness. And as for Amber, make her blind for a week. Perhaps she'll see better—and pay closer attention to her surroundings—in the future." With that, King Drakkar rose from his throne, inclined his head, and took his leave.

CHAPTER SEVEN

LATER THAT EVENING

Amber got home from work around 5 PM.

The house was still empty—thank heaven for little favors—which meant she had some rare time to herself: time to change her clothes, unwind, and eat; time to read a book or catch a movie; time to just sit and think and forget her day.

Her strange, unsettling, disturbing day.

She dropped her keys in a small black wicker basket sitting on a console table inside the front door, slipped off her shoes, and headed for her bedroom: A long, hot shower would feel heavenly. Slipping out of her sleek gray pencil skirt and peeling off her pantyhose, she started to head for the en suite bathroom—and then she swiftly spun around.

The duvet was wrinkled.

The door to her master-closet was open.

And her jewelry tree was facing the wrong direction on her nightstand.

What the hell?

Her heart started to pound in her chest as she surveyed the room more carefully.

"Hello?" she called, retrieving her bathrobe from a hook beside the closet. "Is anyone here? Is anyone home?" Other than Amber's Jaguar—a gift from Tony that she actually hated—the carport had been empty.

No, no one was home.

But someone had definitely been there.

She tiptoed to the tall cherry armoire, opened the top drawer, and reached behind several lacy nightgowns, retrieving her loaded LC9. She pulled back on the slide to chamber a bullet and held the gun, down and away, from her thigh. "Hello?" she called again as she padded out of the bedroom, down the hall, and in and out of each doorway.

She checked the theater, the laundry, the sunroom, and the game room.

The kitchen pantry, the hall closet, and the guest half-bathroom.

Nothing.

No one.

Just a sinking feeling...

That, and the fact that someone had definitely been in her bedroom.

True, Tony could have sat down on the edge of the duvet while he was home, but he rarely watched TV outside of the living room or the theatre, and he *always* sat on the upholstered bench beside the sliding glass doors when he changed his shoes. He absolutely never touched Amber's jewelry tree—the expensive stuff was in the closet, locked in a safe—and the two had separate compartments.

So who the hell had opened Amber's door?

She returned to the bedroom, went back into the closet, set down the gun, and unlocked the safe. Maybe Tony had bought her a new piece of jewelry—maybe he had gone into her closet to put it away.

Nope.

No new, sparkly earrings, dangling necklaces, or flashy rings.

"Hmm," Amber wondered aloud. Maybe she had messed up the duvet, left the door to the closet open, and moved the jewelry tree herself this morning. She absently thumbed her favorite pair of earrings—two simple sapphire studs set next to a pair of small diamonds—they were each resting snugly in her ears. She shook her head and murmured, "Shit." She hadn't gone near that tree this morning; she didn't remember sitting on the bed; and she never left a closet door open. It was a childhood quirk that had carried over: shutting all the boogeymen out and such.

She sighed, still unable to shake the feeling.

That man...

The one with the smoldering eyes filled with flames.

The one who had read her thoughts—the one who knew her full name.

She had given the stranger her address.

"Shake it off, Amber." She spoke aloud. "Do you really think anyone is going to screw with Zeik, Grunge, or Tony? And heaven help whoever does." Feeling a little bit lighter, she reached inside her purse and retrieved her slender silver smartphone. *Where are you?* she texted, sending the message to Tony, then staring down at both her phone...and the gun. "Put that shit away," she whispered, "and just set the alarm." They rarely used it—they didn't see the need—but maybe tonight would be an exception.

Just rolled up to the bar; Tony's reply shot through. *Why? Feeling lonely? Need some company?*

Amber rolled her eyes. *Just checking,* she texted back. *What time will you be home?*

Not late, Tony answered. *Maybe seven or eight.* Then, *WHY?* All caps. *You okay?*

I'm fine, she texted quickly, *just wondered where you were...* Shit, now he would come home horny...oh well.

Be home soon, he shot back. *Keep the bed warm* (smiley face).

Yep, she knew Tony Rossi like the back of her hand.

Later, she texted, shutting off her phone.

Well, at least one thing in her life was still predictable, and in a sense, it meant she had nothing to worry about: Whoever had been in the house was long gone; Zeik, Grunge, and Tony would be home by eight; and tonight would be like any other night... long, boring, and uneventful...including the sex with Tony.

* * *

Jace Saphyrius was famished when he returned to the lair that evening. He marched straight into the kitchen, hightailed it to the enormous oversized refrigerator, and opened both stainless-steel doors.

"Can't wait until dinner?" Zane asked him.

Jace peered over his shoulder.

Zane and his mate, Jordan, were sitting at the large mission-style table, enjoying a pre-dinner snack of their own.

"Looks like I'm not the only one," Jace said, inclining his chin at Jordan. "Is someone eating for two?"

Jordan slammed down her fork and glared at him. "Are you saying I'm getting fat?"

"No!" Jace exclaimed. "Absolutely not. I'm just"—he turned his desperate gaze on Zane, hoping for backup, but when none was forthcoming, he continued—"it's just that Zane mentioned that the two of you might be...*trying*. You know, for a little one. That's all I meant."

This time, Jordan pointed her exasperated expression at her dragyri mate. "Zanaikeyros!" *Yikes, she was using his consecrated name.* "Is nothing sacred...or secret...in this house?"

Zane's eyes grew wide, and he shrugged his shoulders, feigning like he suddenly forgot the English language.

Jordan punched him in the arm, and then she turned her attention back to Jace. "If...and when...there is something to report, you'll definitely be the *last* to know. Got it?" She picked up her fork and dug back in to what looked like some kind of Caesar salad.

Jace laughed.

"By the way," Jordan continued, her voice growing imminently more serious, "is Axe still planning on bringing his dragyra home tonight?"

Jace snatched a leftover rotisserie chicken, a container of mashed potatoes, a side of macaroni and cheese, and three slices of homemade sourdough bread out of the refrigerator and headed for the cupboard to get a plate.

"You do know dinner is at six," Zane said. "Levi will be cooking in your place in forty-five minutes."

"Yeah," Jace grunted, grateful to pass on his usual culinary duties to his more-than-capable lair mate. "And I'll be ready to eat again by then." He turned his attention back to Jordan. "Haven't heard from Axe since 11:30 this morning. I'm assuming his plans haven't changed. Oh, and Zane—"

"What's up?"

"Remember that license plate number he gave me?"

"Yeah, what about it?"

"Well, I tried to run the plate number while I was out. I stopped by the local police department, slipped in incognito, and whispered a few sweet nothings in this cute little dispatcher's ear, laced with a significant amount of compulsion, of course. She looked it right up."

"And?" Zane asked.

"And then she got the world's worst headache, suddenly forgot what she was doing, and tried to move on to another task."

Zane sat back in his seat and crossed his arms over his chest, raising both eyebrows in question.

"I repeated the process three more times. I gave the girl a new command to pull it up again, watched as she either rubbed her temples, or grimaced, and got up from her desk. I was about to ask her a fourth time, but—"

"That is really cruel, Jace," Jordan cut in. "Did it ever occur to you that you could've given her a brain hemorrhage or something? I mean, I get that the Dragyr don't think all that highly of humans, but sheesh, have some compassion next time." Her voice held a hint of teasing, but just the same, Jace caught her drift.

"First of all," he said, "you didn't let me finish. I was just about to say: I was going to ask her a fourth time, but I didn't want to push it, wasn't comfortable with the cerebral reaction. Second of all," he gibed, "unless I missed the memo, you've come and gone from the temple, which means you're no longer human yourself. Welcome to the world of the Dragyr. And incidentally, I believe that's why you and Zane are now capable of having a baby—I think you oughta get to it."

Jordan snickered, flipped him the bird, and went back to eating.

"So, what gives?" Zane asked, following up on Jace's story. "You thinking what I'm thinking?"

"Yep," Jace said. "Cult of Hades. That plate number was protected by a ward. Oh, and it wasn't just the headaches: Every time she tried to enter the number, her screen went black, like a not too subtle message from the cosmos: *Look away...think again... nothing to see here, folks.*"

Zane nodded and rubbed his chin in contemplation. "Damn, then Axe was right; something ominous is going on with his dragyra."

"Yeah," Jace said, and all the humor left his voice. "Back to Jordan's original question—does Axe plan to bring the girl back to the Pantheon later tonight? I think the entire lair needs to stay put...stay home. And frankly, the later it gets, the more prepared we should be: It might not be such a bad idea to have our battle gear on—blades sheathed, firearms loaded—you know, just be ready." He paused to consider his next words. "I don't know...just in case... I have a real bad feeling about this, Zane."

Zane cleared his throat and inclined his head. "Couldn't agree more." He turned toward his dragyra, smiled, and placed a loving hand on her back. "And you know, angel, when he does bring her back, you might have the most instrumental role to play."

"How's that?" Jordan asked, her large hazel eyes darkening with interest.

"My guess," Jace interjected, "is she's not gonna be very happy to be here."

"Axe is playing this one close to the vest," Zane added. "He's not taking any time to meet her, get to know her, explain a little bit about the Dragyr or the Pantheon ...our world, what's happening, or what she can expect going forward."

"Nope," Jace added, "not Axe's style. And with all the creepy dark shit revolving around her, I can't say that I blame him. But still..."

"She may need a softer touch," Zane said. "A more gentle approach from someone a little less intimidating. I mean, it's not our place to interfere with Axe's claiming, but just the same, you might want to be ready as well."

Jace finished loading his plate, grabbed a fork and a knife from the cutlery drawer, and headed back to the refrigerator for a drink and some creamy homemade butter. Indeed, this claiming might *take a village* of Dragyr to pull off.

CHAPTER EIGHT

7:55 PM

True to his namesake, Ghost Dragos emerged from the portal, slinked into the shadows of a dark, dingy alley, and melted into the masonry of the surrounding brick architecture, complete with graffiti, scattered trash, and unidentifiable stains in the concrete and mortar.

Technically, he wasn't supposed to travel through the portal alone.

None of the original, first-generation-born dragyri were.

At least not since Zane Saphyrius had been attacked by a rogue band of pagans in a human gangster's front yard. The act had been rare, brazen, and a sign that the underworld was growing increasingly restless. From that night forward, the Seven had taken unusual measures to protect their original offspring: They had forbidden solitary travel for all Genesis Sons.

No matter.

Ghost was only five minutes early, and Axe would be there to meet him in a few...

Besides, it wasn't like some psychic pagan enemy was going to anticipate Ghost's travel, meet him in the netherworld—the gateway between dimensions—in some disembodied state, and attack: molecules seeking molecules, ether targeting anima, a pagan traversing the elusive portal, moving faster than space and time, and wrapping its wicked claws around Ghost's thick, corded throat.

Nah...

Wasn't going to happen.

And the way Ghost saw it: As long as Axe was there to greet him, give or take a few, the timing was just a technicality—

Either Lord Dragos would understand, or he wouldn't.

And either way, who gave a shit.

A deep, guttural growl rumbled in Ghost's throat even as he glanced askance at the rising moon and felt his hunger intensify as if the two were feeding off one another.

Ghostaniaz hadn't fed in a while. His beast was ravenous, and his fire was waning. The dragyri was yearning for fresh human blood, essence, and heat—for simmering embers to kindle the blaze—to light his fire anew, so to speak. A few more days of putting it off—*feeding*, that is—and Ghost would not be responsible for the carnage: His dragon was capable of anything.

And beyond that gruesome fact, Lord Dragos could be a pain in the neck. The darkest of the seven dragon lords had been known to insert himself into Ghost's private business, and immortal spirits knew, the last thing the dragyri needed was an unwelcome flyby—an *up-close-and-personal*—with his black-hearted father.

No, thank you.

He ducked beneath the dark, soiled archway of a back-alley nightclub, assuming Axe would figure out where he'd went, and wrenched the heavy iron door open with his fist. His palm began to vibrate from the force of the thunderous music, the pulse of a dozen subwoofers causing the panel to shudder and hum, and he was immediately met by an ice-cold glare: a large, muscle-bound bouncer with narrow, beady eyes and a shining bald dome. The human was practically dripping with perspiration—hell, if he sweated any harder, Ghost would need an umbrella just to get around him.

The bouncer's taut, skinny lips drew back into a scowl the moment he took a gander at Ghost. "Club's full," he barked, puffing out his chest and sidestepping into the dragyri's path to block Ghost from entering the nightclub.

Ghost swiped his bottom lip with his tongue, even as his top lip twitched. He flashed the barest hint of fangs and snarled—and the bouncer froze, backpedaled, and ushered Ghost forward. Ghost snorted and headed deeper into the club, drawn by the dark, pulsing music.

An iron staircase intersected the main dance floor, snaking up the side of the wall and ending at an overarching balcony. The dance floor itself was full of hot, sweaty bodies, undulating humans, high on everything imaginable, desperate to find a hookup for the night.

The club wasn't exactly high-end material.

No VIPs or prominent athletes.

No *who's-who* in Denver's political, economic, or social network.

And the more Ghost looked around, the more he figured: Half the men were probably wanted for some felony or another; the other half were likely on parole. And the scantily dressed women were either tethered to the men in some sort of sick, unfortunate domestic situation, or they were working the club for cheap, easy money—hell, they were likely to be on probation themselves.

Yeah, it was a real classy establishment.

But whatever.

Ghost could get in and out without any drama.

He could feed from a half-dozen brawny men, and if the

mood struck him—if the surge of heat, the reanimated fire, and the momentary intoxication of fresh crimson blood aroused him just so—he could slake a few other needs while he was at it. It wasn't like the Dragyr could catch herpes or syphilis, and it sure as hell wasn't like Ghost to bother with conversation, some inane attempt at seduction, or to waste any more time than necessary consorting with a human female.

Feeding was a necessary evil.

As for sex—that was just a release—an occasional itch even Ghost had to scratch, a welcome distraction from time to time, especially when *time* for a Dragyr was an eternal prospect.

He took the iron staircase two stairs at a time, heading for the overarching balcony. There were about twelve inebriated humans crowded into the space: eight males, three females, and one *who could tell*. He could move in and out and feed like a specter.

As he made his swift approach toward a good-looking redhead, a woman with an ample bust and a thick, rounded ass, the female tossed back her head and laughed, thumbed her left earring, and fingered her bracelet—and just like that, Ghost was somewhere else...

Catapulted in an instant to another place and time.

Hurled into another dark, grungy alley.

Ghost was five years old, hunting with his sire, Lord Dragos, and the two were ensconced in a thick London fog. They were prowling down a cobblestone street that still gave off the scent of fresh mortar.

The dragon lord was in amalgamated form, just a mere wisp of his primordial serpent, and he bent low to whisper in his young progeny's ear. "Ghost, can you hear them? There are two human prey approaching the alley. If you listen closely, you can hear the male's heartbeat—it's about eight to ten beats slower than the female's. She's laughing—how melodious—and she's thumbing her ear while playing with a bracelet full of trinkets and charms. While I can't hear the earring, I can sense that she's rubbing it—it is a diamond after all—the vibration is in here." He tapped the left side of his chest three times. "If you are wily and prepared, you can catch them both by surprise."

Eager to both appease and impress his immortal father—hell, his divine creator—Ghost closed his eyes and sharpened his senses, tuning in, unerringly, to the unsuspecting couple just as his father had instructed.

Yeah, the couple was relaxed and unaware.

They were joyful and gay, blissfully ignorant of their surroundings, and drawing ever closer to the mouth of the alley.

Their reflexes would be slow.

The surprise would be absolute.

And Ghost could already strike like a bolt of summer lightning: quick, lethal, and out of the blue.

Yeah, he would be both wily and ready.

But then, unlike his father, he heard another distant sound, a strange, subtle echo, faintly reverberating: *pitter-patter, pitter-patter, faster, faster*...faster still. A third recognizable heartbeat, twice as fast as the woman's.

The human female was pregnant.

Ghost drew back in surprise and tugged on Lord Dragos' arm. "Father," he said meekly, "I think the woman is with child. If I take her blood...her heat...and her essence, won't that harm the baby?"

Lord Dragos replied with a snarl. "You are an immortal Dragyr, Ghostaniaz, the first-generation offspring of a dragon god, and more prominently, you are my son...my youngling...my own flesh and blood. Dragons do not show mercy, nor do we consider the plight, fate, or well-being of human prey. You must *feed* to live—it is the third of the four principle laws—and your obedience is not optional. You will take from this couple, Ghostaniaz; do you understand me?"

Ghost gulped. "Very well."

But he did not understand his father.

He did not understand any of this.

However, he had lived long enough to understand—full well —that it was a fool's errand to defy his sire. As it stood, Lord Dragos would expect him to exterminate the male, to drain him until his heart beat no more. If he were to show mercy to the female now, his father would likely order him to kill her too—and that would extinguish the child.

Why was murdering an innocent babe necessary for a Dragyr to feed?

His mind raced wildly, weighing his options: He could kill them both, and his father would be pleased; or he could drain the female, just short of expiration, and hope that the fetus survived. "I don't like their smell," he blurted clumsily, hoping to get away with an *option-number-three*. "I think her...condition...will alter her taste. Father, can I wait for someone more palatable?"

If nothing else, Ghost hoped Lord Dragos would appreciate the fact that he had dedicated himself to his studies. At five years old, Ghost already spoke three languages—and he wasn't using divine cognition nor mental telepathy to do it—his command of their native tongue was exceptional. Hell, he was using his sense of hearing, just as he had been taught, and he was requesting a special privilege as a Genesis son—maybe his father would be impressed.

The vitriol in Lord Dragos' voice was enough to make Ghost's blood run cold. "From this day until your eighteenth birthday, you will refer to me as Lord Dragos, *never* as Father. And as your lord, I will remind you—just this once—*thou shalt pledge thy eternal fealty to the sacred Dragons Pantheon,* and *thou shalt feed on the blood and heat of human prey in order to reanimate your fire.* Kill the male, Ghostaniaz. Drain the female. And if you hold back on the woman, you will be severely punished."

Ghost curled inward.

He knew the laws, and he knew his father—he knew *Lord Dragos...*

And the dragon's punishments were severe and ruthless.

Yet and still, he also knew magic—he had powers even Lord Dragos didn't know about.

Perhaps...

Just perhaps...

He could pull this off.

The couple rounded the bend, and Ghost pounced, more feral than he had ever been. He bit so deeply into the human male's jugular that the man's trachea collapsed before he died of exsanguination. And then he turned his attention to the female. She tried to scream and run, but Ghost was way too fast...

He clasped her wrists, tugged her down to her knees, and shackled both her slender arms behind her back with one implacable fist. And then he snatched her by the hair, yanked her head to the side, and sank his fangs deep into her throat, the whole time snarling to please his father.

He lapped and he drank.

He gulped and he gorged.

And all the while, he remained tuned in to that tiny, racing pitter-patter...*pitter-patter*...making note of the moment when it began to slow down. "Sleep," he growled in the female's ear, pouring every ounce of compulsion he possessed into the command, and she fell to the ground, unconscious.

Pitter-patter.

Pitter-patter.

Both heartbeats remained.

Ghost turned to Lord Dragos and smiled.

And that's when a deafening roar filled the alley; an ungodly heat wrenched the air; and a stream of orange-and-red flames scorched the humans, cremating both male and female on the stones where they had fallen.

Ghost gasped and faced his father, both terrified and enraged, but he never had the chance to voice his protest.

A second blaze of fire, stronger than the first, washed over him like a wave of acid.

And the gods save his soul, Ghostaniaz burned...and burned...and burned.

* * *

"*Ghost.* Ghost! *What the fuck!*" Axeviathon's thick, gravelly voice pierced a din of shouts, and screams, and humans scrambling, and then the powerful male straddled Ghost's body, locked his hands around Ghost's jaw, and burrowed his thumbs into the joints between his mandible and maxilla. "Ease up, Dragyr!" Axe shouted. "Back off...chill out...and ease the hell up."

Ghost blinked two or three times and stared at the human male lying on the floor beneath him—or at least, what was left of the guy. His throat was torn out; there was blood pooling every-where; and Ghost was straddling the man's body like a rabid dog. "What happened?" Ghost snarled, trying to speak around the fingers still lodged in the corners of his mouth. For all intents and purposes, Axe was astride Ghost's back, and the ball of Axe's knee was about to break Ghost's vertebrae. "Get off me," he hissed.

"You were heading toward the redhead—I assume you were about to *feed*—when she turned toward you, batted her lashes, and smiled. Apparently, her boyfriend didn't take too kindly to it because the asshat snatched her by the hair and punched her.

Yeah, *her*—not you. Next thing I know, you're on top of this guy, doing your best with your teeth. His throat is a pound of hamburger, blood is spraying everywhere, and the human-freakin'-onlookers are pitchin' an unholy bitch-fit. What did you think was gonna happen, Ghost?"

"Get off me, Axe."

"Are you gonna bite?"

"Get off me!"

"Bite me, and I'll bite you back. Got it?" Axe snatched his hands away from Ghost's jaw, flew backward at least a half-dozen feet, and immediately began to deal with the humans: barking out orders, calming them down, and scrubbing a host of memories.

Ghost ran his hand through his jet-black hair and surveyed the mess he'd created. *Well, shit*, he thought, staring down at his steel-toed boots—the tips were soaked in blood, and the leather was ruined. Not to mention, he still hadn't had a chance to properly feed.

He surveyed the alcove, trying to find the redhead: She was trembling in the corner, and she appeared to be in shock. *Three birds with one stone*, Ghost told himself. He could clean up the black eye with some silver fire; wipe her memory clean of the dead guy; then pull her into the corner, shroud her in shadows, and *feed* like he had originally meant to.

CHAPTER NINE

Amber nestled into the soft, inviting sectional, snuggled under a warm throw-blanket, and reached for her buttery bowl of popcorn just as the front door to the foyer swung open.

The alarm went off.

Zeik, Grunge, and Tony stumbled in, Zeik dragging Tony beneath his arm.

And Grunge stopped to key in the passcode and disable the security system.

What the heck?

Not only was Tony bloody and bruised—his nose was broken and his lips were swollen—but the three were promptly followed by a string of bizarre and terrifying-looking strangers. The first was a giant of a man, at least six-foot-five, with luminous copper eyes and long, wavy golden hair. The giant was missing his left hand, yet his arrogance was striking—and as for the dudes that followed him? They were creepy as hell: tall and slender with skeletal features, sunken eyes, and long, wispy manes. They looked like a brigade of slinking shadows, and their pupils glowed an eerie scarlet red.

Amber spilled the popcorn as she leaped from the couch, spun around, and glared at Grunge. "What's going on—who are these guys?" she demanded. She turned her gaze on Tony and blanched. "And what the hell happened to him?"

The husky, one-handed giant rolled his head on his shoulder in an eerie, serpentine motion before flashing a wicked smile at Amber. "You must be Tony's girl?" he murmured. "Amber Carpenter, right?" He didn't wait for a reply. He pointed at Tony and shook his head. "I'm afraid your boyfriend got into an accident—he had a collision with my fist and the toes of my boots." His wicked smile morphed into a scowl; his copper eyes darkened; and he took a generous step in Amber's direction, crossing the living room in three long strides.

To hell with this shit!

Amber snatched a heavy clay vase off the coffee table, raised it above her right shoulder, and backed up several paces, prepared to swing it like a bat if she had to. "Don't come any closer," she warned the marauding giant. "Zeik!" she shouted, her voice now trembling. "What the fuck is going on?" Forget asking Grunge or Tony, when Zeik had always been the de facto leader. *Why did you let them hurt Tony?* she wanted to ask as well, but common sense warned her to stay silent—the same brute who had done all that damage was more or less commanding the room...

And that didn't make any sense!

Zeik Craven was like a cross between a badass Viking and a modern-day Navy SEAL. He was a lethal adversary and a savage fighter. He could do things with his bare hands that were nothing short of astonishing, and when the guy chose to use a weapon— any weapon—the ensuing carnage could chill one's blood. Amber had seen it happen more times than she cared to remember—so why had he invited these assholes into their home, and why was

Tony practically pulverized when Zeik didn't have a scratch on him?

What kind of control did the giant have over him?

Just then, Amber heard a rustle in the kitchen—or maybe it was a clatter—something clanging from the other side of the island, and then two things happened at once: She felt a firm, aggressive pressure on her hips, like two strong, invisible hands grasping her waist from behind, and two of the tall, waiflike skeletors dove at her from the foyer.

She never even saw them move.

They tunneled through the air like billowing pillars of smoke, only they traveled at the speed of lightning, and just like that, one of the silhouettes shackled her by the arm, even as his partner wrenched the vase out of her hand and grasped her other bicep.

The pressure on her hips vanished, and the giant stalked toward her. "Can you smell that shit?" the giant snarled, glaring at the two spectral men.

"Stinks like a dragyri," the one to the left of Amber hissed.

Both Zeik and Grunge started scanning the living room. *What the actual fuck?* Why weren't they helping her?

"Zeik!" Amber screamed as the giant stopped in front of her, cupped her face by the jaw with his one good hand, and bent to give her a kiss. She gasped in fright as his hard, cruel mouth fastened to hers, and then someone turned out the lights and the living room went black.

Amber blinked her eyes.

Once, twice, three times in quick succession...

She could hear the occupants speaking—the giant, Zeik, and Grunge—they were grunting foreign words in some foul, guttural language, but she couldn't see a thing.

And then it hit her like a ton of bricks.

She hadn't blacked out.

And this wasn't a nightmare.

AXEVIATHON - SON OF DRAGONS

Amber Carpenter was blind.

Panic seized her soul. She tugged wildly against the knobby, skeletal fingers still shackled around her arms. And she screamed...and screamed...and screamed.

* * *

Axeviathon stood in the back of the kitchen, watching as Amber toggled through the remote, selected another movie, and snuggled under a throw-blanket, hugging a bowl of popcorn. She was truly a strikingly beautiful female, and every impulse in his immortal body screamed: *Just take her—take her now. Get her out of this blasted residence, carry her outside, and take your dragyra back through the portal.*

He had finished his business with Ghost almost forty-five minutes earlier, and he had been standing in Amber's kitchen for nearly half as long, silent and invisible, while studying, watching, and waiting for her enigmatic roommates, or her boyfriend, to come home. As much as he wanted to whisk her to the Pantheon —snatch his *fated* and get the hell out of Dodge—he needed to exercise patience and let the night play out.

He wanted to watch—and listen—scrutinize the discourse between Amber and her mysterious housemates, learn all that he could before they departed. And that's when the door swung open, and all hell broke loose...

The three males from earlier, those who had pulled away in the Cadillac, stormed into the foyer, the blond-haired guy named Tony—the same one who had been in the picture frame with Amber—being dragged across the threshold like a broken slab of meat. Someone had beaten the shit out of the guy, and the other two males, the ones from the Cadillac?

Well, there was nothing human about them.

Holy.

Hell.

So Amber Carpenter's buddies were pagans!

And they were being followed into the house by a one-handed giant of a demon and a long line of nasty shades.

Instinctively, Axe drew back into the shadows.

Despite the fact that he remained invisible, he slowed his breathing, dimmed his heartbeat, and immediately opened a telepathic bandwidth to his lair mates on the other side of the portal. He began to quietly and systematically relay information: what he saw, what he heard, and who was who. But he was careful to tell the aggressive Dragyr to stay put, at least for now. Amber was so very close to two evil ones—way too close for Axe's liking. One false move, and they could snatch her heart right out of her chest or crush her throat in an instant.

If the pagans got wind of why the Dragyr were interested in the female, Amber would become target-enemy number one, and the pagans could destroy Axe, a powerful, immortal dragyri, just by annihilating the frail human woman: If Axe failed to present Amber to the temple by the end of the ten-day claiming, Lord Saphyrius would be forced to remove his amulet, the life-giving ornament that tethered his life to the Pantheon and anchored his soul in his body.

Nope.

Axe wasn't about to take a chance with his dragyra's life.

No sooner had the corrupt ones entered the foyer than the room erupted in chaos. Amber jumped up from the sofa, spilling her popcorn; the one-handed demon took several steps in her direction; and Amber snatched a heavy clay vase in a white-knuckled grip and hoisted it over her shoulder like a club.

Axe moved so quickly to get behind Amber that the currents he left in his wake rustled a row of overhanging copper pots. *Oh well...* He fastened both palms of his hands to the small of her waist and prepared to wrench her backward, to snatch her out of the giant's reach, but the shades moved just as quickly. They surrounded Amber, shackled her arms, and wrenched the vase out of her hands with ease.

Axe withdrew his hands, let go of his dragyra, and backed up, as silent as the night—he wasn't willing to make Amber a wishbone.

"Stinks like a dragyri," one of the pagans hissed, and if they could smell him, that meant they'd be scanning for his energy. If they homed in on his location, they would tear Amber's arms right out of her sockets, rend her limb from limb in a millisecond.

What's happening, Axe! Zane's gravelly voice, booming across the telepathic bandwidth.

Two shadow-walkers are restraining Amber, Axe barked back.

And then the giant demon—the one leading the shades—bent to Axe's dragyra and covered her mouth with his.

Axe's heart nearly leaped out of his chest.

He was going to gouge that one-handed bastard's eyes out, seize his intestines through his guts, and wrap them around his convulsing throat—so he could hang him by the living room ceiling.

Easy, Jace cautioned, clearly sensing Axe's rising tension. *Squash the emotion, soldier—focus on strategy. How many pagans are there, Axeviathon?*

Axe was just about to say, *Too many,* when his dragyra began to scream.

And scream...and scream...and scream.

CHAPTER TEN

"**W**hat the hell, Trader!" Zeik's caustic voice.

"Penalty kiss, courtesy of Lord Drakkar," the giant snarled.

Amber sucked in air like an industrial wind-tunnel, clearly on the verge of hyperventilating. The bastards holding her arms released her, and she brought both hands to her eyes and scrubbed them frantically. "I can't see!" she shouted. "Oh my God!" she cried. "Tony, I'm blind! *I can't see anything!* Zeik! Grunge! Somebody, help me!" She was sobbing like a baby and choking on her words.

"Penalty for what!" Grunge demanded in the background.

It sounded like Tony moaned, but Amber wasn't sure. "Call 911!" she pleaded, still gasping for air.

The one-handed giant—the one Zeik had called *Trader*—snorted derisively. "Did you really think Lord Drakkar was going to be A-okay with the shit that went down at the bank? A dragyri marching in, strolling past the tellers, and leaving a gift, wrapped in an insult, on Warren Simmons' desk? You're lucky you and Zeik got off so easy—I lost my fucking left hand!"

Amber trembled at the venom in Trader's voice.

Zeik grunted. "Is that why you beat the shit out of Tony?"

"Lord Drak's orders," Trader snarled. "That, and the girl's eyesight."

Amber shook like a leaf, her heart recoiling. *Who the hell was Lord Drakkar? And what kind of a man could remove someone's eyesight with a kiss?* "Zeik!" she screamed, her terror overcoming her. "What the hell is he talking about? Who the hell are these guys? And why aren't you *doing something* to help me!?"

* * *

Axeviathon scrubbed his face with his hands, then leaned forward to brace his elbows on his thighs. He sucked in several gasps of air and snarled...

He had left the living room.

He had abandoned his dragyra.

He had transported outside the bay window in order to clear his head.

It wasn't that he was afraid to throw down, to take on every blasted pagan in that house, but if Amber screamed one more time—if he had to both hear her distress and *feel* her terror—he was going to lose his shit, and a feral, irrational dragyri could do more harm than good.

Axeviathon was a lethal combatant.

He could move like the wind and strike like a scorpion; hell, he could dispatch three enemies before they knew he was there. But even an immortal dragyri like Axe couldn't best a room full of pagans. And Amber was so damn vulnerable. He needed to keep his wits about him. He needed to think like a soldier and calculate like a general.

What had Trader said?

Lord Drakkar Hades had ordered the demon to beat the crap

out of Tony and take Amber's eyesight—*to freakin' render her blind!*—and the bastard had done it because of Axe's intervention, his special delivery at the bank. His fire sparked, his fangs elongated, and he sank both canines deep into the flesh of his hand in frustration. *Zanaikeyros,* he snarled across the telepathic band. *We have to go in.*

Zane's already on his way to the temple, Levi responded. *How many pagans and how many humans?*

What? Axe retorted. His vision was swirling in eddies of black and red.

In the house, Axe, Levi reiterated. *How many humans and how many shades are in the house right now?*

Axe peered through the double-paned window. *Hard to tell for sure—those shadow-walkers are some shifty bastards, flashing in and out like ink blots, but my guess is twelve, maybe fifteen shades. Three demons if you count Trader, Zeik, and Grunge. Tony and Amber are the only humans.*

Got it, Levi said. *Just sit tight for a minute. As I mentioned, Zane's on his way to speak with Lord Saphyrius and Lord Ethyron; he's asking for permission to utilize the Emerald Lair as backup. All four dragyri are home this night, and they can mobilize as quickly as we can. Give us five...maybe ten...and we'll have nine dragyri against fifteen pagans at the least, eighteen at the most. But what we need in the meantime are screenshots—fast, accurate, and keep them coming. The furniture, the layout, where each male is standing, and if all you've got is ink blots, then send those too. Nakai and Jace are already working on tactical operations. The way we see it: quick in and out. Materialize in the living room; strike to kill before they even know we're there; take your dragyra and get the hell outta that house. We may have to leave a handful of pagans standing, but eliminating the enemy is not the mission— you and your fated are all we're about.*

Axe nodded his head, and his vision seemed to clear...just a bit.

Levi was right, of course: This wasn't about payback or wholescale annihilation—it was about getting Amber out of that demonic cesspool of a residence. Who lived and who died would depend on where each male was standing at the moment the dual lairs went in. *Got it*, he replied. *Just tell Zane to hurry. Because if anyone threatens Amber—her life or limb, not her eyesight or feelings—I'm going back in alone.*

Levi sighed across the telepathic link. *If that happens, Axe—if you have to go back in, sooner—Jace, Nakai, and I will be right behind you, and that changes the mission: We fight like hell until Zane and our emerald brothers show up.*

Axe swept his hand through his hair, uncaring that he was streaking the dirty-blond locks with blood. He didn't bother to answer his lair mate—his assent was implied—and besides, he was too busy snapping mental screenshots through the window from the interior of the house and sending them back to the Pantheon.

CHAPTER ELEVEN

Z ane Saphyrius took the white marble steps to the temple two at a time, making a beeline for the sacred fountain to cleanse his hands before he entered, as was required by the Seven.

He didn't get the chance.

Lord Saphyrius and Lord Ethyron appeared in an instant, their amalgamated energy wrapping in and out of the seven giant pillars—they did not appear as magnificent serpents with horns, scales, and lethal spiked tails, but rather as bright prisms of light, reflecting the colors of their primary gemstones: sapphire and emerald. Their figures were large silhouettes in mostly human form, yet translucent and ghostly to the touch, and their glassy eyes were glowing with both intensity and purpose.

One upward glance, and Zane fell to one knee.

He averted his eyes and bowed his head.

"Greetings, Father," he said with reverence. "Thank you for granting me an audience, Lord Ethyron."

Lord Saphyrius waved his hand through the air, and a rainbow of purple-and-blue light followed the movement. "Salutations, Zanaikeyros; you may rise and dispense of all formality. I understand that we don't have time for pleasantries."

Zane paused, waiting to hear a word from Lord Ethyron...

While Zane's Genesis lord was his primary master, and Lord Saphyrius certainly had the right to release him from formal protocol, Lord Ethyron was the second dragon god along the progressive hierarchy, only one step above Lord Dragos. And that meant he was also the second most depraved of the lot. Unlike Lord Topenzi or Lord Cytarius—the seventh and sixth in the spiritual pecking order—Lord Ethyron could not be counted on to proceed with kindness and altruism, to simply embrace Zane's request for an audience or Axe's need for immediate intervention out of benevolence and generosity. He may very well desire something in return, especially if he was going to offer his Genesis Son, Jagyr, in battle.

An awkward silence hovered for a moment, and Zane got the impression Lord Ethyron was enjoying the uncertainty and the tension. Finally, the dragon snarled, releasing a puff of smoke. "You may rise, boy—let's get on with it."

Zane stood to his full warrior's height and drew back his shoulders, releasing some taut, nervous energy. "Thank you, milord."

Lord Ethyron nodded, and his glowing emerald eyes narrowed at the pupils. "From what Lord Saphyrius has shared with me, your lair mate Axe has found himself in a...situation... surrounded by demons and shadow-walkers on Earth and unable to retrieve his dragyra. Is this the long and short of it?"

"Yes, lord," Zane answered. No need for extra verbiage—it would only irritate the caustic serpent.

"I see." This time, the dragon lord sounded bored. "And, alas, the Emerald Lair is home this night, so you would seek permission for Caleb, Rio, Valen, and Jagyr to help extricate both Axe and his female from the sticky situation?"

Zane struggled to keep his facial expression neutral. Lord Ethyron already knew all of this; what was the point of repeating it?

"It would be seen as a personal favor to me," Lord Saphyrius interjected, "a show of political goodwill and an act of solidarity." His voice betrayed no emotion; however, a hot red flame trailed his last exhale of breath, demonstrating his obvious frustration.

Lord Ethyron smiled. "Your mate, Jordan, she is a gifted artist, is she not?"

Zane's stomach clenched, and he nodded.

"Speak up, boy; I didn't hear you."

Lord Saphyrius snarled.

"She is, milord," Zane answered. "My dragyra is extremely gifted."

Lord Ethyron caressed his luminous jaw with an equally translucent thumb and forefinger. "The mural in my temple chambers has faded a bit over the centuries; do you suppose your dragyra would be generous enough to restore it to its original luster?"

Zane bristled, and Lord Saphyrius shifted anxiously in place. This time, the sapphire dragon didn't even attempt to hide his aggravation. "Don't be ridiculous, Lord Ethyron. Such a project would take weeks to complete, if not longer. There are plenty of beautiful human servants to festoon your chambers if you are in need of a female's companionship." His voice rose to a deafening bellow. "Zanaikeyros' dragyra—my daughter—is not one of them."

Well, talk about getting straight to the heart of the issue, Zane thought. Yet again, he kept his thoughts to himself. None of the dragon lords would violate a sacred dragyra, at least not carnally, but where those lines were drawn depended upon the dragon in question. And there was no way in hell Zane was sending Jordan, alone, to spend day after day—or worse, night after night—in

Lord Ethyron's chambers. Jordan was exquisitely beautiful, and her presence would become an overwhelming temptation quite quickly.

"Hmph," Lord Ethyron harrumphed. "Well, at some point I imagine Zane and Jordan will give the Pantheon a son—we could simply all agree now that when the child reaches the age of consecration, he will be assigned to the Emerald Lair as his permanent residence...and gemstone. He will become one of my faithful mercenaries." His gleaming eyes lit up with interest. "The progeny of a Genesis Son would be a welcome addition to my powerful coven."

At this, Lord Saphyrius snorted and crossed his arms over his chest, a chest that was beginning to don sapphire scales. "You are wasting precious time, brother," he snarled. "And your second suggestion is even more ludicrous than the first. Zane is not asking for a year-long commitment from his emerald brothers; he is simply requesting a quick, targeted, and efficient extraction of a human dragyra from a pagan-infested domicile. Keep talking... keep lingering...and the matter may soon be moot."

"True," Lord Ethyron bantered. "Well, if not Jordan or the firstborn child, then what are you offering in return for the use of my soldiers?" His shoulders rippled, his brows furrowed, and his nostrils curled in defiance. "Make no mistake, *brother* Saphyrius, pagans always pose a significant risk. One of my mercenaries may die tonight, no matter how quick, targeted, or efficient the mission."

Lord Saphyrius turned to face the emerald dragon directly. "What do you want, Lord Ethyron?"

Lord Ethyron shrugged one shoulder, as if giving up on his true aspirations. "The female in need of rescue belongs to Axeviathon, so let him pay for her liberation in flesh, blood, and bone."

Zane grimaced, but he still held his tongue.

He couldn't help but remember, less than two weeks earlier, what Lord Ethyron had done to the son of his own lair, Calebrios: As punishment for failing to execute a mission as swiftly as the emerald dragon desired, Lord Ethyron had Caleb flayed and humiliated—the dragyri had endured fifty spiked lashes.

Lord Saphyrius finally capitulated. "You will not torture Axeviathon, indefinitely, simply for an afternoon of amusement. Two pounds of flesh, three pints of blood, and no more than four bones broken. And the son of my lair will have permission to heal the injuries immediately."

"Seven pounds of flesh," Lord Ethyron countered, "seven pints of blood, and no more than seven broken bones. And the son of your lair will wait seven hours before he regenerates. He has forty-eight hours from when he arrives through the portal, assuming the mission is successful, to turn himself over for... payment." He held up two fingers to silence any protest before he was finished wagering. "And if one—or more—of my dragyri die this night in aid to the Sapphire Lair, well then, all will be forgiven, and no debt will be incurred. I think it is a just and equitable proffer. We all have skin in the game, so to speak."

Lord Saphyrius turned his attention to Zane. "Son?" he inquired. "What say you? Axeviathon is not here to accept these terms, so it is up to you to speak on his behalf."

Zane closed his eyes and shuddered.

What the fuck was wrong with those sadistic dragon bastards?

Why did Lord Dragos and Lord Ethyron always get off on watching others suffer?

It really didn't matter.

Axe was in a bind, and if something happened to his dragyra, Amber; if the girl didn't make it out of that house alive; or if Axe got killed trying to rescue her solo—if the Sapphire Lair alone was not enough to dispatch the pagans—then a few broken bones and a couple of pounds of missing flesh would be the least of the dragyri's worries. Axe would end up in the Garden of Grace as a glorious but inanimate pillar; a sapphire statue erected in his former image; an eternal soul bound by sapphire—dead, for all intents and purposes.

Axe was an immortal Dragyr.

His body would heal.

And to Zane's way of thinking, the male would gladly choose torture over risk and uncertainty—allowing Amber to remain any longer in that house. He would pay seven times over to relieve her trauma and end her current suffering.

"Axeviathon will pay his debt," he said evenly. "But we need the Emerald Lair's assistance, *right now*."

Lord Saphyrius nodded, and Lord Ethyron smiled. "Very well," the latter barked, his demeanor shifting instantly to that of a general. "Return to your lair, Zanaikeyros. Caleb, Rio, Valen, and Jagyr will meet you on the balcony in under five minutes, and rest assured, they will each be prepared for battle. Many pagans will die this night, and should this...*dustup*...provoke any form of retribution by Lord Drakkar and his minions—should any of these demons or shades continue to pursue Axeviathon—then my emerald children remain at your disposal. You need only ask them directly for further assistance." He turned to Lord Saphyrius and inclined his head with deference. "And when Axe finally regenerates his injuries, you may give him this as a token of my affection." He held out his hand, splayed his fingers, and drew a circle in the center of his palm with a claw. As the fresh abrasion started to boil and spew blood, it was quickly coated in a hard emerald scale. Lord Ethyron blew silver-and-blue fire over the raised, hardening lesion until it began to glow like a shimmering gemstone. Then he handed the discus to Zane. "Have your lair mate swallow this emerald just moments before he attends to his injuries."

Zane accepted the discus and almost gasped.

Every dragyri male was born with the gift of fire. If he was a Genesis Son, then he retained much of his father's pyrotechnic powers, but if not, then he inherited his gifts from his parents and the lair he was born to. At age eighteen, he would be given increased abilities, commensurate with his new, principal lair, along with his permanent amulet.

Axeviathon was originally born to the Citrine Lair, but he was consecrated to Lord Saphyrius. Now, with this gift from Lord Ethyron, the moment Axeviathon swallowed the emerald medallion, he would possess the powers of all three lairs: citrine, sapphire, and emerald. His fire would burn brighter; his dragon would become even stronger; and he would be able to draw from the energy of all three lords in battle.

Zane wasn't sure he had actually seen what he'd seen, until Lord Ethyron turned to Lord Saphyrius and placed an ethereal hand on his shoulder. "A personal favor to you, my dragon brother: a show of political goodwill and an act of solidarity."

Zane placed the discus in his back pocket and bowed his head, his thoughts almost swimming in the moment. And *that* was the subtle difference between Lord Ethyron and Lord Dragos, the variance just one level of spiritual elevation made between absolute, base depravity and darkness—and just the slightest hint of compassion and light.

CHAPTER TWELVE

T he moonlit raid on Amber's earthly residence was as seamless, stealthy, and effective as anticipated: Eight dragyri warriors traveled through the portal in silence, some dressed in leather dusters, others in plain, wife-beater tees and jeans, all with heavy steel-toed boots, many with spikes on the heels. They materialized in the front yard of 318 Syracuse Lane as silent as the night around them, as invisible as the dense, earthly atmosphere, and that's when Zane slipped Axe his familiar HK45 and explained succinctly *and telepathically* the price his lair mate would have to pay for the use of his emerald brothers.

According to Axeviathon, Zeik, Grunge, Tony, and Amber had retreated down the hall toward one of the interior bedrooms, Zeik hefting Tony in a fireman's hold and Grunge carrying Amber in his arms. Twelve remaining pagans had spread out throughout the house, a thirteenth pagan—a demon with one hand, named Trader—accompanying the roommates to their private quarters, which was exactly where Zane wanted Axe.

The male's only duty—his only *must-accomplish* mission—

was to keep an eye on his dragyra and make sure she didn't take any crossfire, keep her far away from the hand-to-hand combat.

It wasn't as if Axe would've had it any other way—or allowed any other dragyri to take on that assignment. Where Amber went, Axeviathon would follow. And gods of the Pantheon help anyone who had the misfortune of stepping between them. The male was five shades of royally pissed off by the time his Pantheon brethren had showed up.

So be it.

Zane was far more focused on getting all the warriors in and out swiftly and taking out all the scattered but lethal shades.

Ninety seconds tops.

Sixty seconds preferred.

The last thing they needed was an SOS getting sent to the underworld, and a full-scale pagan-dragyri war erupting in a populated human suburb.

No, thank you.

The warriors weren't there to get acquainted or to play ranger games—they were there to execute their enemy swiftly and hightail it back through the portal. It was up to Axe to follow with Amber, and to that end, they had come prepared: Zane with his Viking style battle-axe, Jace with his beloved katar, and Levi with his typical weapon of choice—nothing but his iron-hard, huge, brutal fists. Nakai had his M4 carbine, so he could do double duty, eliminate more than one shade—and Caleb, the first of the Emerald Lair, had his customary black morning star, a wicked-looking implement with a heavy, spiked iron ball at the head.

Rio brought his Japanese katana, a one-and-a-half-pound curved sword, and he would likely take out two enemies, by himself, in one clean, seamless, double beheading. Valen had his solid gold shield with the head of a lion carved into the plate, the edges filed down to a razor-fine point. And last but not least, Jagyr Ethyron—that amped-up, hot-headed son of a bitch—had his simple but effective, heavily weighted mace: a blunt medieval weapon reminiscent of a club, with a stout bronzed head at the tip. Jagyr preferred to bludgeon his prey to death and scrub his hands in their blood as they expired.

Whatever.

The Emerald Lair would fight as if Axe was one of their own, and that was all that really mattered.

Allowing the molecules in his right hand to coalesce into a semi-visible image, Zane made several hand signals to the dragyri warriors, then gently inclined his chin. Even as Axe transported into the master bedroom, the remaining eight Dragyr transported into the house at once, their invisible personas slowly shimmering into view as they emerged behind, in front of, or beside a pagan enemy and struck like a nest of vipers.

* * *

Isolated from his sapphire and emerald backup, Axeviathon remained invisible in the master bedroom with his HK45 tucked inside the waist of his jeans.

He shifted his weight to his toes and dropped into a squat beside Tony and Amber's bed, balancing like a leopard about to leap forward. For all intents and purposes, the human male—Tony—was out for the count, his injuries and fatigue finally getting the best of him. Zeik and Grunge, two obvious demons, were huddled in the corner discussing the night's events in a fevered pitch, even as Trader Vice—*yeah, that was the sin-eater's last name, the one who had blinded Amber*—had helped himself to the master en suite's shower in order to luxuriate beneath the opulent jets. Although Axe wanted to kill the demon-bastard even more than he wanted to hurt Tony, he had to concede that Trader's self-indulgence was serendipitous: one less enemy for

Axe to contend with immediately...one less obstacle between the dragyri and his dragyra's ultimate safety.

Amber's safety...

The poor, golden-haired beauty was still panting and shivering, even as she lay back on the bed, knees up, both hands draped over her eyes, a steady stream of tears pooling from beneath her trembling fingers.

Axe couldn't think about that right now.

He had to remain both aware and alert.

He closed his eyes, just for a couple of seconds, and felt for the subtle shift in energy, the slightest change in the barometric pressure—*and yes, there it was*—the Dragyr had entered the residence. He tilted his head to the side, listening intently: a battle-axe splitting through bone; a Japanese katana slicing through flesh; fists pounding organs; and a high-pitched whir, just seconds before Caleb's morning star found an unsuspecting skull.

Curiosity got the best of him, and Axe opened his eyes, engaged his x-ray vision, and peered through the numerous layers of framing and plaster for the span of ten, maybe fifteen seconds. Although the images were dark, skeletal negatives of the original view, he could still make out what he was seeing: A shadow-walker had grasped Jagyr's mace, immobilizing the dragyri's brutal weapon, but the son of Lord Ethyron had recovered quickly, gouging both of the shade's eyes out with his thumbs, wrenching his fist sideways, and opening the enemy's head like a coconut. Having vanquished one pagan already, Rio walked up the side of a wall, scampered quickly along the ceiling, and dropped down atop an unsuspecting pagan, piercing the soul-eater's cranium with the tip of his katana before driving it home— down through the skull, beyond the throat, and deep into the body, effectively skewering the ink blot. Valen was tussling with another nasty vermin, and the hand-to-hand combat was wicked-quick, violent, and almost impossible to follow, until Valen dropped low, swept his leg along the back of the shadow-walker's knees, sweeping the pagan off-balance, and came down hard with the edge of his shield against the pagan's throat, slicing through flesh, bone, and sinew.

Enough already.

Axe couldn't afford to watch or waste time...

Furthermore, he wanted nothing between himself and Amber, and he was expending precious energy trying to maintain a state of invisibility. Radiating into view, he leaped from his perch beside the black-and-gold bed, snatched Tony by the bloody collar of his undershirt, and hurled him over his head, flinging the human male through a double set of sliding glass doors. Alive or dead? *Who knew?*

Amber screamed like the devil himself was assailing her, and Zeik and Grunge leaped to attention—but not before Axe withdrew his weapon and unloaded the clip into both demon torsos.

Son of a bitch!

They shimmered out of view.

The fucking pagans had evaded the bullets, and they were either regrouping, while invisible, waiting to strike back, or headed into the living room to get their comrades' backs. No doubt, they were keenly aware of the savage commotion by now.

Axe looped the gun over his thumb, allowing it to hang by the trigger, and he splayed all ten fingers wide, palms hovering—and circling—as he slowly tested the air. He was feeling for warmth, a telltale heat signature, the subtle taint of brimstone that always emanated from demonic souls.

Nothing.

The bedroom was empty.

Zeik and Grunge were gone.

He twirled the gun like a Space Age gunslinger, snapping it, lightning quick, back into his waistband, and then he headed toward the en suite bathroom to deal with Trader Vice. He could only hope and pray that the demon was still oblivious, perhaps lost in the sensory overload of a surging shower. True, Axe's first instinct was to scoop Amber from the bed, get the hell out of the residence, and bolt—but it was the second part of that sequence that gave the dragyri pause: He *had* to take the female outside, away from the confines of an interior building, in order to usher her into the portal, and Axe was keenly aware of how fast a demon could move...way too damn fast for his liking. The last thing Axe needed was to turn his back on Trader—with Amber in his arms, no less—and get caught unaware.

Not even for a millisecond.

He couldn't take that chance.

He started toward the bathroom, silently stalking his prey, when all of a sudden, his left ear buzzed.

Axe ducked, and a set of sharp, jagged claws swiped through the air, barely missing his jugular. He came up with a lightning-fast upper-cut, buried his fist in Trader's gut, and twisted to break as many ribs as possible.

The demon snarled with fury.

His taut lips drew back, and he hurled some sort of acidic spittle, aiming for Axeviathon's eyes.

Axeviathon coated both irises in scales.

In a movement so swift, the motion was a blur, Trader whipped a white towel away from his waist, twirled it into a rope, and summersaulted over Axe, landing behind him as he wrapped it around the dragyri's throat. He reached for both ends to tug it into a noose, but the left side fell limp and just hung there.

Axeviathon spun around, shook the towel off his shoulder, retrieved his HK45, and shoved the barrel against the demon's forehead. The pagan's luminous copper eyes grew wide. They shot from the barrel of the gun to the towel, now bunched on the floor, and then slowly drifted upward to the end of his arm. The son-of-a-jackal glared at the stump where his hand should have been, seemingly shocked that the limb was missing. *Well, no wonder he had not been able to draw the towel into a noose...*

Axe squeezed the trigger, and the demon vanished, both events occurring at the exact same moment. "Shit," Axe growled. He was *never* this careless—the freakin' clip was empty.

His dragyra's bloodcurdling screams must have made him sloppy.

And that told him all he needed to know.

To hell with the battle, and to hell with the pagans.

He needed to get his *fated* out of there.

CHAPTER THIRTEEN

T he darkness was like a living, breathing entity, the mouth of an enormous killer whale swallowing Amber whole. Fear had turned to anguish; anguish had blossomed into panic; and panic had risen to unrelenting terror, a violent squall that would not let Amber—or the whale that had taken her—go.

She couldn't stop screaming.

Her vocal cords felt abraded, her throat felt raw, and her heart was pounding so violently it felt like it might explode. What the hell had happened to Tony? So much broken glass! And the giant—that monster, Trader—where was he lurking now? Zeik had given Amber a sedative, and Grunge had carried her to bed, offering some pitiful explanation about the Cult of Hades and her eyesight returning in time.

What the fuck was that supposed to mean!

And then the bedroom had detonated into terrifying sounds —the entire house had burst into chaos: grunts, growls, furniture breaking—the nightmare just got worse and worse.

Amber wanted to get up and run.

She was finally ready to flee the state altogether—to hell with her bondage to Tony, Zeik, and Grunge; to hell with the extortion and the threat from her past—but the entire world was encased in darkness, and she no longer possessed the courage to even crawl across the bedroom floor.

"Shit," someone growled, and she grasped the coverlet with what had to be white-knuckled fingers, choking back her sobs—and her screams—long enough to grow quiet.

And listen...

Who was that?

Who was in the bedroom now?

Thump-thump; thump-thump; thump-thump...

Her heart was throbbing in her chest, and the muscles were constricting around her aorta. Amber was going to have a heart attack. "Who's there?" she whispered, turning her head swiftly to the left, then the right. "Zeik?" No answer. "Grunge?" Still silence. *Where the hell was Tony?* "Trader?" The word was a bitter curse on her tongue, and she immediately kicked at the covers, backpedaling as fast as she could until the crown of her skull struck the bulk of the headboard. "Ouch!" she cried out, biting down on her lip. *Who the hell was in the room?* "Stay away!" she panted. "Don't come near me!" She swiped her hand wildly in front of her, wishing like hell she had a weapon to fire.

"Shh, sweet angel." A deep, gravelly rasp.

Her ears perked up, and her throat constricted. "Who are you?"

"Amber..."

"Who are you!"

"Ambrosia, calm down—"

"Who the hell are you!"

"Just breathe, sweetness; I'm not gonna hurt you."

"Zeik!"

"Amber..."

"Grunge!"

"Listen..."

She didn't know his voice...or maybe...maybe...*what was it?* There was something familiar in that gritty sound. "Tony, where are you?" Her voice was quivering. The man crossed the room— she could hear his weighty footfalls, and the nearer they came, the more crippling her terror. "Don't come any closer," she begged him.

"I am *not* going to hurt you, Amber."

The coverlet rustled, and the mattress depressed as the stranger settled his heavy body beside her, heat radiating off him in waves. He leaned in closer, and she struck out with her fist, but her knuckles collided with a rock-hard chest. "Get away from me!" she shouted.

She punched him again!

Only this time, he caught—and held—her wrist. "Be still."

She shivered all the way down to her toes. "My boyfriend has money—he can pay you."

An eerie silence, and then it sounded like he *snarled...*

She instinctively jerked back and cowered, tucking her head inward like a turtle. "Please don't hurt me," she whimpered. She tugged on her arm in a futile effort to free her wrist from his iron grip—*holy shit, the man had the strength of a python.*

"Shh," he repeated, trailing his fingers from her wrist to her open hand. He grasped her more gently, placed his thumb in the center of her palm, and began to rub slow, methodical circles against her sensitive skin. "Listen to my voice, Amber girl. Shut everything else out, and just tune in to my words. Breathe... again...that's it...in and out; let your chest rise and fall while the world slips away. I'm going to carry you out of this bedroom, and you're not going to resist or scream. Your eyes are growing heavy; your heartbeat is slowing down; and you don't feel anything but peace and tranquility."

"Who are you?" She sighed the words, her voice growing drowsy—Zeik's sedative was definitely kicking in.

"Axeviathon," he said.

What a peculiar name.

"Axe...what?" She tried to repeat it, but her lashes were too heavy; they were steadily fluttering downward. "Where's Tony?" Something was wrong, terribly wrong—something didn't make any sense. She wasn't supposed to leave the house—she wasn't allowed to go out on her own—at least not without Zeik's or Tony's permission.

They would kill this guy.

Hell, they might kill Amber.

At the very least, they would finally turn her in.

"The bank," she murmured, feeling terribly loopy.

"Later," he whispered, "there'll be time to talk, later." He drew back the covers, encircled her waist, and slid one arm beneath the bend in her knees. And then he scooped her up like she was virtually weightless and carried her across the room. "Lay your head against my chest, sweet angel. I've got you."

All wrong...

This entire thing was all wrong!

But the sedative had completely taken over.

Lay your head against my chest, sweet angel...

He had also called her *Ambrosia...*

The bank!

The tall, muscular menace with dirty-blond hair...

The one with the swagger of a jungle cat and the aura of a Viking, the stranger with pupils ringed in sapphire.

What time do you get off work?

Where do you live?

Amber Carpenter *did* know that voice.

The air around Amber suddenly turned cool as the crisp

smell of grass and the clean scent of evergreen wafted to her nostrils on a summer's breeze.

And then, *snap!*

A distant whir...

A faint, droning whistle...

All at once, Amber felt like she was sailing through a long, endless tunnel: traveling, speeding, transcending time, traversing a thousand lands and a dozen lifetimes, encased in peace and endless tranquility...

And then the drugs took hold, once and for all, and the world became as vacuous as her eyesight.

CHAPTER FOURTEEN

TEMPLE OF SEVEN

Axeviathon watched with both interest and trepidation as Lord Saphyrius took Amber from Axe's arms, crossed the sanctuary in a dozen long strides, and waded into the center of the Oracle Pool, traversing deep into the pearlescent waters that ran along the northern end of the inner sanctum.

Axe had originally hoped that a strong, steady stream of healing silver fire would be enough to restore the female's eyesight, but he should have known instinctively that her blindness wasn't physical. The way Lord Saphyrius had explained it, it was a curse—a blight—a demonic abomination that had been tethered to her soul. The power behind the black magick had been granted by an all-powerful dark lord, and the spell would have to be unraveled by an equally omniscient deity.

Thus far, she had remained asleep—Axe's compulsion was still holding steady—but the moment she was submerged in the undulating currents of the living water, the diamond, emerald, sapphire, amethyst, onyx, citrine, and topaz waves, she would undoubtedly come awake.

And wasn't that just shit on top of shit...

Insult on top of injury and terror heaped on fear.

The female had been through more in the last twelve hours than the most courageous soul could withstand in a lifetime.

Lord Saphyrius brushed a partially translucent hand, coated with sapphire scales and presenting long, jagged claws, over Amber's limp body, and her pajamas vanished. *Son of a jackal!* Axe grimaced inwardly. *He could've at least allowed her the dignity of her undergarments.* But elements were elements—and energy was king. Who knew what might interfere with the dragon lord's shamanism...or with the Oracle Pool's healing tides?

Like metal drawn to a magnet, Axe's eyes swept along the length of Amber's body—it wasn't intentional, and it made him feel like a lecher—but her skin was so flawless, so smooth...so perfect. And her curves were so soft and supple—

"*Shit.*" He squinted and turned away, but not before cataloging the fact that Amber's deep, golden eyes and her equally radiant hair were indeed a part of her true, hereditary coloring.

"Axeviathon," Lord Saphyrius called, his powerful voice echoing in the lofty temple. "Come closer, dragyri—she will be frightened when she awakens."

Ya, think? Axe almost blurted, but he knew better than to get sarcastic with Lord Saphyrius. As the third deity along the dragon hierarchy, the dragon was a helluva lot better than Lord Dragos or Lord Ethyron, and he loved every male in the Sapphire Lair like they were each his natural-born hatchling, like they were each a Genesis Son, but he wouldn't hesitate to correct them or exert his almighty power if one of his servants forgot their place.

Axe had no desire to get tossed across the temple.

As it stood, he refused to even think about his upcoming date with Lord Ethyron. He would cross that unconscionable bridge when he came to it.

"Yes, Father," he replied, addressing the dragon as the sire of his lair. He stepped forward to the edge of the pool and watched as the dragon slowly lowered Amber—toes, then ankles; legs, then hips; waist, back, and shoulders, then finally her head—into the swirling waters.

* * *

Amber came awake with a start.

It felt like something soft, warm, and silky was undulating around her legs—*what the hell!*

Her eyes shot open *to utter darkness*, and she started to flail her arms.

Her head dipped below a waterline, and she opened her mouth and gagged.

Something drew her upward, lifting her head out of the water: something huge, something terrifying, something with hard, powerful, scaly hands. She spit out a stream of liquid and screamed at the top of her lungs, choking all the while, as she kicked...and kicked...and kicked, trying to swim backward, trying to get away...

From this thing...

From this nightmare...

From the rising tide of terror: a pitch-black world with disembodied hands.

And then she started to remember—she *sort of* remembered—Tony coming home, all beaten and bloody; that giant named Trader planting a kiss on her lips; the world going dark...

The blindness!

The sedative...

The chaos in the house.

Broken glass and someone approaching the bed...

Axeviathon.

The man from the bank, taking her from the bedroom.

She lashed out wildly, twisting and turning, continuing to flail her arms and kick her legs, as she blinked over and over...and over. And then the blackness became gray, and shadows appeared: soft, blurry outlines; a high-cathedral ceiling; swirling vortices of translucent colors, fading in and out as fissures of light.

The water was emerald, and sapphire, and purple.

The waves were onyx, and citrine, and topaz.

And all of it sparkled like shimmering diamonds.

She shut her eyes, drew a deep breath, and tried to quell her trembling.

She was still asleep—she must be dreaming. "Wake up, Amber," she whispered softly. "Wake up, wake up, *wake up.*" She slowly reopened her eyes and recoiled, too paralyzed by fear to move: Standing before her—above her, and all around her—was a massive creature radiating sapphire light. His enormous outline was that of a man—a huge, terrifying, all-powerful presence—and he was flanked by the silhouette of a dragon: a beast with horns, a scaly snout, and almond-shaped eyes that glowed like two cauldrons of fire. He was massive, haunting, and staring straight through her.

Her jaw fell open, and she started to back away.

"Amber." Someone to the left of the dragon called her name, and her eyes shot in that direction, but she didn't dare turn her head. "Sweetness, don't be afraid."

It was him!

Axeviathon.

The man in her bedroom...the man from the bank...and her chest started to rise and fall in desperation. The Viking was terrifying in his own right—he had scared the shit out of her earlier, both in her room and at the credit union—but faced with what was looming in front of her, he seemed like the better of two horrific options. She glanced down at the water, her eyes drawn by an ascending wave, and realized for the very first time that she was standing in a large framed-in pool.

The air whooshed out of her, and she gasped.

Holy shit!

She was also completely naked.

Her hands shot to her breasts, and panic virtually engulfed her: Where had the Viking taken her? And what the hell were they planning to do to her? "No," she muttered in a desperate voice, finally finding the courage to rotate and flee.

"Do not!" the dragon bellowed, and she froze in her tracks.

"*Amber...*" Axeviathon's voice again. "Be still."

As if by its own accord, a puppet held stationary by a marionette's strings, her body froze, then glided back around, until she was once again facing the dragon. And then her head lolled forward in slow, measured increments, dropping into a silent, reverent bow. *What the hell...what the hell...what the hell!*

"Ambrosia Leanne Carpenter," Axeviathon said—*and how the heck did he know her full name?*—"I present you to Lord Saphyrius, third deity of the sacred Temple of Seven, ruler of Dragons Domain, creator of the dragon sun, the dragon moon, and the Dragyr race, and keeper of the sacred sapphire: god of my pantheon, father of my heart, and master of the Sapphire Lair. He has just healed your blindness as a favor to me. Honor him with your spoken appreciation, and then show him your esteem with silence."

As if the puppeteer had just released her, Amber felt her muscles relax; and while every cell in her horrified body urged her to turn and swim, something deeper—something wiser—told her she had better stay put.

Exactly where she was...

Exactly *as* she was.

Her mind raced to grasp hold of something...*anything*...she could process that might make sense. This was way too...wrong...

overwhelming...unnatural to be real. But if it was still a dream, then she didn't know how to get out of it: *He has just healed your blindness as a favor to me. Honor him with your spoken appreciation...*

She swiped her bottom lip with her tongue and kept her eyes averted, downward. "Thank you," she whispered. It was the best she could do.

A hand snaked out of the silhouette, curving through the air as it grew closer—claws, scales, and sapphire veins—appearing in her subordinate vision.

Her subordinate vision...

Amber could see!

Her eyesight was perfect—it hadn't really sunk in until that moment.

"Thank you." She said it again, only this time, she meant it.

The creature stroked her cheek with the back of his claws. "You're welcome, my daughter." And then he waved his "hand" along the outline of her body, and she was suddenly clothed in a sapphire robe. "Axeviathon, take her home."

Amber's nostrils flared, and her eyes grew wide.

My daughter...

Axeviathon, take her home...

From where she stood in the otherworldly pool, it was deep enough to swim in, yet shallow enough to wade in...to walk if she really tried. But somehow, all she could think of—as if a dragon, a crazy dream, and a terrifying Viking were not enough to consume her—was a small, dirty, and hot convenience store on a terrible August day: walking away with Tony Rossi and entering a whole new, chilling life.

Why did she have the sinking feeling that it was all happening again?

Only this time...*only this man*...would make Tony look like a lamb as compared to a lion.

She raised her chin and turned her head, finally taking in Axeviathon's appearance: messy, dirty-blond hair, a bloodstained muscle-shirt, nothing but sinew, iron, and muscle. He had a thick upper lip, angular cheekbones—the overall appearance of a savage warrior—and once again, there were those deep-black pupils, framed in sapphire irises: intense, brooding eyes, staring right back at Amber.

He held out his hand, and she gawked at it.

He crooked his fingers, and she shook her head.

"Go with the son of my lair, Ambrosia Carpenter," the dragon creature commanded.

Holy shit. Amber sighed. *You can do this, Amber; you've done it before. Just put one foot in front of the other and pray that it's only a nightmare.* Rotating her hands in a circular motion to displace the water in front of her, Amber leaned forward, let the pool accept her weight, and began to swim toward the terrifying Viking.

CHAPTER FIFTEEN

2:00 AM

Tony Rossi groaned in agony as he tugged on the IV cord and tried to turn on his side in the stiff, uncomfortable hospital bed. He was surly, confused, and in a boatload of pain: *What a freakin' shit storm this night had turned out to be.*

First, that crazy-ass bastard Trader had stepped up to him at the bar and dragged him from his bar stool, across the crowded dance floor, and out into the alley, where he had beat the living shit out of him. Tony never knew what hit him. One minute, he was throwing back a beer; the next, he was caught in an iron choke hold; fifteen seconds later, he was outside in the alley, trying to fend off a jackhammer fist coming so fast at his face, the movement was nothing but a blur, and that was to say nothing of the granite-hard leather boots stomping his internal organs and cracking his ribs like chicken bones.

The beating felt like it had gone on for hours, but in truth, it had probably lasted ninety seconds, two minutes at the most. Try as he might, Tony had not been able to block a single devastating punch or to deal his attacker a single counter-blow. And Zeik and

Grunge had let the whole thing happen, which was almost as shocking as the random, brutal beat-down.

But the nightmare hadn't ended there.

Somehow, Tony had ended up back at home—he really didn't remember much, other than lying in his bed beside Amber; drugged, but still in an ungodly amount of pain; and dressed in his skivvies and undershirt—when someone had snatched him by the collar, tossed him into the air as if he was virtually weightless, and the next thing he knew...

Bam!

Smash.

A loud and stunning explosion—glass flying everywhere.

Panic, terror, and confusion.

And then waking up in the hospital, high on morphine: stitches, IVs, a neck brace, and a shit-ton of confusion. Just what the hell had happened? And where was Amber? Where were Zeik and Grunge?

No sooner had the thought crossed his mind than a large burly figure—with dark, narrow eyes and a skull-trim so faint he could've been bald—stepped out of the shadows as if emerging from the half-drawn curtains. Suddenly, Zeik was flanked by Grunge, the latter's flame-red beard glowing in the light of all the blinking monitors.

Tony rolled back onto his back and cursed—the pain was indescribable. "What the hell, Zeik?" he grunted.

Zeik stepped up to the bed. "You're lucky to be alive, Rossi."

"No shit," Grunge blurted, dragging a chair across the sterile floor and plopping into it like he was too tired to stand any longer. "We all are."

Tony furrowed his brows. "What the hell happened?"

Zeik bit his bottom lip and snarled. "Brother, there's a bunch of shit you don't understand, and up until now, you've only had half the picture...the Cult of Hades...the boss we've referred to as

Lord Drakkar...what's really going down at King's Castle Credit Union on a much, *much* deeper level."

Tony's stomach knotted. It wasn't like Zeik to sound so cryptic, and who knew—maybe it was just the drugs, but it looked like the guy's pupils were glowing, blazing a hell-fire red.

"Gotta get you the hell outta this hospital room," Grunge added. "That was never supposed to happen, but—"

"Nosy neighbors called the police." Zeik finished his sentence.

"What?" Tony mumbled. "Who..." He struggled to keep his eyes from closing. "Where's Amber? What happened at the bar —*what happened at the house?*"

Zeik reached for the IV line and yanked it out of Tony's arm, even as Grunge sighed, leaned forward, hefted his weight onto his over-developed thighs, and started working on the oxygen tubes and then lowering the guardrail. "Don't talk. Just listen," Grunge ordered.

And just like that, the males went to work.

They untangled Tony from all the medical contraptions while spitting out a story so outrageously bizarre, Tony knew he had to be hallucinating: The Cult of Hades was more than a criminal sect, and the whole religious piece—the ritualistic worship of dark, evil spirits—was more real than Tony could have ever imagined. Zeik and Grunge were demons, not humans, and they had both been *feeding* off Tony's sins for years: his pride, his greed, his lust, and his envy.

The guy in the bar, also a sin-eater, was named Trader Vice, and Lord Drakkar—the Pagan King—had ordered both Tony's punishment and Amber's blindness.

And the shit that had gone down at the house?

It was more unbelievable than the rest. The freaky dudes with the slinky, shadowy bodies were also called pagans, only they fed on human souls, rather than sins; and somehow—for some reason Zeik and Grunge still didn't get—they had drawn a host of dragon-enemies to the house, and that was the commotion Tony remembered hearing. That was how—who, what, and why —Tony had been tossed through the glass patio doors.

"No, not dragons! *Dragyr*," Zeik corrected Tony for the tenth or eleventh time. "They're sons of dragons, the offspring of gods. They live in a world beyond a portal, and their fathers—and ours —were cut from the same ancestral cloth."

Tony would not have believed any of it.

Not one single word...

Except three things caught and held his attention. One, the loathing and *fear* in Zeik and Grunge's voices: Tony had never heard such reverence for "Lord Drakkar" or fear of any enemy in either male before, and it somehow just made sense—all the years together, the shit they got away with at the bank, the way they controlled other people and fought like they were damn near supernatural...

Apparently, Zeik, Grunge, Trader, and a couple of shades— two, to be exact—were the only souls left standing, still alive, after the Dragyr's lethal attack, and Zeik and Grunge had only lived by retreating, fleeing the house and the master bedroom like a couple of whimpering cowards. Tony had only lived by accident; he had lived because the dragyri hadn't cared enough to check his pulse after tossing him through a thick pane of glass.

Two, both Zeik and Grunge's eyes were glowing while they spun their tale and worked on Tony—*worked to close his wounds and remove his stitches; to heal his organs and fix his broken nose* —using nothing more than their fingertips, some freaky incanta-tions, and a thick black serpentine smoke.

And third, Amber *had* gone blind.

Tony had heard her screaming and felt her panic.

This night might be unthinkable, but it was definitely real.

And that brought Tony, front and center, back to the most

terrifying revelation of all: The Dragyr must have taken Amber, because her body wasn't at the house, a blind girl couldn't just take off and run, and Zeik and Grunge had only been able to track her scent as far as the backyard—as far as a dragyri would've had to go before he could open "the portal."

Amber Carpenter was missing.

Tony's girl was gone.

And it didn't sound like Zeik and Grunge were too terribly interested in getting her back, like the demons or the pagans —*whatever the hell these entities were*—were willing to pursue their dragon enemies in order to rescue Amber.

"No, not dragons!" Zeik corrected him again. "*Dragyr*, Tony. They're called Dragyr."

Tony blinked three times as if coming out of a murky dream. "Then Amber...whoever took her...whichever Dragyr...he'll either rape her or kill her on the other side of this portal? We'll never see Amber again?"

Grunge stroked his beard. "Nah, I don't think so—that's not how a dragyri works."

"Dragyr...dragyri...sons of snakes...who gives a shit what they're called?" Tony murmured, letting off some steam.

"When they want human women for pleasure," Grunge continued, ignoring Tony's groaning, "they take them here on Earth. They only take them through the portal for one reason."

"To keep them," Zeik supplied. "She'll either serve the Seven in the temple, or—shit, who knows?—it seems impossible, but she could be the male's dragyra."

Tony's heart constricted in his chest. "What the hell does that mean? Serve in the temple? *Serve, how?* And what the hell is a dragyra?"

Grunge held out his hand, clasped palms with Tony, and drew him out of the hospital bed. "It's a female mate, someone chosen by the dragon lords to bear dragyri sons for the Pantheon, a *wifey*, if you prefer human speak."

Tony blanched.

"He'll be back," Zeik grunted.

"Who?" Tony asked, gingerly following his demonic room-mates to the hospital door. "We're just gonna walk right down the hall?"

Grunge chuckled. "Humans only see what we want them to see, Tony. We'll do whatever the fuck we please. And yeah, I agree with Zeik. If Amber's a dragyra, her mate will be back."

Tony's head was literally spinning, whether from the over-load of irrational information, the lingering morphine, or an unhealed head injury. He didn't know, and he didn't care. "What makes you think so?" His voice reflected his hope.

"Because at some point," Grunge said, "the dragyri is going to glimpse Amber's memories, and when he does, he'll be gunning for a handsome shit-bag of an Italian human."

"He won't rest until you're six feet under," Zeik supplied. "What we did to Amber that day in the store...what we've done every year since...you can bet your ass he's coming for you, brother."

Tony visibly recoiled. "But...but you guys have my back, right? I mean, nothing has really changed between us? This god, the king of the underworld"—he absently rubbed the tattoo at the back of the neck—"I'm one of his followers, right? Even if I didn't completely get it before tonight? Lord Drakkar isn't just a...a crime boss...he's...he's a freakin' savage god?"

This time, it was Zeik who laughed, and his voice was absent of light, humanity, or even amusement. He spun around so quickly, Tony never saw him move, and then he snatched the human by the throat, lifted him three feet off the ground, and slammed him against the nearest wall.

His eyes were more than glowing.

They were hate-filled, feral, void of a soul.

"Let's get one thing straight," he snarled in a guttural tone. "Lord Drakkar had a message for you: *Let him know that the lord of the cult he worships is terribly displeased with his laziness.* You are *nothing* to Lord Drakkar." Zeik extended five claws from his unencumbered hand and drew a line, trailed in blood—from the curve of Tony's chin, down the center of his throat, to just below his collarbone, with the tip of one talon—and then he dipped his head and lapped the blood with his tongue. "And as for me and Grunge? You're chattel, prey, *dinner.* You will live or die at our whim. You're alive right now because we're waiting for a word from Trader...a word from our sovereign. Do we kill the human bitch because he knows too much, erase some of his memories and keep him to do Lord Drakkar's earthly bidding, or do we use the worthless bastard as bait to draw out the dragyri in question. Lord Drakkar is not going to take kindly to twelve dead pagans; if you're lucky, he will demand revenge, in which case your piteous human life still has value. Are we copacetic, Rossi?"

Tony trembled all the way down to his toes.

What the hell had just happened?

When he had woken up that morning, he had a very sweet life: a shitload of money, a beautiful girl, and a bad-ass arrangement that nearly guaranteed a life of decadence, invincibility, and power. And just like that, the tables had turned.

Tony was now on the bottom of the food chain.

And nothing—*absolutely nothing*—was as it had seemed.

What a freakin' shit storm this night had turned out to be...

Indeed.

* * *

Ghostaniaz Dragos stared at his heavily coffered ceiling, counting the glistening reflections in the beams and the paint as he crossed his ankles on the oversized mattress and squinted against the light of the dragon moon.

"You went through the portal yourself!" Lord Dragos had reprimanded him earlier, pissed over five or ten insignificant minutes, the time between Ghost's arrival on Earth and Axe showing up at the nightclub.

What-the-fuck-ever.

Would the madness never quit?

And now, because the dragon lord owed Lord Ethyron a favor, he was loaning Ghost out as payment...and punishment...as if Ghost gave a shit either way.

Ghost owed Lord Dragos.

Lord Dragos owed Lord Ethyron.

And Axeviathon Saphyrius—the male who had just found his mate—owed seven pounds of flesh, seven pints of blood, and seven broken bones to the emerald god, for providing the use of the Emerald Lair's mercenaries.

Talk about your Game of Thrones.

These jackasses needed a hobby.

So be it.

The way Ghost saw it, he was getting off easy—instead of getting whipped, or beaten, or tortured, himself, he was to be used as Lord Ethyron's weapon. Ghost would deal out Axe's torment, and everyone's sadistic impulses would be satisfied—all debts would be paid.

And once again, Lord Dragos would try to teach Ghost a lesson.

The same infernal lesson he had been teaching him since that childhood night in the alley: *Thou shalt pledge thy eternal fealty to the sacred Dragons Pantheon*, and mercy doesn't pay. When Daddy orders you to hurt someone, to annihilate someone, to make a sport out of torture—or to dine on one's heart—you do it with gusto, or else.

Got it, Ghost thought, rolling his eyes and turning his attention back to the shadows on the ceiling. If he stared hard enough at one particular beam of moonlight, it almost looked like a snake, coiling back to strike.

Huh, he thought; shadows could be interesting.

And comforting.

And Ghost had no problem uncoiling that snake.

He would strike Axe so hard—and so swiftly—the male would never know what hit him, and Daddy wouldn't get the satisfaction of watching Ghost sweat.

The male had stopped sweating centuries ago.

CHAPTER SIXTEEN

3:00 AM

A xeviathon Saphyrius—but he went by the name of Axe
—occupied the entire lower level of the Sapphire Lair.
And just who called their residence a lair, anyway?
The garden-level apartments were immaculate and modern,
reminiscent of an urban warehouse with their exposed brick
walls, wooden crossbeam accents, and plush, luxurious furnish-
ings. There was an elegant kitchenette woven seamlessly into the
contemporary architecture; a palace-sized bathroom fit for a five-
star spa; and rows and rows of garden-level windows, all framed
in arched black ironwork, stamping the suite with a gothic appeal.

Now, as Amber sat on the edge of Axe's oversized sofa, her
feet tapping nervously on the wide-planked floors, she gripped
the mug of hot mint tea between her fists and tried to make sense
of what was happening:

Axeviathon was a dragon...

No, correction—he was a dragyri male, a member of the
Dragyr race.

He had lived for over 225 years in a world he referred to as
the Pantheon, beyond a portal that linked to Earth, a portal he

had taken Amber through when he had removed her from her house on Syracuse Lane. And if that wasn't farfetched enough, he had explained that Zeik and Grunge were demons, pagans who came from the underworld, but temporarily resided on Earth. More than likely, they had been feeding on Tony's sins for decades and doing the bidding of some horrific dark lord. And as for Tony, he belonged to the Cult of Hades, which was something Amber had always known; only, she'd had no freakin' idea what it really was.

The tattoo engraved on the back of Tony's neck was not what Amber had once believed: The witches' pentacle on the pommel of a sword, with a reversed numeral seven just below the cross-guard, had never been a leftover insignia from an old motorcycle gang, a crew Tony had run with before he had met Amber—before he had hooked up with Zeik and Grunge. According to Axe, it was a pledge of devotion and a mark of ownership: a stamp placed on the followers of the pagan lord.

Only Tony thought the pagan lord was a crime boss—or had he always known?

Her temples throbbed for a minute...

Was she getting all this right?

She couldn't be sure.

As far as Amber was concerned, Axe may as well have told her that Dorothy wasn't really from Kansas—she was from Chicago—and Toto wasn't really a dog. He was a three-headed serpent who lived in Poseidon's sea, and Axe had taken Amber to a hotel on Mount Olympus, where she would have to do more than click her heels three times to find her way home.

The lion was really a warlock; the scarecrow was actually a ghoul; and the tin man wasn't missing a heart—he ate them when he wasn't skipping clumsily down the yellow brick road!

It would have been every bit as plausible as Axe's story...

The tale he was spinning to frighten her—or confuse her—which one, she didn't know.

But a few things about the psychotic tale were resonating in her gut, niggling at the back of her mind, and beginning to gain a tiny foothold in the realm of reality—outrageous reality, but reality just the same: First, the bank, King's Castle Credit Union; Warren Simmons had the same tattoo as Tony, and the man got away with murder on a daily basis. There was no way KCCU should have been able to embezzle so many funds, to launder so much money, or to work with so many criminal enterprises in broad freakin' daylight.

And Zeik and Grunge...

They had always seemed superhuman in their own right: all-powerful, nearly invincible. Humans didn't fight like that. And the giant, the one called Trader, he had stolen Amber's eyesight with nothing more than a kiss. *And oh,* lest one forget that enormous beast—*the godlike being*—that had loomed over Amber in that indoor swimming pool, the one with claws, scales, and sapphire veins...

If dragons actually existed, then *Lord Saphyrius* sure fit the bill.

But why Amber Carpenter?

Why some golden-haired girl from nowhere with such a tragic history and an equally pathetic past?

Why would Axeviathon Saphyrius, son of the Sapphire Lair, want Amber so badly?

Why had he acted so brazenly that day in the bank?

"Amber girl." He called her name from across the sitting room as he perched on a dark leather ottoman, and his voice, as usual, was like smooth, melted butter...butter being spread over shards of glass. "You feeling any better?"

She blinked several times. Now, wasn't that just the question of the century. She was feeling like she was about to pass out, and she was so very tired—she needed to sleep—but she didn't dare close her eyes in this...dragyri's...lair. "I'm fine," she muttered, lying through her teeth, but she wanted to keep him as far away as possible. She didn't want him anywhere near the sofa.

"I know it's a lot to take in," he said.

She took another sip of her tea. "Mm hm."

"*Amber*," he prodded, "look at me."

She stared into the center of her mug.

No way.

Those eyes—those strange, mystical, fire-rimmed pupils; those sapphire irises—she didn't want to see them again. They were too real, too haunting, too powerful. And they threatened to bring her entire world crashing down...forever. Because if this was real, then Amber was truly up shit creek without even the hope of a paddle. She grimaced and closed her eyes. She would have never thought she would miss Tony Rossi or long for the mundane life she was stuck in, but in this moment, she would've given almost anything to turn back the hands of time... to be safe at home, her feet up on the sectional, watching a movie next to her long-ago captor...assuming he was even still alive.

A deep, nearly inaudible growl drew Amber out of her musings, and her eyes shot open and fixed on Axe. "Did you love that man?" he asked her bluntly, and she almost spilled her tea.

"Who?" she whispered.

"Tony," he grunted, and then he tilted his head to the side and paused. Amber felt a tickle beneath her scalp, like a feather penetrating just beneath the surface, before he added, "Rossi. The guy in the picture frame that says *Amber and Tony*. Are you in love with him?"

Amber gulped. She bent to set her mug on the floor before she spilled it, and folded her hands in her lap, and then for the very first time since he had entered the bank, she allowed herself to really study Axe, to scrutinize his features, beyond those mystical eyes: his expression, his coloring, his body language.

To, once and for all, take it all in...

At first glance, she was stunned by the obvious—and it wasn't like she hadn't noticed it right away, but she hadn't fully absorbed it. Axe Saphyrius was quite possibly the most gorgeous *anyone*, male or female, she had ever seen in her life. He had the kind of good looks that screamed playboy or billionaire, the kind of guy who might travel around Europe in a Lamborghini with a different supermodel on his arm every week, with one glaring exception: Axeviathon wouldn't fit in a Lamborghini, and he was rugged and earthy from the top of his beautiful head to the tips of his sexy toes. He would probably fit more comfortably in a five-thousand-pound pickup truck, and he would be far too restless to engage in the mundane, bored out of his mind with a superficial woman.

Her eyes swept over his hair.

Again, it was striking...flawless...the way it framed his face, yet on closer observation, not one single strand was in place. It just fell in random sweeps and lifts that happened to look perfect: the top, kind of up and to the side; several dirty-blond fringes falling forward into his eyes; still other wisps of thick, unruly tresses framing his sharp, angular jaw like it had been layered to accentuate his eyes. It was just shy of shoulder length, and some of the ends curled under, while others curled out. It was wild, but tame. Unruly, yet stylish. It was rugged and multilayered, just like the man.

His skin wasn't exactly dark or light, but the perfect satura-tion of melanin, and maybe it was because he hadn't been home in a while—he hadn't had a chance to follow his usual routine—but there was a definite shadow around his jawline, his chin, and his lips, where a slightly darker shade of hair had grown in: his chiseled jawline, his strong, almost arrogant chin, and his well-defined lips, which looked like they had been sculpted by the hands of an artist. Perhaps dragyri were simply cut from a different cloth.

And as before, his eyes were magnificent, and it wasn't just their extraordinary color. Even if they had been brown...or green...they would have been stunning because of their narrowing, oblong shape, the way they followed the set of his brows so seamlessly.

Amber shifted restlessly on the couch.

Humans were not that flawless.

Their features were not that symmetrical.

And even when they had deep-set eyes, they weren't mesmerizing in their intensity.

It was as if all the years of his very long life were reflected in those sapphire flames.

She stared down at her fingers.

"Is that a *yes*?" he murmured, and she almost jolted.

"Excuse me?"

"Rossi. The human. The nature of your relationship."

Amber's nostrils flared, and she bit down in annoyance. "It's none of your business," she said in a whisper.

He chuckled then, a deep, gravelly sound, and swept his fingers through his hair. It fell right back into that perfect, haphazard shape. "Oh, Amber girl, I don't mean to frighten you, but everything about you is my business."

Her eyes shot back to his. "Why?" She couldn't believe she had the courage to question him—not now, not here, not while she was completely at his mercy—but what she didn't know could definitely hurt her, and Amber would rather have all the facts.

He sighed, and then he slowly nodded. "Every dragyri male has a fated dragyra, a human female who is meant to be his mate. And once he finds her, he has ten days to claim her, to present her to the lords in the temple. That morning in the bank, when I passed by your station, my amulet heated up—it burned me." He absently thumbed a gemstone necklace hanging loosely around his throat. "And just for an instant, your eyes turned deep, dark blue...sapphire...matching the color of my ruling lair. For me, for my kind, it was a sign from the Seven—from the dragon lords that rule the Pantheon. It meant that you, Amber Carpenter, are my *fated*. The woman I have waited centuries to find."

Amber's jaw dropped open as she tried to make sense of his words.

To at least put them in context, even if she couldn't comprehend them.

To draft a roadmap and devise a plan. If she couldn't break through his psychosis, she could at least play along with it—humor the guy until she figured a way out of wherever she truly was.

But this was way too much.

She closed her mouth and pursed her lips, yet her muscles twitched, her nerve endings grew sensitive, and her heart began to beat like a drum in her chest.

Fight or flight in full effect.

To hell with it.

She rose slowly from the sofa, turned her head to measure the space between the living room and the nearest exit, and then leaped onto the cushions, hurdled the backrest, and sprinted like a gazelle trying to outrun a cheetah as she dashed toward the door to the suite.

CHAPTER SEVENTEEN

A xe cursed beneath his breath.

Well, that had gone over well.

Shit...

He didn't possess a communication style beyond blunt and way too candid.

He rose from the ottoman and stroked his chin: He could stop her with his voice, take command over her body, chase her down like a wild animal, or try to call her back.

As if...

He focused his full attention on the large wooden twelve-panel door to the suite instead: dropping the latch, holding it steady, and waiting as she pried...and pried...and twisted at the handle.

"Amber girl..."

"Stay away from me!" she shouted.

"Amber." He took several long, steady strides in the female's direction. "Calm down. I'm not going to hurt you."

She spun around, and her eyes were wild; her throat was

actually convulsing. "Let me go!" She pressed her back against the heavy door and began to tremble from head to toe.

Axe tried to gentle his voice—he really did. "Amber, just breathe." He placed both palms against the wooden panel, laterally, behind her—one to the left of her shoulders, the other to the right—and he leaned in closer. She looked like she was going to faint. "Relax." He repeated the sentiment, only this time, he laced his voice with power, adding a dash of mind-control to the suggestion.

She swayed to the side, and he caught her by the arm, gently setting her upright. "Even if you could get this door open, there's nowhere for you to go. Come back; sit down. Better yet, try to get some sleep—we can speak some more in the morning, hash it all out in the daylight."

Her frantic gaze shot across the suite, fixing unerringly on the raised king-size bed in the corner, and she rapidly shook her head. "No way."

Axe's head fell forward until their foreheads were touching, and his dirty-blond hair mingled with her rich golden bangs. He knew it was too intimate, both brazen and intrusive, but he also understood something she didn't—the strength of their inherent bond. He had the power to comfort this woman with his touch, to steady her with his nearness, and the way he saw it, hands were out. If he cupped her jaw or stroked her cheek, she might actually try to bite him. As it stood, he was pinning her in, but he saw it more as a shelter than a cage. "Listen, Amber girl, and not just to my voice—listen to what you're feeling inside. You're tired, you're overwhelmed, and you're not going to process any of this unless and until you get some sleep. I'm not going to harm you, and you know that deep inside. Listen to what your intuition is telling you."

She peered up at him through thick golden lashes, the long

tips wetted by teardrops. "I think you're crazy," she whispered. "That's what my intuition is telling me."

He pulled back a couple of inches and locked his gaze with hers, still leaning into her slender body. "No, you don't," he argued. "If anything, you're terrified that I just might be sane."

She blinked three times, and a tear escaped, rolling softly along her delicate cheek. "I want to go home, back to my room-mates. Back to my life...where I'm safe."

Shit...shit...and double-shit.

To hell with it—she was breaking his heart.

He placed his hand on her jaw and brushed away the tear, gently, with the pad of his thumb. "Back to your roommates?" he rasped, though he was genuinely trying to soften his tone. "Back to Zeik and Grunge, *the demons*, and Tony? The guys who invited a host of shadow-walkers into your living room? The guys who stood there and did nothing as Trader took your eyesight... cursed you with blindness...the roommates who stood back and watched you panic...and suffer? The ones who just let you scream? Or the ones who gave you a sedative and put you to bed, leaving you to suffer in darkness and terror?"

Amber bristled. "You took me from my home."

Axe nodded and dropped his hand. "I took you to the temple, to Lord Saphyrius."

She raised her chin and held his stare. "You handed me over to some, some dangerous creature who could've killed me."

"And yet, he restored your eyesight." Axe bit down on his lower lip and sighed. "You might not get this, you might not understand it...yet, but I heard you scream in that living room— and I understood full well what was happening. I did what I had to, to remove the threat and to get you away from Trader and those pagans. And I took you someplace where you would finally be safe, and while you might not trust me, at least you can see me with your own two eyes. And unlike Tony, Zeik, and Grunge, I'm exactly who the hell I say I am. The way I see it, Amber girl, I'm the only person in your world right now that you *can* trust."

She rolled her eyes and scoffed. "Trust? You're kidding, right? *Trust?*" In an act of courage that was honestly impressive, she planted both hands squarely on his chest and shoved.

He didn't budge an inch...

And not because he was being defiant, but because it felt more like the tickle of a butterfly's wing than a serious attempt to move him.

He took a step back out of courtesy, and she placed both hands on her hips, the fear in her eyes betraying the insincerity of the confrontational posture. "I don't trust you, Axe, and I don't want to be here. And even if everything you're saying is true, you don't know me...you don't know my life...and you don't know my story." Her jaw tensed in anger, and she nearly ground her teeth. "And you have no idea just how much you have in common with Tony, *the man that I love.*" Her eyes shifted up and to the right as she spat those last words with venom, and Axe knew she was trying to goad him—she was smart enough to pick up on his inherent jealousy, his innately possessive nature, and bold enough to try to strike where it would hurt.

Amber Carpenter was a fighter, through and through.

Whatever her life's story, it had taught her to be brave, to be defiant, to go down fighting, rather than retreat. And as for those beautiful, dark, amber-colored eyes, the pupils glazed over with anger, fear, and moisture; they had shifted at the exact same moment her blood pressure, pulse, and respiration had spiked— they had mirrored her electrodermal response, an automatic increase in her sweat gland activity, and Axe had read it all like a book...

Amber wasn't just stretching the truth, she was out-and-out lying.

So, she *hated* Tony Rossi...

What gives?

"What did he do to you?" Axe grunted, trying to keep his own physiological reactions in check.

Amber blanched. "What? *Who*?"

"The man *that you love*," Axe echoed, with equal sarcasm. "What do I have in common with Tony?"

She faltered, but only for a moment, her hands falling from her hips, her shoulders curling inward, and her fingers gripping the sides of the mystical sapphire robe she was still wearing. She looked off into the distance, beyond Axe's shoulders, and her smooth, arched brows curved down into a frown. This time, she was accessing a memory, and despite Axe's best intentions —*damnit, he had already invaded her privacy far too much and too often*—he couldn't help but glimpse the scattering of images, the random, crisscrossed projections hurling through her mind:

A hot August afternoon, walking into a convenience store, and then earlier this night, staring up at Trader...right before he had kissed her.

A green-and-blue blanket, a baby stroller, and an uneven stack of potato chips, empty boxes, and doughnuts—all contrasted against the sounds, smells, and feel of Amber's living room, watching Zeik and Grunge walk in with a battered Tony Rossi.

"Don't move! Don't speak! Don't even breathe!" Zeik barking orders at a handsome cashier.

Then, "Penalty kiss, courtesy of Lord Drakkar," Trader snarling.

The images were moving in and out, fast and furious now: Grunge shimmying behind a security camera, Tony perusing an aisle like a stalker, all three males concealed in hoodies—then the inky, terrifying silhouettes of the shadow-walkers as they entered the foyer on Syracuse Lane.

Amber experiencing the same fear and dread.

"Looks like we may have just found a teller for King's Castle Credit Union," Grunge snorted; she was back in the cramped convenience store...

"Did you really think Lord Drakkar was going to be A-okay with the shit that went down at the bank?" Trader snarled...back in the terrifying living room.

"*Shit*," Axe mumbled as the remainder played out, Amber's memories bouncing back and forth between the past and the present—*she had only been fifteen fucking years old when Tony had abducted her*. She was twenty-five now, and the way she saw it—it was all happening again.

He stepped toward her, placed his pointer and middle finger against the hollow in her temple, and sent a small pulse of energy into her medial temporal lobe to stop the flow of images, to halt the horrific, incessant memories in their tracks—enough was enough.

She jolted and stumbled back.

He caught her, placing one hand at the small of her waist and tunneling the other in the back of her hair. "With the gods as my witness"—he bent to whisper in her ear—"I swear to you, Amber girl, this isn't the same. Rossi wanted to own you, to use you, to keep you like some pet. I want nothing more than to honor you and make your life worth living...celebrating. You had no choices, no power, no free agency. You were only protected as long as you did Tony's bidding. In time, you will come to know power and choice beyond your imagining here in the Pantheon, and I am the one who will live to do your bidding. Tony and I have nothing in common. I will never, ever hurt you, Amber. You are not my pet; you are my greatest treasure. And I will cherish you, if you will let me."

Stunned by his words and overwhelmed with emotion, Amber squirmed out of his arms and took several paces to the side, her eyes darting around the room in panic. And then she pressed both hands to her ears as if trying to shut it all out.

She was exhausted.

Overloaded.

And her mind was reeling.

"You can read my mind?" she muttered, weakly.

Fuck.

"Yes, and I'm sorry. I didn't mean to invade your—"

"That shit Trader said," she interrupted. "*Penalty kiss, courtesy of Lord Drakkar...that, and the girl's eyesight.* Then it's true, isn't it? Trader was...he *is*...a demon?"

"Yes," Axe murmured.

"And you; you really are a...a dragon?"

"A dragyri," Axe said.

She shook her head. "And Warren's tattoo...King's Castle Credit Union..."

"It's a shell company, an arm of the Pagan Underworld, heavily staffed by members of the Cult of Hades."

She doubled over and gagged, and he leaped forward to steady her, placing the palm of his hand on her stomach to keep her from retching. "Breathe, Amber girl; just breathe." He used another electrical impulse to quiet her stomach muscles before he scooped her up in his arms and headed toward the back of the apartment.

Her exhaustion must have been all-consuming because she laid her head on his shoulder and wept. "Everything," she murmured, as he pulled back the covers on his oversized bed and placed her gently beneath the sateen sheets, "everyone...and everything...has been a lie. My entire life has been nothing but a lie."

He had no words as he reached for a pillow and slid it softly beneath her head.

"I know that people call it Stockholm syndrome," she

rambled listlessly, "feelings of trust or affection from a victim toward a captor, but I really thought that, at least over time, Zeik and Grunge had my back." She barked a hollow laugh, and it was as cynical as it was empty and heart-wrenching. "And I thought, at least in the only way a sociopath could, that somewhere in his broken soul, Tony actually loved me. That it wasn't *all* just possession."

Axe closed his eyes, willing the irises to remain sapphire, praying his pupils would remain deep black—because all he could see was deep, blood-red rage, and his fangs were pressing against his gums, threatening to extend against his will. His dragon's fire was blazing like a torch, and he wasn't sure if he could contain it much longer. "I think he lost his soul to the darkness, long before he met you." He paused and grit his teeth. "But if he could have...loved...if there was any remnant of a sentient soul left in him, I'm sure he would have...must have...loved you. Maybe that part of him did." She would never know what those words had cost him. Axe wasn't a male to bleed empathy and kindness, but Amber was hanging on by a thread. "Sleep, Amber girl." He used another compulsion, but hell's bells, what else could he do? Axeviathon was wrung out, himself, and his beast was practically clawing to get out.

As her eyes drifted shut and she sank into the pillow, he bit into the flesh of his hand.

Tony Rossi wasn't just lost to the darkness.

He was marked.

He was chattel.

He was a dead man walking...

If he wasn't already deceased, then Axe was going to end his miserable existence. If the flight through the glass doors hadn't already claimed him, Axe would feed on his fear before he strung him up by his own intestines and scattered what remained of his ashes to the wind.

Axe might not be able to get to Zeik and Grunge, not without starting an all-out war between the Dragyr and the Pagans, but Tony was human—or at least he had been—and that meant he was either six feet under or he was still earthbound.

It was just a matter of following up.

And then it was just a matter of time...and opportunity.

CHAPTER EIGHTEEN

THE NEXT DAY – PAGAN UNDERWORLD

Beneath the thick, murky haze of the underworld's sky, Trader Vice paced atop the gothic castle battlements until he came to a naturally concealed dark gray parapet and perched on the edge of the stone. Requiem Pyre, Lord Drakkar's chief sorcerer and most esteemed member of congress, seemed to appear out of nowhere as he emerged from the fog, linked both hands behind his back, and narrowed his steely deep-blue eyes on Trader. "Soooo," he hissed, his long, dark hair flapping in the wind, causing the numerous plaits of bones and ancient fox shells to clamor against one another, "your little escapade on Earth cost us the lives of how many shades, again?"

Trader bit his bottom lip.

It was a rhetorical question.

It had to be.

Besides, he only had one hand left, and Requiem was renowned for setting traps. Trader wasn't walking into this one.

"And with the exception of two shadow-walkers, Zeik, Grunge, and yourself, of course, are the only pagans who survived, demons, all the latter." He cracked his knuckles behind his back.

Trader didn't bite.

"Ah, yes, and two worthless humans: Antonio Rossi, who now knows of our kind, and Amber Carpenter, the human's female pet." He unlinked his hands and held two fingers up as if he were testing the wind. "Ah, but then she is no longer Antonio's female pet; she is now a ward of the Pantheon. Am I leaving anything out?"

Trader cleared his throat.

"From what you surmise—from what we *all* surmise—Axeviathon Saphyrius delivered the box of chocolates to the bank, which means he most likely came into contact with Amber the same day. And it was the Sapphire Lair, after all, accompanied by their emerald brethren, who slaughtered our shadowed kinsman. So, either the seven lords desired this utterly random human female as a servant in the temple, or Axe and his lair mates had another, more intimate purpose for taking her through the portal. And while Lord Drakkar is terribly vexed at the loss of his loyal patrons, *you* feel all is not lost entirely? Have I summed this up correctly?"

Trader suppressed the urge to hock up some phlegm and spit it at the sorcerer's feet. Nonetheless, the condescending diatribe was getting old.

"Have you lost your voice as well as your hand?" Requiem inquired.

Trader averted his eyes. "I can speak just fine." He didn't see the backhand coming, but he felt the burn against his cheek and tasted the blood on his tongue. *Shit*; Requiem must have knocked out a tooth.

"Let me tell you what *I* am going to do for you," Requiem continued, as if the insult had never happened. "What Lord

Drakkar's chief sorcerer and an ancient practitioner of demono-latry is going to give you in order to appease our king."

Now this caught Trader's attention: *So, they were going to let him live?*

"First, you might have killed the dragyri male Axeviathon if you hadn't been missing a hand." He flicked his wrist in a dismissive gesture, making it clear that the limb would not be restored. "So, we do see that while your punishment was appropriate, it may not have been...most practical. I will give you...*something*...to take its place, if only in battle, if only to seek revenge. And as for the latter sentiment —vengeance, that is—we can only hope and pray to the darkness that the dragyri male returns through the portal to finish what he and his lair mates started. Antonio survived. Zeik survived. Grunge survived...as did you. Perhaps these are loose ends the son of Lord Saphyrius will wish to close. Perhaps Zeik and Grunge are correct in assuming the male will seek some sort of chivalrous retribution on behalf of the simple girl." He shrugged. "Who knows." And then his deep blue eyes turned glassy, crimson, and unambiguously demonic.

He took two fluid steps backward and held out both hands, flingers splayed, horizontally, to the deck of the battlements. His claws curled inward and began to drip blood, each droplet sizzling like grease in a skillet as it made contact with the ancient granite.

And then the blood began to coalesce.

And the coagulated film became like fog.

The fog grew dense, sticky, and granular until it mirrored liquified soil.

Trader gasped. Though he had only seen the substance a half-dozen times in his five centuries of living, he would recognize the grisly quicksand anywhere. The pernicious substance could trap and hold anyone—for a time—even an immortal dragyri, rendering the body unusable; the supernatural powers inaccessible; and destroying the captured one's ability to fight back. Requiem had chosen to conjure an incredibly powerful spell, which meant only one thing: Lord Drakkar was well and truly pissed.

The king wanted revenge.

Requiem smiled, and the grin was as wicked as it was devious. "Our lord wants Axeviathon Saphyrius. For the insult at the bank, for the insult at the house, for the incessant, vexatious battles the Dragyr continue to wage against the Horde. Kill a few demons here...kill a few shadows there...never wage war against the underworld, but strike like cowards, over and again, in these petty little skirmishes, hidden in the dark. And for what? Usually in the defense of human women." His voice grew to a thundering crescendo. "Enough!" he bellowed. "Our lord has had enough."

He flexed his hands in the quicksand like a baker kneading bread, and then the colorful, creative bastard withdrew one hand from the mixture, reached behind his back, and retrieved a living, squirming, turquoise-and-black tiger snake out of thin air.

"Shiiiiit!" Trader leaped back.

Requiem's smile broadened. "Cat finally released your tongue? Good." He tossed the snake into the viscous, granular concoction and continue to stir it with his hands.

Trader shook his head.

Being a demon was one thing—they all had dark, supernatural powers—but the chief sorcerer freaked him out. He watched as Requiem practically bathed in the substance, immersing his body up to his chest, and all the while, the fiend ignored the crazed, infected snake who was whipping around in a frenzy, striking at imaginary ghosts, and snapping its tail like a lash. The tiger snake was mad with the desire to kill, possessed by the need to secrete venom...

And then just like that, Requiem reached out a long, spindly arm and grasped Trader by the back of his neck, drawing him closer and closer to the thick concoction and the perverse, frenzied snake. Trader tried to draw back, to wriggle free, but the sorcerer's grasp was immovable. Requiem recited several short incantations in the ancient pagan language, and Trader's jaw fell open, his mouth opening wide.

The snake dove inside the cavity and tunneled down Trader's throat.

The quicksand rose like a geyser, exploding from the earth, and followed the tiger snake's trajectory, burrowing into the demon and filling Trader's body like a badger fleeing an enemy, scrabbling into an underground tunnel.

Trader choked and gagged.

He flailed and jerked.

He felt like his sternum was going to explode and his intestines were about to fall out. And worse—so much worse—he could feel the tiger snake slithering, in and out, around his rib cage. He opened his mouth to scream, but no sound came out.

And then the world was quiet, and his body quit resisting.

Everything settled, and Trader stood up, tall.

Requiem threw back his head and roared with laughter. He paced several tight circles around the demon, then shackled Trader's right wrist, held it in place, and swiped at the demon's face with five bloody claws.

Trader jerked back, extended his left arm, and caught the sorcerer's strike before it could land—

He caught the sorcerer's strike!

With what?

His left hand?

No, not his left hand—he caught it with the mouth of the tiger snake, the head of the snake—the serpent was now an extension of Trader's wrist.

The snake sank its fangs into Requiem's palm and, at last, excreted its venom.

Requiem Pyre moaned like he was having an orgasm, and then he shook out his hand, took a step back, and the snake-head disappeared back inside Trader's left arm. "You will never have a left hand again, Trader," the sorcerer purred. "Our king does not retract his punishments, but the next time you need the limb to fight, your reptilian servant will be available to strike for you." Pleased with his work, he once again linked his hands behind his back and brought the conversation back, full circle, to where it had begun. "Your little escapade on Earth cost us the lives of too many shades, but there is yet a prize to be salvaged. The next time you vomit—and you can do so at will—your body will release the quicksand, and at least for the next two to three minutes, your prey will be immobilized...paralyzed...utterly helpless and absent of power." He narrowed his gaze and lowered his voice, wanting to emphasize his next words. "Be very clear, Trader: This gift is not a reward—it's an obligation. If you can grasp your enemy while he is caught in the sand, I can pull both of you through to the underworld. Can you even imagine what a gift that would be for our king, a dragyri male to torture for all eternity? The ability to strike at the hearts of the Seven so effortlessly, so frequently? Recompense for all these trifling battles..." He sighed and nodded his head. "But, as we all know, the Dragyr rarely travel alone, so if faced with a choice—to claim a prize for our king, or to exact vengeance by destroying an immortal dragyri—you are free to choose the latter. Take the male's head, remove his amulet, and return the talisman to the king instead. Axeviathon's death would be an acceptable substitute if you cannot deliver the dragyri to our world. Are we clear?"

Trader whistled low beneath his breath, recognizing the true, reciprocal nature of the gift he had just been given. "Crystal," he said, because yeah, he got it.

He understood what his dark lord wanted.

Moreover, he was burning to seek vengeance himself.

Trader didn't know how long it would take, whether he would have to follow Tony, Zeik, or Grunge, whether he would have to wait for Amber to emerge once more from the portal, or whether a decade or more would pass before Axeviathon Saphyrius set foot on the third planet of the Milky Way galaxy, but Trader could be a patient demon—and he would wait forever if he had to. "I *will* deliver the dragyri to our king, one way or another," Trader reassured Requiem, knowing full well that he had just pledged his word, and if he failed, Lord Drakkar would end his existence, retract his immortality.

Requiem sucked in a sharp breath of air and appraised Trader more thoughtfully. "Very well, then. I would say our business is concluded."

"Almost," Trader argued, raising his left arm. "There is still the matter of my new left hand. What do I owe you, Requiem?"

The sorcerer bowed his head and grew quiet. After a moment of pensive silence, he whispered, "The tiger snake was spawned from my magic. As such, I can feel his rage and desperation. I will know when he strikes, when he excretes his venom, and as before, I will always find it exquisitely pleasurable. Use him often, Trader, with yourself, with women, in every creative way you can imagine, and I will derive secondhand satisfaction from each depraved act you—and the serpent—engage in."

Trader averted his gaze.

Yeah, the chief sorcerer really freaked him out.

So Requiem wanted Trader to use the snake, both in battle and *sexually,* on women's bodies—*on men?*—for self-satisfaction. There was just some shit that should be off-limits.

But whatever.

In for a penny, in for a pound.

Trader had gone too far to turn back now. "It will be as you wish," he murmured, stifling a shudder.

CHAPTER NINETEEN

A mber awakened to the aroma of freshly brewed coffee wafting through the apartment and a golden ray of sunlight streaming over her cheeks. She sat up abruptly, pulled back the covers, and rubbed her eyes, trying to get her bearings.

Where was she?

This wasn't her bedroom.

And she wasn't wearing her familiar pajamas; rather, she was dressed in a huge, draping white T-shirt that fell all the way to her knees. *A man's undershirt.* She shook her head to clear the cobwebs. Hadn't she fallen asleep in a sapphire dress —no, a robe—a mystical, ethereal, almost gossamer robe, one that had been placed on her body by an equally mystical dragon?

Yeah, she remembered now...

Like the golden rays streaming through the garden-level windows and highlighting the rustic ironwork frames, the memories flooded in: Axeviathon taking Amber to the temple; the dragon god healing her eyes; returning to Axe's suite—to his lair—

and learning the truth about Zeik, Grunge, and Tony. Amber falling apart and Axe carrying her to his bed.

Sleep, Amber girl, the dragyri had said...

And that was the last thing Amber remembered.

Axe must have changed her clothes while she was sleeping, or maybe the enchanted robe had magically faded. She cringed at the thought of the dragyri seeing her naked, even as she swung her legs over the side of the mattress and placed both bare feet firmly on the floor.

"Good morning," a female voice called out.

Amber jumped from the bed and spun around, startled to find a beautiful, auburn-haired woman, about five-foot-eight, smiling from behind the galley-style island, making herself at home in Axe's kitchenette.

What the hey?

"I brewed some fresh Kona coffee—I hope you like it strong— and I have some bagels, cream cheese, and fresh fruit as well," the auburn-haired lady continued. "Jace, Axe's roommate, cooked a huge breakfast this morning, and we saved one of everything for you...just in case. So, if you prefer bacon or eggs, sausage or pancakes, or even cinnamon rolls, just say the word."

Amber combed her fingers through her tangled hair and frowned. "What time is it?" Considering all that was happening, it was a nonsensical question, but it was the first thing that came to her mind.

The woman set the coffee, bagels, and fruit on a silver tray, then placed a knife, fork, and napkin beside the food, and slid the tray forward on the counter. "It's about 10:30 AM. You slept the morning away, and I can't say that I blame you." She stepped out from behind the island and lightly tapped her hand to her chest. "I'm Jordan, by the way, Zane's mate. My...*husband*...is another one of Axe's roommates. He is also a dragyri male and a member of the Sapphire Lair."

Amber didn't want to be rude.

After all, this was the first halfway normal person she had run into since Axe had brought her through the portal, and for all intents and purposes, the woman was being really, *really* friendly. But strange was strange, and the shit was too real...and too messed up...to ignore. "Where is Axe?" she asked Jordan, hating that the words came out clipped. "What are you doing in his apartment? And forgive me for asking, but what exactly are you... What kind of a thing..." She paused in an effort to rephrase the question, to sound more polite. "Are you human or what?" It was the best she could do.

This time Jordan sighed, and her expressive hazel eyes darkened with compassion. "Axe wanted to give you some space, but he didn't want you to wake up alone. Thus, the reason I'm here. He's upstairs in the la—in the house—and I am a dragyra, just like you."

Amber gulped, trying to process the woman's words: *I am a dragyra, just like you.* No, Amber highly doubted that, but she chose to leave it alone. "You were about to say *lair*, weren't you?"

Jordan nodded. "Yes, but there's no need to make a difficult situation even worse; some words are more...intimidating...than others, when they really shouldn't be. House...lair...this is a lovely home, and the difference is purely semantic."

"Right," Amber blurted. "Semantic. Like dragon, dragyri, and dragyra. Just a matter of degrees—or scales, horns, and spiky tails —because all of this is really normal. Nothing to see in this...*lovely home.*"

Jordan's demeanor grew altogether serious, even as her brows curved into a frown. "You're right, Amber; there is nothing normal about this. There is nothing familiar about where you are, what we are, or the last twenty-four hours you've lived through. And believe me, I don't mean to make light of any of it. I was in your shoes less than three weeks ago—yep, tomorrow will be week three—and just like you, I was a normal human woman living a boring, everyday life. I had a good-paying job, friends I saw on a regular basis, my own condo, and a ton of future plans. Needless to say, none of them included Zane or the Pantheon—so yes, you're correct, and I get it."

Amber slowly nodded.

So, Jordan wasn't one to bullshit—she told things like they were.

Good.

In a rare act of reciprocity, Amber opened her mouth, and her next words just kind of spilled out. She told Jordan everything— the fact that she had grown up in so many foster homes; what had happened at the convenience store on that hot August afternoon; how she had lived with Grunge, Zeik, and Tony for so many years; and what it was like working at the credit union. And unlike the night before, when Axe had read her scrambled memories, the story was clear, succinct, and in chronological order—she had simply blurted the CliffsNotes version as if she could no longer hold it in.

She didn't know why she did it.

She had never done anything like that before...

Perhaps she was losing her mind, the stress was getting the best of her, or some infinitesimal part of her soul still believed she was dreaming...

"So, as you can see," Amber concluded, "my life was anything but normal, and I didn't have any future plans. My job sucked— everything I did was illegal—and I didn't really have any friends. In fact, as it turns out, I was living with two demons and a cult worshiper and working for...for the Pantheon's enemies."

If Jordan was shocked by Amber's confession—or her total lack of boundaries—to her credit, she didn't let on. Her complexion grew pale, but only for a moment, as she listened without interrupting. Finally, she brushed the palms of her hands over her jeans and said, "I have no idea how much Axe knows about you, your life, or your past, but he didn't tell me any of that. Just the same, I had already pieced some of it together: The other night, Zane fought along with Axe and the other males to get you out of your...your unfortunate circumstances." She patted the top of the counter. "Please, sit down. Have something to eat. At least have a cup of coffee. It won't do you any good to starve yourself or to refuse our hospitality. That was a lot to disclose, first thing in your morning, and you're going to need your strength to get through the rest of the day." She pointed at a large blue duffle bag sitting on the floor beside a barstool. "Besides, I brought some women's sweats, some jeans, and a couple of T-shirts that might actually fit. There's some socks, underwear, and toiletries as well —the typical female line-up." She smiled, and her eyes nearly sparkled with empathy. "It's not what you're used to, I'm sure, but it'll do for now, at least until you can collect your familiar belongings. Because by the way—and just so you know—you will be allowed to collect them, or someone will do it for you. I still have my condo, my friends, and many of my future plans. Your life won't come to an end just because Axe has claimed you— mine didn't."

Amber stared at the bag and winced.

Your life won't come to an end just because Axe has claimed you...

What the hell was that supposed to mean?

So, Axe was planning to keep her...forever?

Even as the thought crossed her mind, an ember of hope warmed in her chest: If Axe allowed Amber to collect her belong- ings—if her life didn't end, here and now, in this apartment—then that meant she would someday go back through the portal.

Eventually, Axe would take her back to Earth.

And when that happened—*Holy Mother of Mercy*—Amber could still escape.

She could still get back to Zeik, Grunge, and Tony, assuming all three were still living, and the powerful trio could help her, hide her...get her away from Axeviathon. *Yeah, she got it!* she argued with her subconscious mind, as something deep in her stomach twisted at the thought of returning to that horrible bondage. After all, everything Axe had said was true: Tony had stolen her...used her...kept her like a plaything or a pet all these years, and neither Zeik nor Grunge had lifted a finger to protect her from that bastard Trader.

The Cult of Hades, whatever it truly was, had taken advantage of a fifteen-year-old girl in order to staff their corrupt credit union.

No, Amber wasn't an idiot.

She got it—she really did.

But she also got the power of the *familiar*: the comfortable duvet on her king-sized bed; the feel of snuggling beneath a throw on the living room sectional; the sound of hard, plastic pool balls breaking on the table when Zeik, Grunge, and Tony relaxed in the rec room during a Friday night game...the warm burn of a shot of brandy flowing down Amber's throat. She had learned to live the life she had been given, and she knew how to play the hand she'd been dealt. Her routine was familiar; her life was comfortable; and love her, hate her, use her, or betray her, she knew Zeik's deep voice, recognized Grunge's flared nostrils, the way they twitched when the guy got angry, and she knew the feel of Tony's strong hands. Even if his touch was sometimes caustic, she knew it better than she knew herself. And the fact that Zeik and Grunge were demons? The fact that Tony worshipped some underworld god?

What could Amber say...

They were the same men...the same males...she had known for a decade.

Nothing but the context had changed.

Hell, she couldn't explain it, and she didn't want to—Amber's life was hers, and hers alone. And over the years, she had made her peace with it. She didn't want this unfamiliar world. She didn't want Axe and all his words of compassion...tenderness...or desire. Frankly, his passion and intensity scared the shit out of Amber. She knew coldness and darkness, how to be somewhere—and with someone—yet remain inherently alone.

The aroma of fresh coffee overwhelmed her senses, and Amber felt drawn to the kitchen, even as she felt exposed.

Too exposed.

She had said too much...divulged too much...when she had no intentions of making this place her new home. She would have to keep her deepest thoughts to herself, going forward.

Ambling to the kitchenette, she climbed onto a barstool, picked up the fork, and forced an amiable smile. "Thank you," she said softly. "For the breakfast and the company."

Jordan took several wary steps back and leaned against an interior counter. "What just happened?" she asked. "The sudden shift in your demeanor?"

Amber raised her brows and then quickly spread some cream cheese on a bagel and stuffed it in her mouth. She couldn't talk if she was eating, and hadn't Jordan encouraged her to eat? Jordan crossed her arms over her stomach and stared, but Amber pretended not to notice. She continued to sip her coffee and take slow, careful bites of the assorted fresh fruit.

"Trauma bonds," Jordan finally blurted.

Amber set down her fork. "Excuse me?"

Jordan closed her eyes and nodded, and when she opened them again, they were dark, serious, and fixed on Amber like she was staring straight through her, to her soul. "Trauma bonds," she repeated. "That glassy, faraway look you just got in your eyes; that sudden defensive posture in your shoulders; the way you appeared to be pining for home—"

"Were you reading my thoughts?" Amber interrupted, her voice growing icy. Of course, she was pining for home—anyone would be. Hadn't she just been kidnapped?

Again...

"No," Jordan insisted. "I would never do that, Amber, but then again, I didn't have to. Do you think I didn't want to get the hell out of this Pantheon? You think I didn't actually try to escape?" She waved a slender, elegant hand through the air, her fourth finger adorned in the most exquisite ring Amber had ever seen, and gently shook her head. "Before Zane...before all this...I was a prosecuting attorney for years, and in that capacity, I saw a lot of things, met a lot of people, and I learned a few things about victims...and crisis." She pushed off the counter, took several steps forward, and bent over the bar, resting her upper-body weight on her elbows. "Amber, when someone is thrust into a crisis, when their entire life becomes a high-stakes venture—all about chaos, turmoil, and self-protection—when you never have control, and your well-being is constantly threatened, whether physically, emotionally, or otherwise, the mind and the body find a way to adapt."

Amber leaned back on her stool and stared at her plate, even as her stomach began to curdle. She didn't like where this was going. Despite her impulsive confession earlier, this woman still didn't know her, and she didn't want to hear Jordan's...*insight*.

"There are actual chemicals released in the brain every time we experience trauma," Jordan continued, "epinephrine, norepinephrine...cortisol...and like a roller coaster that goes up and down, the body changes its chemistry to adapt to the never-ending ride. It gives us what we need to survive in a crisis, but when that crisis never ends, it turns it into a drip-line of sorts. It spikes or dilutes on a regular basis, depending upon the level of stress, until we literally develop an addiction...or a physical need...to use those chemicals to get through our daily lives."

Amber rolled her eyes. "And I suppose you call those *trauma bonds*," she mocked.

Jordan nodded. "When *being afraid* wakes you up every morning; when being hurt, or used, or mistreated defines your afternoon; when lying beside a man you really don't want to sleep with, night after night, is always on the menu; yeah, your brain creates a brilliant chemistry to get you through each terrible event. Hell, just to get you through each day. Problem is: Over time, you need those chemicals every bit as much as someone on meth needs their next fix. You need it to wake up, to get through the morning, and as crazy as it sounds—you need it to feel sane, to feel safe." She stood up straight and shrugged her shoulders. "All I'm saying, Amber, is if you're feeling homesick...if you're idolizing your life...if you think that going back where you came from would be better than Axe and the Pantheon, then part of that, at least some of it, might not have anything to do with what you're processing here, or how you're weighing your newfound circumstances." She held up two fingers to halt any protest, before she'd had a chance to finish. "Don't get me wrong: I'm not implying that you liked the trauma, deserved the treatment, or preferred the betrayal you were living—I can't imagine what that was like for you. I'm just suggesting that part of what you're feeling...experiencing...is withdrawal, a need to have your daily fix of the chemicals you've relied upon to survive for so long."

At this, Amber picked up her fork, slid the tray across the island, and threw the utensil. She didn't aim the fork at Jordan, though it came fairly close to the woman's head, and she didn't mean to make such a clatter as the silver tray—and all its contents—tumbled to the galley floor and spilled all over the hardwood.

Patient as a saint, Jordan didn't flinch. "Those trauma bonds, and the need for those chemicals, are every bit as strong as your need for food, air, and water."

Amber practically snarled. "So, what happened in my house Monday night—that demon who stole my eyesight; Axe taking me away from my life and whisking me into some foreign portal; you standing here, now—a total stranger—lecturing me about something you know nothing about"—her voice rose with her angst—"that's not trauma? That's not abuse? That's not going to make my fight-or-flight chemicals shoot through the roof? Who the hell do you think you are?"

Jordan stepped up to the island and placed her hand over Amber's. "Why are you crying?"

Amber sniffed. "I'm not crying; I'm angry."

"You should be," Jordan said softly, and then she slowly removed her hand. "But as long as we're putting everything out on the table, there's something else I think you should know. It's something Zane asked me *not* to tell you, but I get the sense you're tougher than you look. You've survived a hell of a lot more than the last thirty-six hours..."

Amber blinked away a reservoir of pressing tears and bit down on her lower lip, which was trembling. She wasn't sure she could take much more of this, and she was a little bit ashamed of her outburst.

"When Axe saw you in that house," Jordan continued, "when Trader took your eyesight...the dragyri almost came unglued. You were surrounded by pagans, demons, and shades, and they could've killed you in an instant, faster than Axe could've moved to stop them. So, he called out to his lair mates to ask for backup, but there were too many pagans in that residence. Axe needed a second lair, just to be certain. Some of the males who fought that night—*who fought to get you safely out of that dangerous situation* —were from another lair, and their lord, their ruling god, charged Axe a pretty heavy tax for their assistance."

Amber blinked three times. She had no idea where Jordan was going with this. "What kind of tax?" she whispered. "What are you talking about?"

Jordan grimaced, and for the first time, her eyes reflected some real discomfort. "Axe has forty-eight hours—well, more like thirteen or fourteen now—to turn himself in to the temple in order to *pay up*. He has to be there by midnight." She made air quotes with her fingers as she spoke the words *pay up*. "He owes Lord Ethyron, the ruler of that other lair, seven pounds of flesh, seven pints of blood, and seven broken bones as payment. And trust me, Lord Ethyron is going to collect." She paused to soften her tone, even as her throat visibly convulsed. "I just want you to think about something the next time you're missing home: What have Zeik, Grunge, or Tony ever sacrificed on your behalf? What would they be willing to give in order to keep you safe? What would they have traded for your protection...or your eyesight? And I also want you to think about this: Even when you answer those questions, you're still going to want to go back. And that's fine. I get it. No one is saying you should feel happy right now—you would be crazy to feel anything other than trapped, panicked...confused...even desperate. You're nowhere near being ready to give Axe a chance this soon, not at this juncture; you're still just coming to grips with all that has happened... But what I am saying is that the desire to go back... Amber, that may be something altogether different, and at some point, you're going to have to deal with the trauma bonds as a completely separate issue. For the record, I think Axe could regulate your body chemistry—he could heal that imbalance for you, if you ask him...if you let him. And I know for certain that Lord Saphyrius could do it. You have a boatload of shit to contend with going forward, more than enough to consider and think about; fighting a powerful addiction doesn't need to be part of the mix. And hate me if you will, but one woman to another—*no one deserves the hand you were dealt.* If I can help you with what's happening here and now, please, just reach out."

As if on cue, three brisk knocks resounded against the twelve-panel door, and Axeviathon turned the handle and strolled in. He took several long, purposeful steps toward the kitchenette, then stopped dead in his tracks and frowned. Unerringly, his eyes swept over Amber, ostensibly making note of her pressing tears, even as he studied Jordan's protective posture—and then his gaze surveyed the mess on the floor, and the tips of his canine teeth crept down beneath his raised upper lip. "What's going on here?" He spoke in a chillingly calm and even voice.

Jordan forced a tentative smile, rounded the corner of the island, bent over to retrieve the blue duffle bag, then hefted it onto the counter. The moment she released it, she placed her hand on the small of Amber's back. "Probably not what you were hoping for," she said, politely, to Axe, and then she immediately turned to Amber. "Women's clothes, basic necessities, and fresh undergarments...let me know if you need anything else. And Amber?"

Amber met Jordan's hazel gaze and waited—there was nothing but true compassion, if not friendship, in those eyes.

"I know I could've handled this better. Heaven knows, I didn't mean to preach, but I took one look at you, recognized your character, and I just knew I needed to keep it real. If nothing else, you've had more than enough bullshit to last several lifetimes. I'm sorry if I added to your distress."

Amber stood up from the stool and backed away.

She wasn't sure if she was retreating from Jordan, from Axe, or from the whole damn situation—she just knew she needed some space. Still, there was one thing she wanted to clarify, and it was probably best that Axe didn't hear her words. She crooked her fingers at Jordan and waited.

The woman stepped forward silently. She bent her head and

angled her chin, placing her delicate ear just inches away from Amber's mouth. "What is it?"

"The flesh, and blood, and bones," Amber whispered, "that wasn't just an analogy, right? You actually meant he's going to be tortured?" She didn't know why she cared. She didn't know *if* she cared. She only knew that she had to be certain.

Jordan mouthed the words: "It's literal."

Amber raised her chin. "Then keeping it real...no bullshit, right?"

"Right," Jordan said.

"He has to have skin in this game," Amber murmured. "There's something he wants, something he needs, something that only I can give him—is that true?"

"Yes," Jordan said. "That's true."

"Will you tell me, later...whatever it is?"

Jordan stood to her full graceful height and slowly shook her head. "No. I can't do that, Amber—it's not for me to tell. But Axe will tell you everything when the time is right."

Amber cleared her throat, then took a slow, deep breath.

She knew Jordan had told the truth earlier. Amber had heard about Stockholm syndrome, and she knew the brain produced chemicals to deal with stress and fear—she wasn't so naïve as to believe she had come through the last decade unscathed. Yet and still, the nightmare behind her—the life she still preferred to return to with Tony, Zeik, and Grunge—seemed to pale in comparison to the nightmare before her, the fate she was facing with Axe.

Dragon gods...

A hidden realm...

Supernatural warriors—or mercenaries—creatures unlike anything she had ever known.

And this one, the dirty-blond standing ten feet away, staring at Amber with such an intense, piercing gaze, he was strong enough—determined enough—to offer his blood, his flesh, and his bones in exchange for a stranger's freedom, for Amber's freedom...

Only to bring her here.

What in the name of these dragon lords did Axeviathon want from Amber?

Just what the hell had she gotten into?

CHAPTER TWENTY

Axeviathon watched as the door swung shut behind Jordan, and Amber made her way silently to the couch. He strode into the sitting room, picked up the ottoman resting in front of an adjacent oversized armchair, and plopped it down in front of her. And then he took a seat, leaned in toward Amber, and rested his elbows on his knees, his chin on his hands. "What the heck just happened here? You copacetic?"

Amber visibly blanched and leaned as far away as possible, pressing her back into the cushions behind her and folding her arms around her stomach. "No, Axeviathon—"

"Axe is fine," he interjected.

"No, *Axe*, I'm anything but copacetic right now."

He studied her tired features, the weariness in her dark amber eyes and the hard set of her beautiful mouth, and he wished he could give her more time...more space...leave her alone for a day or two so she could process what she'd learned so far. Problem was: They didn't have a whole lot of time. It was already day three in the ten-day cycle—Axe had seven days before he had to take his dragyra to the temple for conversion—and almost worse than that, he had to meet up with Lord Ethyron before midnight.

By eleven fifty-nine, to be exact.

But who was counting?

The point was: When the emerald dragon got through exacting his seven pounds of flesh, seven pints of blood, and seven broken bones, Axe would be out of commission for the next seven hours, if not longer. Lord Ethyron had forbidden the dragyri from healing his wounds any sooner than that time span; and that meant Axe wouldn't be available to comfort, teach, or get to know his dragyra...at least not until he had fully recovered.

He would be no good to Amber.

And whatever had happened during her conversation with Jordan—the tray of shit strewn across the floor was a small indication—if there was something he needed to repair, he had to do it now...today. True to his supernatural nature, he had heard the ladies whispering. He hadn't tried to eavesdrop; he had even tamped down his hearing. But there it was—he had heard every word. So Amber knew about Axe's upcoming torture, and she also knew that the dragyri wanted her for a very specific and selfish purpose: *Thou shalt propagate the species by siring dragyri sons and providing the Pantheon with future warriors. In so doing, thou shalt capture, claim, and render unto thy lords whatsoever human female the gods have selected to become dragyra. And she shall be taken to the sacred Temple of Seven—on the tenth day, following discovery—to die as a mortal being, to be reborn as a dragon's consort, and to forever serve the sacred Pantheon.*

Okay, so she didn't know the latter...

But the question would eat away at her until she did.

And Axe wasn't quite ready to divulge that much.

Still, he needed to make some inroads...now.

"Your conversation with Jordan was rough?" he asked her, knowing it was a rhetorical question. "Anything I can do to help?" He flipped a wayward lock of unruly hair out of his eyes with a sweep of his fingers and waited.

Amber made fleeting eye contact, bit her bottom lip, and stared down at her lap. "I told Jordan a lot...things about myself... the kind of things you saw in my memories about Tony, Zeik, and Grunge, what happened when I was still a teenager."

Axe nodded slowly, reached out to squeeze her hand, then just as quickly withdrew his touch. "All right." What else could he say?

She sighed. "And Jordan told me about that green dragon god, the shit—*the stuff*—he's going to do to you. That it's happening because of me."

At first, Axe chuckled at her reference to a green dragon god—Lord Ethyron would lose his cool if he heard that, but all the same, Axe's stomach clenched. "The Emerald Dragon Lord," he corrected, not because he gave a damn about her vernacular, but because it was never too early to instruct his female—it was Axe's job to keep Amber safe, to initiate her into life at the Pantheon, and learning how to avoid offending one of the Seven was always a good place to start. "As for the shit he's going to do to me," he added, "and you can say *shit*—or worse—around me, Amber; I've lived for 225 years, and I've never been a gentle or proper male. Trust me, my language gets worse than that. As for anything happening *because of you*: You don't need to worry about my well-being, sweet angel. That's between me, my lair, and our lords. Not your fault. Not your responsibility. It wasn't your doing, Amber. You're *my* dragyra —your safety in that house was my responsibility, and it always will be. Given a choice between suffering or watching you suffer..." He shook his head and snorted. "No contest, sweet lady."

At this, Amber looked up at him and actually held his stare.

Her eyes brightened for a fleeting moment, and Axe registered a real spark of attraction—he felt what Amber felt when she looked at him.

She squirmed in her seat, but this time, she didn't turn away. "Maybe," she whispered, "but I'm sorry just the same." She swallowed so hard, he saw the lump in her throat, and then she added quietly, "And for whatever it's worth, I don't think I ever thanked you; I mean, for the eyesight, fixing the blindness thing." At this, she finally looked away and folded her hands in her lap. "Don't get me wrong: I don't want to be here, and you had no right to take me. And that doesn't mean that I'm...that I'm open...to anything you need from me. I'm just saying that I'm glad I'm not blind, and I recognize that you played a big part in that."

Understanding how difficult this was for her, he reached out to cup her jaw in his hands—he couldn't help it. Almost by instinct—or maybe because she was just so damn beautiful and vulnerable—he stroked her cheeks with his thumbs. "You're welcome, Amber girl," he said with an inadvertent rasp. He had no hard feelings about the other statements: Of course, she wasn't locked and loaded, ready to pull the trigger on their pairing...their mating...so to speak.

She wrapped her hands around his wrists, and her touch was so gentle it was exquisite. Furthermore, whether she knew it or not, she peeked up at him through those long, sexy lashes, and her lips actually parted. *Yeah, there were five gallons of chemistry swirling between them already.* But then again, the gods would've made sure of that when they chose her. To Axe's disappointment, the connection was fleeting—she tightened her fingers around his wrists, lowered his arms and his hands from her face, and pushed them forward, down and away, before refolding her hands in her lap. "You don't know me well enough to touch me like that," she scolded softly.

Axe took a slow, deep breath.

This was the perfect time to back off—or push forward—he

could see advantages and disadvantages in going either way. But time...*time*...the clock was ticking. "Yeah, but you wanted me to touch you, and you felt something pass between us. You liked my touch, Amber girl."

She shivered, and then she bristled. "Don't even think about it, Axe."

"Think about what?"

"You know what."

"I'm afraid I don't. Be more specific."

Her voice grew stern. "Don't think about *anything* when it comes to me—is that specific enough?"

His faint smile grew broader. "It's actually extremely vague—and impossible—but okay, I'll be good. For now."

She sighed then, and it was wholly exasperated. "What do you want from me, Axeviathon?"

"Axe," he repeated once again.

"*Axeviathon*," she said, determined to be defiant.

He placed one hand on her knee, and she stiffened—but she didn't swipe it away. "I know there's something...important...you want, a much larger reason why you took me. What is it, Axe?"

He added pressure to his touch. "I've told you, Amber; *you're my dragyra*. Going forward, we are going to have to...forge a path...find a way to eventually come together as a man and a woman—a male and a female—find our own way in the Pantheon." He shook his head, and the gesture was adamant. "I'm not going to harm you. I'm not going to force myself on you. I'm not going to take anything you aren't eventually willing to give, but I am going to keep coming at you with truth, with answers to your questions, with my touch, whenever I can. Let's just say, we don't have a lot of time to get to know each other because, yes, there's more to the story. The gods have a stake in your existence, your presence here, too. And they aren't known for being all that patient."

Amber slapped his hand off her knee, stood up abruptly, and paced to the other side of the room, where she stood in front of the fireplace mantel and stared at the ancient stones. "You mean that emerald god, the one that wants to hurt you, also wants something from me? Something like—"

"No!" Axe barked, cutting her off mid-sentence. He spun around on the ottoman and stared at her slender back—if her spine got any stiffer, any straighter, she would be a couple of inches taller. *Shit, he was screwing this up. His damn blunt, non-communicative ass was truly making a mess of the entire interaction, and he was scaring the shit out of his dragyra.* "No," he repeated, softening his tone. "It's nothing like that, Amber. It's complicated, but not like that. Ultimately, what has to happen between us involves the gods and the Pantheon; specifically, it involves the manner in which the Seven will welcome you into our world." *Now, wasn't that just the understatement of the century...*

Amber spun around, and her eyes were wide as saucers. "Just what the hell does that mean?"

Axe cringed inside.

"Axeviathon—*Axe*—what does that mean: the manner in which the Seven will welcome you into our world! Who the hell are the Seven?"

Axe concentrated *hard* on lowering his voice and softening his tone. "There are seven dragon lords in the Pantheon. You already met one of them the other night, Lord Saphyrius, the dragon who healed your eyesight. He will want to...see you in the temple...along with the other six. It's a formal welcoming ceremony of sorts, and yes, it can be quite intimidating."

Shit...shit...and more shit!

This was quickly deteriorating from bad to worse...

Axe could do better.

He had to do better.

He needed to take a different tack.

"But the main thing is: You won't be alone. Just like the healing the other night, your time in the pool with Lord Saphyrius, I'll be there to keep you safe. And just like this thing I have to do tonight with Lord Ethyron—another trip to the temple, another ceremony of sorts, payment for bringing you here—the onus will be on me. Anything unpleasant, any crosses we have to bear, I'll be the one bearing them, not you." He cursed beneath his breath—that was only half true. During the sixty seconds of consecration, when the Seven scorched the couple with orange-and-red flames, when they destroyed Amber's mortal body, allowed her to die, then regenerated her, once again, as an immortal, three seconds of unbearable pain would break through. And that was only if Axe was perfect, implacable, capable of shielding his dragyra from the rest...

But there was no way he could tell her all that now.

She'd run for the hills, fight him with her last dying breath— she'd shut down completely, and he would never have a chance...

To earn her love or her trust...

The jig would be up before it began.

What the hell was he supposed to do?

"You're not telling me everything," she said bluntly, even as her amber eyes narrowed in suspicion. She chuckled softly, and it was a bleak, hollow sound, completely void of humor. "I spent the last ten years living with two demons and a cult worshiper—*did I get that right?* I think I know a half-truth when I hear one." She held up one hand to keep Axe silent before she pressed on: "But you know what? In all honesty, I have a half-truth of my own: I asked the question, but I don't really want the answer. I'm not ready to digest anything more. Not right now...I don't want to know."

For the breadth of a second—maybe a little more, a little less —Axe felt like he almost deserved the punishment he had coming at midnight; he felt like the world's greatest cad. "I'm sorry I'm messing this up," he said honestly. "For whatever it's worth, I'm doing my best. I just—"

"What do you know about trauma bonds," she blurted, interrupting his train of thought.

He drew back and paused. "Come again?"

"Trauma bonds," she repeated, completely changing the subject—*thank the gods*. "Have you ever heard that term? Like the psychological chemistry behind Stockholm syndrome?"

He blinked his sapphire eyes several times, trying to make the adjustment with her. And then he grew quiet and pensive...thinking...where was she going with this? "What do you mean?" he asked, wanting to be clear. "Are you talking about neurochemicals, brain chemistry? Cortisone, and that kind of shit? What happens in the body when it experiences trauma?"

Amber nodded slowly, and her face turned ghostly pale. "Yeah, exactly. What do you know about chemical imbalances, like when someone has them in their body?"

Axe furrowed his brows. They could go back and forth all day, but his dragyra wanted something specific—better to cut to the chase. "What do you need, Amber girl? What are you asking me to do?"

She gulped, and this time, it was Amber who was clearly caught off guard by the bluntness of Axe's words. "Well, that was direct," she murmured, and then she wrung her hands together, rubbed her arms as if she had a chill, and shifted her weight nervously from one foot to another. She was trying to muster her courage.

"Just say it," Axe prompted. He still didn't have a clue...

"I think there's something wrong with me," she whispered. "And Jordan said you could fix it."

* * *

Amber felt like she was going to be sick.

She couldn't believe she had just done that...said that... blurted to Axe about the trauma bonds, asked him, more or less, if he could fix them.

She wasn't even sure she bought it all—the whole chemical Stockholm syndrome thing—but of one thing she was very certain: She needed to be whole to get through this ordeal. She needed a clear head to get out of the Pantheon. And whether or not she conned Axe, Jordan, or someone else—a Dragyr she hadn't met yet—to take her back through that portal, making it happen was no longer an option! What was it Axe had said? *"Ultimately, what has to happen between us involves the gods and the Pantheon; specifically, it involves the manner in which the Seven will welcome you into our world..."*

Those were the dragyri's original words, before he had danced all around the subject.

The manner in which the Seven will welcome you into our world...

Oh, hell no.

That dragon in the swimming pool had been terrifying.

What was about to happen to Axe at midnight was unconscionable...

Barbaric!

That temple was eerie, frightening, and occupied by strange supernatural forces—Amber did not care to meet all seven dragons and learn, firsthand, when the time finally got here, what the heck they had in store for her.

She just couldn't do this, any of it.

And that changed her entire battle plan.

If any part of her brain was unhealthy; if her fight-or-flight reflexes were all out of whack; if her judgment was compromised in any way or she wasn't capable of thinking clearly...if she was anything less than 100 percent...then, yeah, she wanted

Axeviathon to fix it. Because Amber was going to need her wits, her brain, and all her reflexes to get out of this alive.

"So, just to make sure I'm straight..." Axe's deep, raspy voice pulled her back into the moment. "You want me to take a look, so to speak, at your neurochemistry...your hormones...your entire composition, and fix anything chemical that's out of balance?"

Amber forced herself to nod her head. "Yeah, I don't want anything to be...off." She paused, wondering for the first time if he could even do such a thing, and then worrying about what might happen if Axe started digging around in her brain. "That's assuming you can even do it," she blurted, "but you can't read my thoughts in the process. My memories, my feelings, and my thoughts are off-limits."

Damn, had she just waved a red flag in front of a bull?

As in, I'm obviously thinking something I don't want you to know—so whatever you do, don't look for it.

A blatant invitation...

How stupid.

"I don't have to read, measure, or test your chemical makeup, Amber," Axe said. "I just need to know where to focus my intent. The curative power of silver fire is far superior to human medicine; it can regenerate cells at the molecular level, reinstate the original genetic codes. Just so long as I send it in the right direction, tell it what I want it to do, it has the living intelligence to do the rest."

Amber's jaw dropped open, and she couldn't reply. *Silver fire?* As in actual flames, that scorching element that burned stuff to ash? "Um, I—"

"And one other thing," Axe interjected.

Amber felt weak in the knees: *What now?*

"You want me to target your hormonal balance...your neurochemistry...that means we've gotta go far beyond skin deep. I can't just bathe you in the curative flames, Amber girl; I need to make contact with your blood."

Her weak legs gave out, and Amber sank to floor, drawing her knees to her chest and encircling her shins with her arms. "Oh," she faltered. Her courage was rapidly waning. "I guess it's not that important, after all. Why don't we just—"

"One bite," Axe said. "One bite. One artery. And I can make it pleasurable, not painful." He locked his sapphire gaze with hers, and she thought she might just pass out. "As soon as your blood begins to flow, I can withdraw my fangs and bathe the wound in fire: thirty seconds or less, the bite will be healed; the chemistry will be balanced; and whatever trauma bonds may have existed...they'll be gone. Your call, Amber girl; but yes, I can do it."

Amber pressed her palm to her stomach, trying to quell the rising nausea. Her neck was sweating, she felt light-headed, and she wasn't sure, but she may have been swaying, tilting, rocking sideways and falling toward the floor. *Oh, Lord, she did not want to vomit!* But fire...*fangs*...one bite to an artery!? Just what the hell *was* Axeviathon?

A dragon, a vampire, or a warlock?

And what the hell was she even thinking...

This was so absurd!

Her stomach heaved, and she rolled onto her knees, tucking her chin to her chest and pressing her forehead against a wide hardwood panel. She needed some ice—or a really cold wash cloth—because she was about to puke all over Axe's beautiful floors.

And then she felt two strong arms encircle her midriff and lift her, straight up, into the air, even as her knees remained tucked to her chest. "Breathe, Amber girl." Axe's soothing voice.

Just as soon, he was striding across the floor.

Carrying Amber like she was feather-light—weightless—then laying her down on the couch.

He reached for her legs, covered her knees with his palms, and stretched both limbs out, vertically. And then he turned her onto her side.

Amber gasped!

The room was spinning...

And Axe was...*crawling?*

He was lying behind her in a spooning position, one hand over her pelvis, the other, in her hair—*what the fuck?*

The nausea subsided instantly, and he rasped in her ear: "I'm not sure why you asked me for this service, but you could spend days thinking it over, hours, getting more and more freaked out, or we could end this in thirty seconds and spare all the drama." He pressed a soft kiss just beneath her ear, but it must have been meant as a distraction because the hand on her stomach rose to her neck, encircled her esophagus, and pressed her chin upward, stretching and elongating her throat.

Axe was both exposing her jugular and pinning her in place!

"Kind of like removing a Band-Aid," he murmured. "By the time you know it's happening, it's over." The hand in her hair curled into a fist, which meant Axe had Amber pinned by both her throat and her head! *Oh, shit, he was going to bite her.*

CHAPTER TWENTY-ONE

mber's body tensed as Axe nuzzled the nape of her neck, laved his tongue across her jugular, and pressed his warm mouth over her cool skin, making a gentle— then aggressive—seal with his lips. She thought she heard a guttural sound, like a grunt or a snarl, and then she felt two razor-sharp tips, fangs pressing against her neck.

She tried to squirm, to wrench her head away, but he still had her hair in his fist—and he didn't hesitate to tighten his grip and hold her head to the cushion.

And then he bit her...

Just two pinpricks at first, before the ivory daggers sank home.

Amber jerked from the shock—yes, there was a moment of excruciating pain, the second his fangs had first pierced her skin —and then like water washing over a river-rock, the pain had been swept away. She felt a tug on her carotid artery—his teeth spanned both vessels—Axe withdrew his bite, and her blood began to flow.

This was crazy.

Insane.

And something...more...was happening to Axe.

Something primitive, something territorial—the male was becoming aroused.

He released his grip on her hair, drew his nails along the back of her scalp, ran his curled fingers through her tresses, yet again, then fisted a new set of locks, even as his left leg came up, bent at the knee, and wrapped around Amber's thighs.

He shuddered, and she whimpered.

He curled forward, bending over her body; dragged his teeth along the base of her throat and moaned; then continued across the swell of her breast, nuzzled her underarm, and slid his mouth down and along her rib cage...

He lifted the hem of Amber's knee-length T-shirt and dragged it upward, grasping and kneading her skin, her muscles, and her ribs as he went along, until her stomach was both quivering and exposed. Whether from fear...or something else... Amber couldn't pinpoint.

Axe dipped his head once more and nuzzled her stomach, laved her belly button with his tongue, then fisted the roundness of her abdomen like a basketball player palming a ball. His large, muscular back arched subtly, and his muscles contracted, then released...

And then the dragyri rolled on top of Amber, forcing her onto her back.

She pressed her inner thighs together—there was no way she was opening her legs.

The dragyri snarled, slid both hands down her sides to her hips, then raked his fingers over her outer thighs, and traced the concave hollow above and around her lower stomach, until he gained access to her inner muscles. He dug his fingers into her flesh, spread both legs apart, and nestled his body against her pelvis...

Holy shit.

Amber's legs fell open—he was just too powerful—and he spread them even wider.

What the fuck...

His hand went back to her throat, and once again, he curled his fingers inward—grasping, kneading, and pressing down ever so slightly, before rotating his thumb over the open puncture wounds. And then he planted his palms on either side of Amber, splayed his fingers against the couch, and pushed up on his arms to raise his massive torso above her.

His sapphire eyes looked wild.

The barely banked flames were both sparkling and dancing—shimmering like wildfire, blazing in his pupils—and his features were stamped with both savagery and lust. He shifted all his weight onto one strong arm—onto one bulging bicep—and placed the other hand, once again, along her throat; only this time, he slid the heel of his hand against the slope beneath her chin, until the pressure under her jaw forced her head backward.

Amber arced her neck like she was exposing her jugular to a predator, her head being placed exactly where Axeviathon wanted it, and all the while, she was helpless to do anything about it—the severe male had completely overwhelmed her.

Dominated her body and her will...

And then his wild eyes grew feral; he threw back his head; his jaw snapped open; and a blazing stream of pure silver fire shot out of the dragyri's throat. Instinctively, Amber jerked back, but there was no escape—nowhere to go—as the blaze found her jugular with unerring precision, snaked around her throat, and seemed to enter the oozing puncture holes.

The sensation was both searing and cooling at once.

The fire felt like a hundred volts of electricity, entering her body through her throat.

But it wasn't painful.

Not at all...

It was soothing, invigorating, surreal...

As the fire began to travel through her anatomy, following the network of arteries and veins, her body heated from the inside out, and her nerve endings were set on fire. Not literally, but maybe *literal* would have been best, because Amber's stomach clenched, her thighs began to tremble, and her breasts felt suddenly heavy and agitated.

Oh...*oh, no*...she was burning with desire.

She was every bit as aroused as Axe...

As if it had a mind of its own, Amber's pelvis rocked beneath the dragyri, seeking deeper and more intense contact, and Axe groaned in response to the invitation, gyrating his hips against her.

She jackknifed on the couch.

He shuddered.

She tried to press her thighs together, to quell the rising ache in her belly, but she forgot that Axe was lodged between her legs, and she ended up caressing—and stroking—his hips.

His arousal swelled instantaneously, filling his jeans and blatantly pressing against her.

Amber moaned...

No, no, no...oh, shit...

He strained against her core, and she unwittingly arched her back.

The flames from his throat retreated, swirling back down his throat, but Amber had an entirely different problem to contend with, next—she wanted this male inside her more than she wanted her next breath.

And he knew it.

His mouth, his lips, his tongue now free, he began to devour her body: first, returning to her jugular, where he kissed, laved, sucked, and bit her, then dragging his teeth down her throat...

Axeviathon feasted on Amber's body: her collarbone, the swell of her breasts, and then her quivering stomach...

Her ribs.

Her belly.

Her sensitive waist and hips...

And he raked his hands along all three zones, even as he covered them with his tongue...lavished them, devoured them... explored them with his mouth.

And then he grasped her by the waist and shoved her forward, sliding her up and along the couch, and latched on to the nucleus—the center of her need—covering the juncture between her thighs with his warm, seeking mouth.

Oh, gods...

He nuzzled her through her panties, and then he engaged his teeth...

"Axe!" Amber cried out, almost in a panic. She wasn't sure if she was begging him to stop or pleading with him to go further.

The dragyri shuddered again.

He crawled up her body, taking what was left of her T-shirt with him as he stretched it over both breasts; cupped both mounds in his kneading palms; and began to do wickedly tantalizing things to her nipples before sucking the right apex into his mouth.

Amber's whimper became a cry, and tears filled her eyes.

She had never felt anything like this in her lifetime: the hunger, the sensation, the yearning ache in her body. The fire that was still consuming her.

And then all at once, Axeviathon jerked back.

He released her breast from his warm, moist suckling and shoved his body upward, his entire upper torso trembling as he slowly leaned back, shifted his weight onto his knees, and ambled off the couch. He swept a large, powerful hand through his dirty-blond locks and panted, trying to catch his breath, and then he took three generous steps backward, away from the temptation.

"Amber girl," he grunted, his voice like raw, gritty sandpaper, "I'm sorry...*I'm sorry*...just give me a minute."

Amber's eyes grew wide as she watched him like a hawk.

Her nipples were hard, her panties were damp, and her thighs were still trembling and aching with *want*—yet he had said he was sorry, like he had done this by himself.

Like she hadn't egged him on.

He placed his hands on his hips and paced across the sitting room, and then he slowly shook his head. "I didn't mean for that to happen, Amber girl. I would never take advantage of you like that."

Amber sat up slowly, pulled the T-shirt back down to her knees, and swung her legs over the side of the sofa. Then she just sat there, feeling both lost and confused. She had never reacted to a man's touch like that before—and she had never felt more exposed.

"You all right?" Axe murmured.

She licked her lips, then pursed them together and nodded. "It wasn't just you," she croaked, feeling mortified. "I kind of—"

"Stop," Axe interrupted, holding one hand up. "You didn't do anything, Amber. The fire...the heat...the passion and intensity... it all streamed into you when I bathed your wounds in the flames. It wasn't intentional, sweetness; it's just—some of my essence was bound to leak through, and I didn't anticipate that happening, like I should have." He paused and glanced away. "My bad."

Amber gulped.

Some of his essence leaked through?

Some.

Not all?

So that was just the tip of the iceberg?

Holy. Hell.

"Then the passion...the arousal"—she cringed at the second word—"that was yours, not mine?"

Axe nodded, reestablished eye contact, and flashed a sly, wolfish smile. "Yep. That was all me, pretty lady."

Amber shuddered inwardly. "But...but it was the fire, the transference that made you do that—*that made you feel that*—right?"

He laughed, and the sound was deep, wicked, and utterly masculine. "Nah, Amber girl; like I said: *all me*. It just happened to leak into the fire."

Amber hugged her midriff in a self-protective gesture.

She didn't know what to say...

So all this time, while Axe was talking to her, teaching her, asking and answering questions, the male was actually horny as hell...

"I see," she whispered, and then she crossed her legs, careful to make sure the T-shirt didn't ride up her thighs. Her body was still feeling achy; her mind was still spinning from his touch; and she was doing her best to process what he was telling her, but she felt like a fish suddenly thrust onto the beach.

Water, please?

She needed to get out of there...

To go clear her head.

As if he sensed her dilemma and understood her stress, he pointed toward the master bathroom at the back of the suite. "Why don't you take the blue duffle bag that Jordan brought for you, go take a shower, and chill out for a bit. Come back when you've had a chance to regroup...collect your thoughts." He lowered his mass onto an ottoman, placed his elbow on his knee, and rested his chin on his fist. "I'm not going anywhere, sweet angel—I can wait. Besides, I could use a minute, myself."

Amber eyed the blue duffle bag still sitting on the kitchen island—he didn't have to tell her twice. She jumped up from the couch, scrambled to the kitchen, reached out to snatch the bag off the counter, and paused. Her eyes swept inadvertently across the floor and the mess she had made a bit earlier: the silver tray, the plate, and what was left of the fruit and the bagel...not to mention the weaponized fork.

"I'll clean it up while you shower," Axe said, following her gaze unerringly. "And by the way, your chemistry is...it's set, sweet angel. The trauma bonds are gone."

Amber felt like a weight had suddenly been lifted from her shoulders, and she knew that the right thing to say—the polite thing to do—was to just whisper, *Thank you*, and move on. After all, the male was actually being a fairly decent person, or dragon —*whatever*. He was doing his best to be kind and respectful, even when he could have taken her, or raped her...had his way with Amber on the couch.

And she would have been none the wiser.

Yet and still, the male had pulled away—Axe had held back.
So why then was she about to push the envelope?

"Axe?" She spoke timidly.

His eyebrows shot up.

"What is supposed to happen in the temple with me and you? What is the *manner in which the Seven will welcome me into your world?*" She placed the last five words in air quotes to let him know she remembered his confession, verbatim.

Axe narrowed his gaze on Amber, and he didn't look away or blink. "The dragon lords will change you to my species—convert you—in order to make you immortal; and all seven will do it, at once, with fire."

She swallowed her fear and pressed on. "But it doesn't really hurt or anything, right? I mean, it'll be like what happened here, just minus the sexual tension?" Her voice faltered on those last three words.

Axe hesitated, but only for the space of a couple heartbeats.

"No, Amber girl, it won't be anything like what happened here. It'll be loud, fearsome, overpowering, and terrifying. That said, you won't feel much of anything for the first twenty-seven seconds, and that's because I will take the brunt of the Seven's fire for you...the burning. There will be three seconds when the flames will break through, when I will no longer be able to shield you from the heat. And after that, the next thirty seconds—*the last thirty seconds*—will be pure nirvana and bliss for you, not so much for me. That's the whole of it, sweetness, the entire truth."

Amber closed her eyes as Axe's words sank in...

But no way, no how, was she going to try to process their meaning—not right here, and not right now. Her mind could only grasp so much.

Not being one to push her luck, and too afraid to test the hands of fate, she reopened her eyes, stared at the duffle bag beneath her fingers, and focused her full attention on the present moment. As it stood, there was another elephant in the living room to contend with, and this time, the secret was Amber's: Axe was dead wrong about something he had said.

That passion—it wasn't *all* him.

Yes, the healing flames and the curative fire had sparked the desire, meaning most of that arousal had come from Axe, but there was something else—something buried just below the surface that Amber had also felt—a connection, a recognition, like coming home from a long vacation.

And that hadn't come from the fire at all.

It had awakened inside of Amber.

As bizarre and impossible as it seemed, there really was some kind of invisible thread linking her heart to his—if only for a moment, she had felt it, sensed the inescapable tug, and the connection had been incredibly powerful. And frankly—in this stark, unguarded moment—that truth terrified Amber more than the temple...

It frightened her far more than Axe's savage lust.

She slid the duffle off the counter, anchored the strap over her shoulder, and walked quietly across the apartment to the bathroom, never speaking a word and never looking back at *her* dragyri.

CHAPTER TWENTY-TWO

T ony Rossi sank deep into the clear, swirling water in the large master-bath jetted tub. The water was way too hot, scalding really—in truth, it should've been too hot for comfort—yet Tony shivered all the way to his bones.

Amber was gone.

That demon bastard Trader Vice had taken up residence at 318 Syracuse Lane for the duration—yeah, he had moved into the Denver house until Axeviathon Saphyrius, or whatever male had taken Amber, showed his cocky *dragyri* face again, earthside.

And to make matters worse, Tony's association with his roomies, his longstanding friendship with Zeik and Grunge, was anything but amiable and usual: It was a shit-show of extraordinary magnitude...

Lord Drakkar had all but referred to Tony as lazy—as a human, Tony meant nothing to the powerful, dark deity—and Zeik had made it abundantly clear: Tony's days on this earth were as good as numbered. As long as he did the demons' bidding, they would allow him to live, but the second he displeased them—or got on their nerves—it was lights out for the insignificant mortal.

You're chattel, prey, dinner...

You will live or die at our whim.

Tony slid beneath the waterline, soaking his short blond hair and allowing the scalding liquid to wash away his fear. If he got too caught up on Zeik's cryptic words, if he went too deep into his head, the fear and the anger would get the best of him. He might say or do something he couldn't take back, forget his newfound position on the bottom of the food chain, and Antonio Rossi wanted to live...

As long as he could.

As long as his demon roommates would let him.

He emerged from the water, ran his palm through his crop, and shook off the feeling of hopelessness and dread. All wasn't lost. At least not yet. There was still a chance he could please the lord of the underworld—there was still a chance he could get Amber back. Zeik and Grunge had finally heard back from Trader, they finally had their "word" from their sovereign, and they knew how Lord Drak wanted them to proceed. According to Trader, Lord Drakkar Hades and his chief sorcerer, Requiem Pyre, were hell-bent on seeking revenge for the loss of their comrades during the Monday-night raid, and they were definitely planning on using Tony as live, human bait.

The way Zeik had explained it: The portal—and the Pantheon—was like traveling through a hidden tunnel and emerging inside a virtual vault. Amber may as well have been locked away in an impenetrable chamber, absent of any doors or windows, with guards so fierce and deadly, not even a gnat could get through to her. But there was also some strange prehistoric kinship between Lord Drakkar and the dragon lords that ruled the Temple of Seven, the dragyris' sovereign rulers. And while nothing got in or out of that pantheon—not a note, not a thought, not a telephone call, email, instant message, or missive—Lord Drakkar had fashioned a small, temporary workaround...

Something about spherical objects or paperweights...

Something about enhancing transmissions with the use of jewels...

Something about creating a globe that would allow a cell phone signal to get through.

The long and short of it was this: Trader had given Zeik and Grunge a multicolored paperweight about the size of Tony's fist, with a flat, level base on the bottom. The moment Tony placed his hand over the top of the sphere and grasped it, the seven gemstones would heat up, and the circle would start to glow. Once that happened, Tony was good to go—he could text Amber to his heart's content, and the messages would go through to the Pantheon. Of course, according to the demons, the dragon lords would know—they would feel it—but so-the-fuck-what.

There was nothing the Seven could do about it.

Sure, they could manufacture a whole new system of transmitting and allowing radio waves and such to move in and out of the Pantheon; they could take Amber's cell phone and bar her from reading—or responding to—her messages; or they could send some of their mercenaries to Earth to destroy Drak's clever creation. But Requiem and Trader, as well as Zeik and Grunge, were banking on the fact that Axeviathon—or whatever male had taken Amber—was as eager as they were to receive the transmissions. The Dragyr wanted to get to Tony as badly as Tony wanted to get to Amber. In short, they would allow the texts to go through, even if they were the ones who were reading them. However, the first few texts—the first time it happened—Amber was as likely as not to see them. The Dragyr would not be expecting it, and thus, they would be reactive as opposed to proactive—they might take her phone after it happened, but they wouldn't think to take it before...

Tony sighed.

What-the-hell-ever...

The details were beyond his comprehension—or his pay grade.

His job was to send a slew of texts to Amber, hope they got through, then wait along with his demon cohorts for the Dragyr to take the bait:

Amber, baby, I miss you so much!

I'm so sorry I wasn't able to protect you.

Please come home.

Please come back.

Zeik and Grunge can help us...

Meet me at the empty field behind the house, the one that follows the dry canal. I'll be there every morning, noon, and night.

12AM.

12PM.

Like clockwork.

Even if it takes months to find you.

And the moment you show up, I promise—we WILL get away. A new home, a new identity, a whole new life. I will protect you from now on, Amber. I love you! You know this...

Baby, please! I'm lost without you.

So, yeah, Tony was doing his duty like a good, obedient human.

He had copied the texts, and with the help of a supernatural sphere, courtesy of the dark lord of the underworld, he had pasted it again and again...and again...into *Messages*, and sent them every hour, on the hour, to Amber.

No one really believed the girl would show up.

No one believed the Dragyr would let her.

But they were betting on the fact that Axeviathon would bite, and when he did, Trader, Zeik and Grunge would be ready.

CHAPTER TWENTY-THREE

LATER THAT NIGHT: THE PANTHEON

I t was 11:30 PM, and that meant Axe had exactly twenty-nine minutes to show up at the Temple of Seven. Amber shivered, even as she shuffled back, trying to camouflage her body beside a massive stone fireplace that separated the Sapphire Lair's great room from the hall that led to the open gourmet kitchen and eating nook.

All five of Lord Saphyrius' progeny, as well as Jordan, were present in the great room: Zane, Levi, Nakai, Jace, and of course, Axeviathon. The latter had just introduced Amber to all of them, and she couldn't help but feel like a bug beneath a microscope, surrounded by terrifying, immortal giants. Levi had been kind when he had greeted her in the most deep, melodious voice; nonetheless, the male had hands—he had fists—like two iron wrecking balls, and not even his light sense of humor could detract from his obvious wild nature. Nakai had been a bit more reserved—like he was more of a thinker than a talker. Just the same, he was equally intimidating, with that small archaic tattoo emblazoned on his left temple, some sort of winged cross in a circle that stood out as a constant reminder: *Forget the gorgeous*

*dark-brown hair, the sapphire irises, or the light-brown pupils; I'm
anything but human, and those wings aren't just symbolic...*

Amber rubbed her hands up and down her arms to try to
generate some warmth.

Jace had been the easiest to relate to, with his warm, capti-
vating eyes and his breathtaking smile. For a moment, Amber had
almost forgotten that he was also dragyri. Yet his sinewy, but
strong, muscular build, coupled with the power that practically
radiated around him, overshadowed those sea-green pupils and
that short blond hair that lay back in perfect waves—no, she
couldn't forget that Jace was also lethal. As for Zane, Jordan's
mate, well, the male was just...something special. According to
Axe, he was a Genesis offspring, a firstborn son to Lord
Saphyrius, and yeah, his rugged, almost medieval good looks did
nothing to hide his savage bearing. Amber had no idea how
Jordan had ever warmed up to him.

And then there was the secret...

The cell phone set to *mute* in Amber's pocket—the thing had
not stopped ringing...

Well, *vibrating*, but just the same: Tony had been texting
Amber hourly, begging her to meet him in the meadow...a field
about a mile and a half behind their Denver residence...swearing
that he, Zeik, and Grunge could help her. They could whisk her
away and hide her. And that meant Antonio Rossi was still alive,
and so were Zeik and Grunge. Beyond that, it meant that the
three of them knew everything: where Amber was, who she was
with, and what it would really take to save her...to protect her...to
get her away from the powerful Dragyr.

Needless to say, she was trying to figure a way to work it out.

Yes, a part of her felt like shit for doing it.

And no, she wasn't eager to go back to Tony...

Jordan had been correct about the trauma bonds—whatever
pull, whatever affection, whatever need had once been there,

however distorted and unhealthy, it was suddenly and irretrievably gone. Amber felt nothing for Tony Rossi, other than loathing. And while Axe had been both generous and kind, checking in on Amber and seeing to her needs, reaching out to talk to her, touch her, reassure her all day, she still couldn't get with the program: She couldn't digest this terrifying fate, and she couldn't embrace this strange, mythical world. She couldn't see herself living in this opulent lair, not even with the gorgeous cathedral ceilings; the thick crisscrossed wooden beams; or the floor-to-ceiling windows showcasing the most breathtaking views Amber had ever seen, not the least of which was a stunning waterfall that provided a soothing, constant, ambient serenade in the background.

No, Amber couldn't live in the Sapphire Lair, and she couldn't become a member of the Pantheon of Dragons. She sure as hell couldn't enter that temple—again—and just stand there as the seven dragon lords scorched her with fire...

Jordan reached out to touch her arm, and Amber nearly jumped out of her skin. "You okay?" the hazel-eyed beauty asked. "I know this has got to be overwhelming."

Amber forced an insincere smile and nodded. "I'm fine; well, I'm trying to be. But thank you."

Jordan reached for Amber's hand and squeezed it, and Amber squeezed Jordan's back.

Amber had already decided to reach out to the hazel-eyed dragyra, to do her level best to befriend the female, and not because she intended to stick around or keep the relationship, going forward. But because she had overheard Jordan telling her mate that she wanted to go to a concert with someone named Macy on Friday night, and she wanted Zane to use his amulet to escort her through the portal—however that worked—to drop her off at the venue's entrance, where she would meet up with her friend for a girl's night out, then return to the exact same spot to be escorted home at midnight.

The country-western concert was less than five miles from Amber's house...

And it was supposed to end around 11:30 PM.

The proximity was perfect, and the timing was impeccable.

If Amber could get Jordan to let her tag along, she could slip away during the concert—or even make a break for it as soon as it was over; hire a driver from one of those transportation networks; hell, even a cab or a town car would do—and have the service drop her off at the field. She could come up with some excuse or another to break free from Jordan and Macy, if only for five minutes—she had to. And then it would be sink or swim, live or die, get into that vehicle and escape, or live the rest of your life in the Pantheon. Amber was nothing if she wasn't resourceful. Somehow...*some way*...she would make it happen, even if she had to cause a commotion, crawl out of a bathroom window, or change her appearance in a bathroom stall in order to sneak past her female companions.

And, thus, the texts she had sent back to Tony:

This Friday night at midnight.

I'll try to make it happen.

But we won't have very much time—maybe five minutes at most.

You have to be prepared on your end for the fact that I might be followed by a dragyra and her human friend, and she may be followed by her dragyri mate—don't hurt them, Tony. Don't hurt anyone. No one else gets involved, or I won't go with you. I mean it: I'll fight you before I let you (Zeik or Grunge) touch the women...

Just get me out of there quickly!

We may only have this one opportunity...

Amber squeezed Jordan's hand a second time before quickly

releasing it, and her stomach roiled inside. Amber was not a duplicitous person, and Jordan had been nothing but gracious, thoughtful, and kind. Under different circumstances, perhaps in another life, Amber would've given her right arm for a friendship with such an outstanding person—talk about a far cry from home, from all she had ever lived with or known—but this wasn't another lifetime, and the circumstances were grave. Amber had one shot to get this shit right. She had one chance to get away from Axe and to avoid that temple.

And *damn it all to hell* if she hadn't spent her whole entire life being obedient, taking care of others, letting herself be used because someone else had an agenda that was more important.

No more.

This time, Amber had to be selfish.

She had to escape the Pantheon and then escape Tony—she had to reclaim her life.

"Are you worried about Axe?" Jordan whispered, clearly picking up on Amber's distress. The beautiful dragyra eyed the enormous pool table beside a well-stocked bar, tucked at the back of the great room, and sighed. "These guys are strong; he'll be okay."

Once again, Amber felt like crap. "I think the whole damn thing is unconscionable," she said, and every word was the truth. *Seven pounds of flesh; seven pints of blood; seven broken bones—* all the more reason why Amber couldn't stay. These immortal beings were both savage and cruel. The lives they lived were beyond imagining.

And then Axe stepped away from the pool table.

He met Amber's gaze from across the room, and her stomach literally clenched.

This was awful...horrifying...the dragyri was about to go through hell and them some for Amber, and all the while, she was plotting to get away from him.

Stop! she told herself, nearly grinding her teeth together. *Don't go there. Just don't. Be strong...stay focused!* She straightened her spine and raised her chin as Axe ambled away from his lair mates, crossed the room in a dozen long strides, and stood before Amber and Jordan. Despite his bearing—his power and his determination—his face was slightly ashen, and his sapphire eyes were cold. There were no flames burning in those depths, no passion, no fire, nothing but resolve. The male was steeling himself for what was about to happen in the temple.

"Amber girl, I have to go now." For a moment, he glanced down toward her pocket, the pocket concealing her cell phone, and Amber's heart skipped a beat in her chest. "You stay close to Jordan for the next twelve hours, okay? I'll be out of commission for a few, but my lair mates have my back...they have your back... and so does she." His gaze met Jordan's, and somehow, he forced himself to smile.

Jordan bit her lip and looked away. She was clearly fighting tears, trying her best not to cry. She stepped toward Axe, threw her arms around him, and gave him a warm, loving hug. "Lord Ethyron is a bastard," she whispered icily.

Axe hugged her back, then stepped away, pressing one finger to his lips. "Shh," he cautioned. "Be careful, Jordan. Gods have ears, and this isn't your drama. Zane would kill me if I somehow got you in trouble. I'll be fine."

Jordan crossed her arms over her stomach, looked down at the floor, and the tears started to flow freely. She took Axe's hand in hers and held it—she stood there, clinging to his hand for nearly sixty seconds—and all Amber could think was that it should've been her: Amber should've been the one crying, consoling him. At the very least, she could at least reach out, maybe say thank you, or try to encourage him, but as it was, she just stood there and watched as another woman—an incredibly beautiful, compassionate woman—tried to comfort the male who was paying a debt for Amber.

"I...I don't know what to say," Amber murmured, feeling like a fool for interrupting the moment, but the awkward silence—and the equally intimate exchange—was unnerving her.

Jordan released Axe's hand, rose to the tips of her toes, and pressed a chaste kiss to the side of his cheek. And then, without looking back, she walked away, heading toward the pool table and Zane.

"That's okay," Axe replied, his tone softer than Amber remembered. "I just hate that you have to be alone right now. I mean, you've got the whole lair and Jordan, but I hate that we won't have more time...at least not for a while." He reached out to cup her cheek in his hand, and for the first time, Amber let him—she didn't pull away or try to remove it.

There was no way she was going to reject him right now.

And truth be told, she needed the contact as much as he did.

She curled her fingers around his wrist and leaned into his touch—it wasn't a caress, but it was close enough. "Axeviathon," she whispered.

He chuckled. "*Axe.*"

She smiled. "I don't understand why this is happening, *Axe.* Any of it. Not why you took me. Not why you want me. And not what I'm doing here. And I especially don't understand what this dragon god wants to do to you—or why you have to go through this." She swallowed her confusion, her sorrow, and her regret and stared into his enchanting eyes. "For whatever it's worth, I'm sorry...about all of it."

He blinked, and the flames in his pupils returned. "Do you understand this, Amber?" He placed his other hand on her other cheek, bent his head, and leaned in to kiss her. Only he didn't press his lips to hers; he just brushed them lightly—a gentle graze over her parted mouth—and hovered above her. "Kiss me, Amber girl."

He wanted her to come to him.

He wanted her to *want* the intimacy.

But most of all, he must have hoped...he must have wanted... for her to feel the strength of their preordained connection.

Amber's heart began to pound in her chest, her knees felt weak, and her palms grew sweaty. Gods help her because, in that moment, she was feeling all of it.

She stared at his lips.

Those perfect, sculpted, full masculine lips...

And she closed the distance between them.

CHAPTER TWENTY-FOUR

H aving climbed the white marble staircase, passed the seven magnificent pillars, and cleansed his hands in the sacred fountain, Axeviathon traversed the foyer in the Temple of Seven, clutched one of the two mammoth stone doors that led into the inner sanctuary, and drew it open with resolution.

He could do this.

He had no choice.

It was just a matter of getting it over with.

Squinting against the familiar blinding light—the reflection of gemstones in the glass floor beneath him projecting mirrored prisms from the high coffered ceilings, which were plated in all seven jewels—he kept his eyes focused forward and headed straight for the octagon dais. He didn't bother to look at the opulent paintings or glance at the pearlescent Oracle Pool; he just climbed the seven stairs, ignored the dual pair of anchored handholds set into the platform—soon, Amber would be kneeling right there—and took his place, opposite Lord Ethyron's empty emerald throne.

He bowed his head and waited.

He shuffled from side to side, linked his hands behind his back, and tried to still his thunderous heartbeat—the sanctuary was so damn quiet...

Too damn quiet for Axe's liking.

And then, to his surprise, Lord Saphyrius materialized first, appearing on the sapphire throne as if out of an ancient mist. "Axeviathon." He spoke Axe's name with kindness...compassion...almost reverence.

"Father," Axe responded, referring to Lord Saphyrius as the sire of his lair.

"Lord Ethyron will join us in a moment," the sapphire dragon said. "I wanted a private word with you before the unpleasant event commences."

Axe gulped.

The unpleasant event—*yeah, that was one way to put it.*

He held his tongue—he may have even held his breath—and waited for Lord Saphyrius to continue. He wasn't at all certain he could speak coherently anyway; the stress was beginning to take its toll.

"Are you aware of the cell phone transmissions passing through the Sapphire Lair?" Lord Saphyrius asked.

Axe frowned and raised his chin. "Come again?" While the dragon lord may have been in amalgamated form, his deep, scaly brows were furrowed, and Axe immediately caught his own error: He might be scared shitless and unable to form coherent sentences, but that didn't mean he could get flippant, or casual, with his dragon lord. "Apologies, Father. Would you please repeat that?"

Lord Saphyrius sighed and leaned back on his throne. "Were you aware that your dragyra has been receiving transmissions from Earth through her cell phone, several throughout the day, actually, and earlier this night, she responded. Look up, son."

Axeviathon raised his eyes toward the ceiling, and an embla-zoned scroll of light unfolded, words appearing on the canvas in bright-orange flames:

Amber, baby, I miss you so much!

I'm so sorry I wasn't able to protect you.

Please come home.

Please come back.

Zeik and Grunge can help us...

Meet me at the empty field behind the house, the one that follows the dry canal. I'll be there every morning, noon, and night.

12 AM.

12 PM.

Like clockwork.

Even if it takes months to find you.

And the moment you show up, I promise—we WILL get away. A new home, a new identity, a whole new life. I will protect you from now on, Amber. I love you! You know this...

Baby, please! I'm lost without you.

And then, beneath it, a new set of words: a text from Amber to Tony...

This Friday night at midnight.

I'll try to make it happen.

But we won't have very much time—maybe five minutes at most.

You have to be prepared on your end for the fact that I might be followed by a dragyra and her human friend, and she may be followed by her dragyri mate—don't hurt them, Tony. Don't hurt anyone. No one else gets involved, or I won't go with you. I mean it: I'll fight you before I let you (Zeik or Grunge) touch the women...

Just get me out of there quickly!

We may only have this one opportunity...

Axe bristled and closed his eyes. Talk about some shit he

really didn't need to see...to know...not right now, and not at this moment. He needed all his concentration to get through what was to come.

But so be it.

It was what it was...

So, despite the trauma bonds being lifted—vanquished—Amber was still trying to get the hell out of Dodge. That wasn't so unusual for a newly acquired dragyra. It wasn't like the Pantheon screamed *Home Sweet Home* to a human woman, at least not at first.

But that kiss...

The one she had given him before Axe had left for the temple.

Amber was in deeper than she knew...

Axe prickled one more time, then opened his eyes. As the clock had just struck midnight, it was now technically Thursday, and that meant Axe had twenty-four hours to heal completely and get his shit back together. He would let Zane know that Amber's plan was a go—go ahead and take both dragyras through the portal, let Amber attend the concert, and give Jordan a heads-up that Amber planned to escape—Axe would be ready for the meet-up. He would follow his dragyra himself. As it stood, unless Zane brought another mercenary with him, he couldn't step out of that portal without an escort of his own—first-generation shit, the Seven had forbidden it—and Axe did not want to let on to Amber that the jig was up. So yeah, he'd follow via a parallel portal or perhaps show up a little early—either way, he would be back to full health by then, and a 100 percent dragyri male was more than capable of extinguishing a duplicitous human male.

"Thank you, Father," he said in a surly tone. "I'll handle the business tomorrow night."

Lord Saphyrius nodded, and then his features grew curious. "And what is your intent?"

"To end the human piece of shit, once and for all," Axe growled. "To kill the worthless bastard."

Lord Saphyrius nodded. "Very well." He paused for the space of several dragon heartbeats and then inclined his head in sorrow. "Son, Lord Ethyron is ready. I regret the unpleasantness of the night's event, but promises are promises—and debts must be paid. However, I will not stay to watch. I cannot. I trust that my emerald brother will not supersede his bargain—take more than he is allowed to take. The repercussions would be epic. Nonetheless, it is not my place to police the matter this night. Be strong, Axeviathon, and know this: At the culmination of your sentence, Lord Ethyron will offer you a sacred discus, fashioned from his own flesh, blood, and scales. You will soon possess the powers of *three* sacred lairs: your birth lair, citrine; your consecrated sapphire home; and Lord Ethyron's emerald magic. Your fire will burn brighter; your dragon will be stronger; and you will be able to draw energy from all three lords in battle. Perhaps such knowledge will strengthen your resolve." With that, the sapphire dragon disappeared. He didn't amble away from the throne or linger—he simply vanished into thin air, retreating to his temple chambers.

And just like that, Lord Ethyron took his place.

He stood in front of his emerald throne and sneered at Axeviathon like he was already deriving enormous sadistic pleasure from the torture to come.

Axe bowed his head, once again; only this time, he resented the hell out of the gesture. "My lord," he murmured, trying mightily to keep his tone respectful.

"Ah, Axeviathon..." Lord Ethyron held out both hands, talons fully extended. "So good of you to grace me with your presence this night. Welcome...*welcome*...to the Temple of Seven. Shall we get on with it, dragyri?"

Axe bit his bottom lip.

That sick, twisted, son-of-a-perverse-putrid-bitch! Axe thought. He felt sorry for his emerald lair cousins; he really did.

A deep, guttural growl filled the throne room, and Axe's heart clenched in his chest—*oh shit, what if the dragon lord had heard him?* What if Lord Ethyron was reading his thoughts?

But oh well...

What if?

What was he going to do?

Torture the dragyri—come at him even harder?

It was doubtful that Lord Ethyron had planned on holding back to begin with.

A grating, creaking noise filled the sanctuary, and Axe glanced upward, over his head, only to see a large metal pulley-system descending from the cathedral ceilings—*what the heck was it attached to?* The medieval-looking contraption came to a halt about four feet above Axeviathon; two sets of thick chains, iron bolts, and wrist cuffs dropped down from the center of the bar; and Lord Ethyron's malevolent voice filled the sanctuary. "Hands up, Axeviathon."

Axeviathon retreated inside: mentally, physically...spiritually.

He crossed his wrists over his head and stretched out his arms, and without preamble, he was floating upward, propelled by Lord Ethyron's power. The iron clasps opened and shut around Axe's wrists, squeezing four to five inches of his forearms like a supernatural fist, and then the dragyri was hanging from the temple ceiling, dangling from the archaic pulley. A large, winding tail whipped out from the emerald throne and zigzagged across Axe's body, whirring through the air as it rent, and Axe's clothing fell from his body, leaving his muscle, skin, and bones exposed, save only his skin-tight, thigh-length boxers.

Axe tightened his muscles and sucked in his stomach, staring dead ahead at Lord Ethyron, waiting for whatever was coming next: a second swipe of the tail, more lethal; a lunge, followed by iron-sharp teeth; or the perverse use of webbed wings, searing flames—whatever. Axe was prepared for anything.

Until the pulley spun him around to face the temple doors.

What the heck?

Axe shuddered and tried to maintain his courage—his grit. So Lord Ethyron was going to strike him from behind? He wanted to add the elements of surprise and blindness to the excruciating, unrelenting torture he was about to dole out...

So be it.

Then the massive, twenty-feet-high, temple doors flew open, and Ghostaniaz Dragos stormed into the sanctuary: The male was dressed in battle leather, his feet adorned in heavy, spiked boots; his fists wrapped in crude, lanced gloves; and his glowing diamond irises—his strange phantom-blue pupils—were as dead as the gaze of a killer shark, as cold as the arctic snow. His muscles were twitching; his lips were drawn back into a snarl; and his jaw was set in an implacable line. For all intents and purposes, the male was empty...soulless...locked and loaded with lethal intent.

"I owed Lord Ethyron a favor." *That was Lord Dragos' hellish voice, echoing throughout the sanctuary!* He had come out from his chambers to watch! "Ghostaniaz is here to make recompense for me," the diamond dragon bellowed.

The words settled over Axe like a winter's frost.

He tried to meet Ghost's barren gaze, to make some sort of eye contact and plead with his eyes: *Brother, dragyri, it's me—it's Axe!—keep your bearings, Ghost! Don't lose it completely. Please.*

Why the hell had Lord Saphyrius trusted Lord Ethyron to play by the rules, to keep to the seven pounds of flesh, the seven pints of blood, and the seven broken bones—as if the emerald dragon lord possessed that much honor? And even if he did, all bets were now off.

Ghost Dragos was a completely different beast...

The broken male did not possess a conscience, let alone a rational mind—he didn't have an *off lever*; he didn't have the capacity to know when to stop.

The male was nothing but pure unfettered rage, darkness, and brutality.

Whatever courage Axe had once possessed swirled down a drain of terror and dread.

* * *

Ghostaniaz Dragos stormed into the temple, tossing the heavy stone doors aside.

He was focused...determined...channeling the devil—he would give Daddy dearest the shit-show he desired. He had practiced the bludgeoning in his mind, a dozen times, prepared to strike swiftly, efficiently, and with exacting precision.

His father wanted savagery—he would accept nothing less—and Ghost was more than prepared to deliver. He had learned that lesson the hard way, more than once. But what he would not give Lord Dragos—or Lord Ethyron—was a mindless puppet on a subjugated, sadistic string.

Ghost was no one's lackey.

He would take the seven pound, pints, and bones so quickly —so ferociously—that the whole damn twisted event would be over as soon as it began. And Lord Dragos could say nothing about it: Ghost would stick to the letter of the law, and then the fucking demented party would be finished.

He strode across the luminescent glass floor like his legs were being propelled by automation; leaped all seven steps to land on the dais; and circled Axe three times.

He was studying the male's physique, his musculature, choosing and marking targets in his mind, even as he made an absent mental note of Axe's horrified sapphire peepers. *Shit*. The dragyri was utterly terrified.

But then...

Good.

Ghost could feed on that fear.

He took a long, deep sniff of cortisol and channeled it through his blood, and then he struck like a scorpion with a blunt, rotated fist—the sternum, two ribs, the upper-left clavicle— Ghost's arms were like two military-grade jackhammers, pounding away at Axe's skeleton. Axe's chest caved in; his body sloped to the side; and his left shoulder dropped at least three inches.

Four bones down; three more to go...

Ghost dropped back, left leg forward, same knee bent, his back foot extended in a perfect straight line, but turned out at an angle. He shifted his weight forward, onto his stationary knee, drew the back leg up to hip level, and snapped it forward like an iron lash, making contact with Axe's right femur. The thigh bone snapped. Maintaining perfect balance with his leg still in the air, he snapped the tibia next—one shin to match—then struck the upper right ilium like a bolt of lightning, crushing the dragyri's hip.

Axe's head fell back, and he roared in agony, his once-strong, muscular body flipping and flopping like a fish out of water.

Ghost didn't give a shit.

The worst was over—all seven bones.

And the fact that Axe was laboring to breathe, in so much pain he didn't know which way was up—the fact that his bones were ruined and crushed—would make the next set of injuries like piss on a forest fire.

So-the-fuck-what.

The damage was done.

Seven pounds of flesh—this part would be easy—just so long

as Ghost could measure the weight...at least somewhat accurately.

Rolling his fingers inside his gloves, he appraised Axe's torso with X-ray vision: the pecs, the glutes, the quads, and the abdomen—these were the largest muscular areas, and they offered the greatest quantity of flesh. He gazed down at his spiked leather gloves and chose to release his talons instead. This way he could strike, dig deep, tunnel his fingers inward, and grasp the largest handful of flesh as he twisted and wrenched back.

Strike, dig, twist, wrench!

Twice to each zone and once to the abdomen.

Ghost worked like a machine, in and out, wrenching, tearing, rending Axe's flesh until the male spit out blood and started to beg for mercy.

Not yet, Axe—not quite yet.

Ghost's fangs descended to their lethal-most length, and the flesh of his lips curled back around them, and that's when the thousand-year-old savage red haze took over.

He lunged for the prolific arteries, one at a time, tearing each open with his jagged teeth, then lapped at the blood and swallowed mouthfuls, which, truth be told, detracted from the overall pints on the floor.

Whatever.

Axillary, brachial, left and right femoral, renal, internal iliac, and finally, the *coup de grâce*: the carotid artery.

Axe's body may as well have been a spurting fountain—or better yet, an exploding geyser—such was the overwhelming spray of gore, plasma, and dark crimson fluid spewing from the dragyri's torso. And in that moment, the experience became transcendent, and Ghost fell to his knees and bathed in the splatter: He ripped off his gloves and lathered his hair in Axe's blood; he scooped up a handful and slurped from his palm; he sniffed it, snorted it, and breathed it in...

And then a strong, harsh elbow thrust him aside. "Enough!" Lord Saphyrius was standing beside Ghost on the dais, in as close to human form as Ghost had ever seen him. He must have entered the sanctuary when Ghost wasn't looking.

The sapphire dragon lord bathed Axe in silver-blue fire—he didn't heal his injuries, and he didn't close his wounds—but he stopped the flow of blood, tore his own radial artery open at the wrist, and poured his life-giving fluid down Axe's throat. The dragyri male was half-unconscious, so the dragon lord stroked his larynx to coax the substance down.

"Ghostaniaz, take Axe home," Lord Saphyrius commanded, and Ghost snapped out of it.

He shook his head to dislodge the cobwebs and stared up at the broken, bloody, hanging piece of meat that used to be Axeviathon Saphyrius.

Swallowing what could almost be described as the hint of *something* akin to an emotion, Ghost rose to his feet, leaped into the air, and grasped the chains above Axe's wrists—he wrenched his fists downward, both tugging and crushing in one brutal motion, and the huge, heavy body fell forward with a moan.

Ghost hoisted it over his shoulder like a fireman.

Refusing to look at Lord Saphyrius, Lord Ethyron, and especially his father, Lord Dragos, the brutal dragyri male turned on his heel and carried Axeviathon out of the throne room.

CHAPTER TWENTY-FIVE

TWO O'CLOCK AM

"You can't go in there, dragyra. Trust me, you don't want to see what's in that bed," Nakai Saphyrius told Amber, his tall, lean frame blocking the door to Axe's suite, even as the arcane tattoo emblazoned on his left temple seemed to glow with thermal light.

Amber got it.

She did.

Axe didn't want her to see him like this, and his lair mates were in there with him, taking care of him, doing gods knew what to try to ease his pain, but the shit wasn't working—the shouts, the groans, the deep, masculine keening—Amber could hear it through the door, and that was worse than actually being in the room...seeing Axe...up close and personal.

Up close and personal...

The thought made Amber pause.

What...why...how?

When had she decided that she wanted to be *close* to Axe, at least long enough to get him through the aftermath of the torture, at least until Friday night?

She couldn't explain it.

Not even to herself.

But something in her heart—something in that kiss—made her kindness, going forward, almost imperative. She wanted Axe to know, once she was gone, that it wasn't about him—what she had done. She wanted him to know that she had glimpsed his soul, and she had cared. She just couldn't live in the Pantheon. She just couldn't *belong* to anyone else...

"Nakai," she pleaded, reaching once more for the handle to the door. "I know he doesn't want to see me. I know *you guys* don't want me to see him, but all of this—it's because of me. I have a right to be in there with him." She couldn't believe her nerve, speaking to the dragyri male that way. Nakai may have been tall and lean, but the male was all hard, unforgiving muscle. And that damn tattoo—it gave Amber the willies.

Nakai sidestepped in front of the handle, jarring Amber's hand away. "Sorry," he said. "No can do. Why don't you retreat to the guest room and come back around 8 AM? By then, Zane will have healed Axe's injuries, and Axe will have had a chance to shower."

Amber stepped back and crossed her arms over her stomach. She couldn't believe she was about to do this, but oh well. It was time to take a different tack. "Call Lord Saphyrius," she demanded.

Nakai's dark-brown eyebrows shot up. "Come again?"

"Can you summon Lord Saphyrius? Ask him what he thinks? Let the dragon god decide the matter, whether or not I should be in there with Axe."

The corner of Nakai's mouth quirked up in a sardonic smile, and he swiped his bottom lip with his tongue. A harsh, masculine laugh escaped his throat, and he brushed the back of his neck with his hand. "No harm, no foul, Amber—I know you're new to the

Pantheon—but trust me when I tell you, that's not how it works. We don't summon the gods; they summon us. And this isn't the kind of matter one brings Lord Saphyrius in on. Seriously, why don't you—"

"*Why don't I what?*" Amber snapped, balling her hands into fists. "Retreat to the guest room, try to get some sleep? I swear, Nakai, if you say one more dismissive, condescending thing to me, I'm going to punch you in your throat."

The male jerked back. And then that sardonic smile appeared once again. In fact, Amber could've sworn he tightened his jaw—and his throat muscles—preparing for the blow that was coming.

"So women like us, the ones you capture—people like Jordan and me—we serve a purpose, but we mean nothing to you? We're like slaves, dogs, worms beneath your feet. That's what you want me to know? That's what you want me to get? That's what you want me to tell Axe *and* Lord Saphyrius?"

Nakai just shook his head.

"My opinion is less important than yours...than Axe's...is that what you're trying to say?"

Nakai met her gaze, and his light-brown pupils nearly blended with his sapphire irises, both refracting a deep, pearlescent light. "No," he whispered. "But you already know this. And if Lord Saphyrius showed up right now, you would be the first to scramble under the nearest piece of furniture. Truly, you don't want to play Red Rover with the gods. As for Axe, he'll understand." He looked off into the distance as if collecting his thoughts before returning his regard to Amber. "*Dragyra...*" He let the word linger. "This isn't an easy time for Axe, either, this claiming...and as for what happened to him tonight? It was beyond brutal, and for reasons you can't possibly understand, at least not yet. Let the male have some dignity; at least give him his pride. I know he'll be anxious to see you when the suffering is over. I'm not trying to deny you anything. I'm just trying to protect my lair mate."

Amber pursed her lips together. "Nakai, I haven't been straight with Axe. And I haven't been kind to him, either. Whatever happens going forward, this thing that happened tonight—in the temple—will be part of our history. His and mine, together. And he will always know that he fought for me, suffered for me, but I didn't fight for him." She almost stumbled on those last words—it was such a load of bullshit—there would be no Amber and Axe going forward.

But Nakai didn't know this...

"At least give him that. Give *me* that," she continued. "And you're right: I don't ever want to see that sapphire dragon god again, let alone actually speak to him. But I'm speaking to you—*I'm asking you*—let me go in and see Axe. I get where you're coming from, I really do. But in the end, it's not your call to make." She stared pointedly at his broad, powerful shoulders and his hard, unmovable chest. "Don't lord your power over me, Nakai. It's not fair. Convince me with your argument, if you can, but don't control me with your strength."

At this, Nakai sucked in a thin gulp of air. "Amber..."

"Let me go in."

"I don't think he's even coherent."

"I know; that's okay."

"Why?" he whispered. "Why is this so important?"

Much to her surprise, Amber curled inward. She pressed her elbows together, tucked them into her stomach, and let her head fall down, onto her fists. She was fighting back tears, and she couldn't explain them. She only knew that every shout, every whimper, every keening moan was pulling at her heart like Axe had looped fish-hooks through the organ, and he was tugging on the line.

It was crazy.

It made no damn sense.

And she didn't understand the what, why, or how of it...

She only knew that, any moment, if the male cried out again, those strings were going to jerk too hard and pull her heart right out of her chest. The truth of the matter was simple and shameful: Amber could barely breathe, and getting into that room was purely selfish.

"Nakai, I can't breathe." Alas, she had told him the truth.

Nakai grasped Amber's wrists and gently pulled them away from her face, and then he studied her features like he was trying to solve an ancient mystery, like he had never seen a woman before. After several uncomfortable seconds had passed, he brushed her cheek with his thumb, twisted his torso, and knocked on the door. "Amber's coming in," he barked through the panel, and then he reached for the handle, cranked it downward, and shoved the door open, about twelve or so inches. He placed his hand on the small of her back and bent to speak in her ear. "I don't know if the dragyri did it on purpose or what, but Ghost didn't touch Axe's face—or his hands. Try to keep your eyes straight ahead, locked on his eyes or his features if you can. If you have to touch him, take his hand."

Amber could hardly believe it.

Just like that, Nakai had given in, and she wasn't about to look a gift horse in the mouth.

Steeling her resolve and pulling back her shoulders, she raised her chin and slowly padded into the apartment.

* * *

Nakai had warned her to keep her eyes focused, straight ahead.

And Amber had thought she could do it.

But the sight that greeted her when she crossed the suite

toward the open master bedroom had done more than steal her breath—it had shaken Amber Carpenter to her core.

Someone had stripped the bed of linens and laid two or three absorbent mattress pads in their place. They had strewn a sheet of heavy plastic over the pads, and Axe was lying, naked, on the top of the plastic sheet. He had underwear on, and he was wrapped in blood-soaked bandages from his calves to his thighs, from his hips to his chest: both arms, both legs, and his stomach.

Levi was pacing like a restless tiger, back and forth in front of the iron-framed windows. Jace was puttering around in the kitchen, brewing something that smelled like broth, and Zane was planted in a chair beside the mattress, in the process of changing the bandages wrapped around Axe's chest.

Amber bit her bottom lip and pressed forward, trying to keep her eyes on Axe's face—on the unforgettable grimace of agony etched deep into all his features, and the utterly silent tears streaming down his tense, sunken cheeks.

She gasped.

Whether in surprise, shock, or horror…

It had never occurred to her that such a powerful warrior could cry.

And as she drew closer to the bed and the blood-soaked wrappings, she would've had to have been blind—again—to miss the fact that there were pieces—whole visible chunks of flesh—simply missing from the dragyri's body: planes, valleys, unnatural divots where sinew and muscle should have been. And Axe's breathing was labored to say the least. His sternum was broken, and so were his ribs. So was his clavicle, his femur, his tibia, and his hip. Those bones that were not protruding or visibly collapsed were twisted at an unnatural angle, making his once-powerful, magnificent frame look more like a gory pretzel, twisted beyond recognition.

Amber's stomach lurched, and she almost heaved.

She stopped walking, held out both palms, and struggled to take a deep breath.

Zane glanced up in silence, his hands still buried in Axe's chest. "Amber." Just one word, maybe a greeting, maybe just an acknowledgment of the fact she was there.

And just what the hell had she thought she could do?

Nakai had been right all along.

Axe's bewitching eyes opened; he turned his head in her direction and groaned.

The motion must have been too much for the dragyri because his abdomen spasmed. Zane leaned forward and rolled him over, onto his side. and Axe started to puke his guts out—at least what was left of them—into a tray propped beside his head. After... during...every heave, he shouted in agony as his broken muscles contracted and released.

Oh, gods of the Pantheon, what had she done...

"I'm sorry," she whispered to no one in particular, and then she turned on her heel to run out of the room.

Three steps.

Maybe four.

And she slid to a halt...

Braced her hands on her knees and caught her breath.

Curling her lips around her teeth and biting down for courage, she drew in three deep breaths and stood up straight. And then she strolled into the kitchen, wet a dish cloth beneath the faucet, and filled the towel with ice. Ignoring the Dragyr who were watching her like circling vultures, she paced to the edge of the bed, dropped down onto her knees, and pressed the ice to the back of Axe's neck. "Shh," she crooned to him softly. "I'm right here, Axe. Breathe, just breathe...in and out." She didn't know how she did it, but she slowed her heartbeat to match Axeviathon's and tried gallantly to breathe with him...*for him.* "In and out—I know it's hard, but you're doing good."

His chest stopped quivering, and he finally stopped retching.

She grasped the edge of the tray, slid it aside, and glanced over her shoulder at Jace. "Will you empty this, please?" She didn't wait for the male to reply. She turned to Zane and narrowed her brows. "Can you roll him back over?" she asked.

Zane nodded and turned his lair mate, as gently as possible, back into a supine position.

Axe grunted in pain.

"Look at me," Amber told him. "Right here." She tapped her cheeks beneath her lower eyelids.

His eyes locked with hers, and she forced a tender smile. Then she cupped his cheekbones in her hands and began to massage his temples. Every ten or fifteen seconds, she slid one hand toward the back of his head, caressed his damp, blood-stained hair, and massaged his scalp in soothing, gentle circles.

Slowly, his eyes fell shut, though he still grimaced, grunted, and winced.

"Shh," Amber continued, pouring all her concentration into the tips of her fingers, while envisioning a white healing light streaming into him. And then, as if out of nowhere, she was suddenly transported to another place, another time, and another broken soul, equally wracked with agony:

Amber was holding, caressing, and singing to an eighteen-month-old girl.

A girl who was hungry, dehydrated, and covered in blisters.

She was humming a lullaby to her foster sister, Tina.

And as the melody returned, and her compassion awakened, she knew that something intrinsic had happened when Axe had healed her trauma bonds—she knew because she hadn't felt anything like this in a decade.

She hadn't felt sympathy...or tenderness...or *love?*

She blinked the thought away—she was confusing Axe with Tina.

Yet, in that instant—that transcendent, singular moment—as the past and the present blended as one, Amber knew one thing for certain: There was nothing she wouldn't do to stop Axe's suffering.

Absolutely nothing.

She had entered that convenience store, so many years ago, for Tina.

And even knowing all that would come to pass, she would enter it again—for Axe—if it would take away his agony.

CHAPTER TWENTY-SIX

Axe stared up at the roaring waterfall, even as he reveled in the feel of his strong, vibrant, *perfect* body. He had never been more aware of his power and never more grateful to be Dragyr. Not only had the emerald discus assisted Zanaikeyros in Axe's healing, but Axe had come out of the ordeal stronger, more powerful, feeling more alive.

And now, all he wanted to do was reconnect with Amber, the golden-haired beauty who had kneeled by his bed, breathed for the dragyri when he couldn't catch his breath, and done all she could to nurse him back to health.

Her kindness had truly surprised him.

And if truth be told, Axe was pretty sure it had surprised her too.

"So, this is the famous waterfall..." Amber's soft, almost lyrical voice floating on a breeze behind him. *Good*—she had seen his note, the one Axe had placed on her nightstand, and she had come to meet him as he had hoped and asked.

Axe turned around and held out his hand. "Dragyra, come closer." He waved her forward.

Amber shook her head and planted her heels in a soft mound of grass.

Ah, so now she was feeling skittish...

In the light of day, she was likely still planning to go...

To still meet with Tony and try to escape.

Following the healing—the expert application of Zane's silver-blue fire and the time it had taken for Axe to regenerate—the two dragyri lair mates had spoken, albeit briefly: *yes, to the concert, to Jordan meeting Macy; yes, to taking Amber along if she asked; and no, to involving the other Dragyr—Axe's extended lair mates. Axe planned to handle Tony alone.* He was itching for the chance to test his new, improved body.

He was yearning to release his claws, tunnel through the human's imploding chest, and retrieve Tony's still-beating heart in his hand. He wanted the merciless human male to see his own pulsing organ dripping blood in front of him as his life-force leaked onto the ground.

"After all we shared this morning," Axe said to Amber, "you're still afraid of me, still unsure of our bond?"

Amber wrung her hands together and shifted nervously in place. "Axe, I...I don't know what to say. Last night, I mean, early this morning, that was different, I guess. You needed my support."

Axe smiled wanly and nodded his head. "Yeah, there's no denying that, Amber girl. But it seems to me, you needed me too: to be close to me, beside me, to see me through the whole ordeal."

She shivered and turned her attention to the waterfall: stream after glorious stream of frothing, crystal water rushing out of several rocky crevices at once, flanked by autumn-colored trees that never changed their colors, growing proudly...impossibly... out of the rocks. And the constant ambient roar was like a natural lullaby, nature's soothing song, serenading the Sapphire Lair. "It's beautiful," she said, cleverly changing the subject.

"Yes, it is," Axe replied, narrowing his gaze on his dragyra's stunning eyes and changing the subject right back. "You're beautiful, and your kindness, your need...last night...was beautiful as well."

Her dark amber gaze met his, and she paled. "Axe, I don't...I don't—"

"You don't what?" he interrupted. "If anyone should feel uneasy...or embarrassed...a little bit off in this moment, it's me, don't you think?"

She smiled then, and the visage was positively breathtaking. "Not embarrassed...no. You had no control over what happened to you." She cast her eyes toward the ground and gently cleared her throat. "Axe, who is Ghost?"

So, she was changing the subject again...

And now, it was Axe's turn to shudder.

Shit, just shit.

That was one subject Axe would rather avoid; it might be years—hell, decades—before he could speak that name again, look that brutal Genesis bastard in the eyes. The freakin' dragyri had bathed in Axe's blood... "Why do you ask?" he finally murmured. It was the best he could do.

Amber shrugged, and the lift and fall of her exquisitely narrow shoulders, her deep-set collarbone, her long, graceful neck drew Axe's eyes—and his appreciation—like a moth to a flame.

"It was just something Nakai said," she replied. "He said he didn't know if Ghost did it on purpose, or not, but that he didn't damage your face or your hands." She quickly equivocated: "I dunno, that just kind of struck me. I don't know if you refer to the dragon lords as ghosts—or what they become when they're violent and punitive—but if I wanted to hurt someone, really degrade or humiliate them, I think I would disfigure their face." She grimaced and shook her head in apology. "Don't get me wrong: I don't have those kinds of violent tendencies." She punctuated the words with an uncomfortable chuckle. "And I'm not making light of what this dragon god did, but it's just...from everything I've ever read in newspapers or seen in documentaries, when someone attacks another person out of rage, out of deep-seated hatred, they always slash or ruin their face." She absently brushed her hand through her hair—she was feeling nervous, or perhaps a bit out of line. "And another thing: At least when it comes to humans, we communicate with all five senses: sight, hearing, taste, smell, and touch. If we don't have a voice—or even when we do—we still connect with others through those perceptions." She sighed in exasperation, as if she felt she wasn't making any sense. "I dunno; I guess I'm just saying that it struck me too that the dragon did so much damage, yet left all five of your senses intact, even down to not touching your hands. To me, if I didn't know better, I would think it was some sort of gesture of mercy, like he wanted to hurt you, but not as bad as he could. He wanted to injure you, but he went out of his way not to insult or humiliate you."

Axe took a step back.

For a moment, just a fleeting second, he felt like he was naked and exposed, yet again, in front of his dragyra, and he was a bit taken aback by the feeling as well as Amber's insight.

What the actual fuck...

She couldn't be right, could she?

Had Ghostaniaz actually held back in the only way he could?

The thought left him mystified and more than a little confused, but he didn't want to go there—not now. His time with Amber was way too precious. They only had five more days before Axe had to take her to the temple, and based upon what was about to go down—the concert, the field, Axe *ending* Tony for good—the next twenty-four hours might be wasted as well. "Ghost," he breathed the word on a shaky inhale, "is the Genesis Son of Lord Dragos, the darkest of the seven dragon lords. The long and short of it: Lord Dragos owed Lord Ethyron a favor, and Ghost is not known for being gentle or compassionate, so Lord Ethyron used the dragyri to dole out the torture." There was nothing else Axe wanted to say, so he let the words linger in the ambiance of the waterfall.

Amber nodded. "I see." She stood there in silence for a couple of seconds before adding, "So, I guess that you and Ghost are friends then? He really didn't want to do it." She made the last sentence a statement, not a question, and once again, Axe was perplexed.

Maybe looking from the outside in, Amber was able to see something Axe couldn't.

He wasn't sure that anyone considered Ghost Dragos a friend, but then, there it was—the male had managed to take seven pounds of flesh, break seven critical bones, and extract seven pints of blood without ever touching Axe's face or hands, without dulling even one of his five senses.

Hmm.

Fodder for another day.

"Come here, sweet angel," Axe entreated once again, extending his hand. She smiled this time, but she still didn't budge—so Axe crossed the grassy ridge and went to her. "We're past this, pretty lady," he rasped. "All this stranger shit." He placed two fingers over her heart. "I think I've seen you, and you've seen me." She started to back away, and he hooked his arm around her waist, drawing her into his body—*to hell with it!* "Thank you for what you did." He pressed a tender kiss against the base of her throat.

She shuddered and turned her head to the side, tucking in her chin.

"Nah," he murmured. "We're not going back there. We've come too far for that bullshit." He grasped her chin lightly and turned her toward him, and then he bent his head and kissed her lightly. He drew back, just a smidgeon, and hovered. "Thank you for what you did, Amber girl," he repeated. And this time, he brushed his bottom lip against her top lip, drew it into his mouth and suckled it, then repeated the ministration with her full bottom lip, also tracing the same with his tongue.

He moaned.

And she sighed, her breath mingling with his.

And that was all the encouragement Axe needed. He drew her in closer, pressed his body against hers, and tunneled his hands in her hair. And then he kissed his dragyra until she was breathless.

CHAPTER TWENTY-SEVEN

"A re you ready, my love?" Zane Saphyrius spoke the words out loud, but their deeper meaning was implied: *Are you ready for an evening with Macy, the country-western concert, and all the drama about to go down with Amber... and possibly Axe?*

As always, Zane's mate looked ravishing: Jordan was wearing a stylish, form-fitting dress that fell just above her knees, with a low-cut zipper-detail at the neckline. Yeah, to his way of thinking, it exposed a little too much cleavage—and the way all those thick auburn waves fell beyond her shoulders, accentuating the hazel-eyed beauty's collarbone? He would've preferred a plain brown gunnysack, but his dragyra had a mind of her own, a brilliant mind at that, and it was one of the many reasons he adored her.

"Ready and excited," she said with a wink, turning to smile at Amber.

Amber was a couple of inches shorter than Jordan, but she had more than made up for it with her spiked-heel leather boots, and that hip-hugging, dark red miniskirt with the contoured black blouse wasn't exactly camouflage material. For a female who was planning to slip away and run, she couldn't have dressed more inappropriately.

Ah, but then wasn't that the genius behind the sexy outfit?

No reason to give Axe anything to suspect...

In fact, since nine o'clock that morning, and since Axe had been healed, he and his dragyra had moved about the lair in relative comfort if not comradery. Zane had noticed the fledgling couple in a corner, on more than one occasion, talking in hushed but amiable whispers. He had seen them eating alone at the bar in the central lair's kitchen. And he had watched them retreat to Axe's private lair for more privacy, Amber's slender hand tucked into Axe's meaty palm.

Zane didn't think the couple had...well...consummated the burgeoning union, and it wasn't because Zane was nosy or thinking about his lair mate's private affairs. It was just that Zane was a dragyri male, a primordial, wild creature at his core, and all the Dragyr had a heightened sense of smell. Again, not something Zane couldn't—or wouldn't—ordinarily tamp down to afford his lair mates some privacy, but like the primitive creatures they were, the Dragyr had a tendency to mark their territory, and scent was a big piece of that picture. Purposeful or not, Axe would've left his...stamp...all over Amber. He couldn't have helped it if he had tried.

"So, I just hold your hand, and there's nothing else I need to do?" Amber's soft, hesitant tone jolted Zane out of his musings. She was asking Jordan about the portal.

"That's it," Jordan said. Then she fixed her gaze on Zane. "Right? She holds my hand, I hold yours, and you take it from there?"

Zane flashed his mate a smile. "Yep," he said, his shoulders falling back. "Hold on until we arrive at the concert, then let her go. That's it; that's all." His pupils narrowed, and he switched to telepathic communication. *Axe will be right beside us in a parallel portal; he's wearing black jeans, his working boots, and a plain gray sleeveless muscle shirt: the dirty-blond in the dark, rounded Dolce and Gabbana sunglasses. He's going to hang back for the entire concert, blend in with the crowd, and keep an eye on Amber. So try not to get caught up in any outside drama—try to enjoy your night out with Macy. I know this is detracting from your plans quite a bit, but seriously, Jordan—Axe will be right behind you. If Amber tries to slip away, let her go. If she pulls that cell phone out of her purse, don't say anything. Axe knows she has it, and he's on top of it. When the concert is over, come back to the same exact spot I drop you off at. I will be there waiting, and the portal will be open. Take Macy's hand, just like we talked about, and step into the portal entrance. We'll transport her home before we head back to the Pantheon, and just a tap on her shoulder, as little mind control as possible, and Macy will be none the wiser. She'll have no memory of seeing me or of the portal—she'll believe she made it home in a taxi.*

Jordan nodded. "You ready, Amber?" she asked, once again, flashing an ingratiating smile at the newest member of the Sapphire Lair, whether the female believed she was staying...or not.

Amber gulped, and her stunning eyes widened with both curiosity and apprehension. "I think so," she said. "This doesn't hurt or feel funny, right?"

Jordan laughed. "It feels a little funny, but no, it doesn't hurt. It's kind of a really cool sensation actually."

Amber shook her head briskly as if dispersing her nerves. "Well, I guess there's no time like the present."

Zane studied her expression—she was definitely tense.

And by the shadowed look in her amber eyes, she was feeling both hope...

And regret.

* * *

As far as country-western concerts went, Amber had to hand it to Jordan and Macy: The band was excellent; the crowd really got into it; and if only for a while, the catchy lyrics, the bass guitar, and the multi-part harmonies almost made Amber forget what she was really up to at this "girl's night out."

Almost...

Texting a car service from a bathroom stall, trying to figure out a way to make a break for it at exactly 11:40, and worrying about Jordan, Macy, and Zane had still occupied most of Amber's thoughts. Jordan was more than just human now—according to Axe, she had been converted in the temple—and Macy, while funny, nice, and fairly easygoing, also seemed like a person who could turn on the hysterics, if given enough drama to run with. As for Zane? Again, Axe had made it clear that Zane couldn't step out of the portal, at least not while he was alone, without another dragyri to escort him—something about Lord Saphyrius' orders, something about a recent mandate from all the dragon lords—so while that made Amber feel a little bit better, it also freaked her out.

What if Zane brought Levi, Jace, Nakai, or Axe with him when he came to pick up Jordan?

As it stood, it seemed too easy by half that Axe had not questioned Amber about her cell phone: the fact that she had kept it—and used it—the entire time she had been in the Pantheon. *And just how the hell did that work, anyway?* There weren't likely to be any cell phone towers littered about the supernatural world, and Amber had never asked for a Wi-Fi password, assuming the Dragyr even used such a thing.

The whole thing was just way too easy.

Way too uncomplicated.

And if Amber had learned anything throughout her troubled life, it was that nothing ever came that easy...

The band's lead singer, a rusty-haired cowboy with wild, unruly locks and torn, faded blue jeans, kicked at the stage with the heel of his boot; strummed three last notes on his acoustic guitar; and raised his cowboy hat high into the air, waving the Stetson at the crowd. "Thank you, Denver! We love you!" he shouted, and the crowd broke into an uproar.

Macy and Jordan were clapping wildly, straining their necks to get one last glimpse, as Amber reached for her cell phone, thumbed it on, and glanced at the clock: 11:35 PM.

Shit!

She had five minutes to get out of the amphitheater, make her way to the curb, find her driver, and jump into the car. Hopefully, the driver had followed her texted instructions to the letter, eager for the $200 tip: *Just so you know, I'm trying to ditch my boyfriend after the concert. Long story, but there's $200 in it for you if you can help make that happen. Please tie an orange ribbon, scarf, or bandana around the driver's side mirror and keep the car running! Unlock and OPEN the backseat door and be prepared to hit the gas the minute I get in. $200 cash if you do all five things!*

What made matters even worse—without knowing why she needed it, Axe had given Amber the two hundred bucks.

Oh, well, she couldn't worry about that now.

She tapped Jordan on the back of her shoulder. "This crowd!" she shouted, shaking her head and grimacing. "The noise! I'm starting to get claustrophobic—I'll meet the two of you out front." She held her breath, knowing this would never fly. There was no way Jordan Anderson-Saphyrius was going to let Amber just wander away. Amber's leg was twitching as she tapped it against the ground, all her senses in high alert. She had already mapped out a snake-like route, the first five or six bodies she would need to weave around in order to make a run for it.

She was just waiting for Jordan to object.

Jordan's bright hazel eyes seemed to cloud over, and something that looked oddly like sorrow flashed in their depths, and then the dragyra slowly nodded her head. "Okay." Drowned out by the crowd, she mouthed the words in an exaggerated fashion: "We'll see you in a few."

And yes...

Yes!

The band was coming back for one last encore.

It didn't get any better than this.

Stunned by what had just occurred...as well as what Jordan had said...Amber slipped her cell phone back into her purse and turned on her booted, spiked heels to get the hell out of the amphitheater.

Too simple.

Too perfect.

Too good to be true.

Nothing in life ever came that easy...

Didn't matter—Amber could think about that later.

Right now, she had a date with a midsized SUV, and hopefully, one with an orange marker wrapped around the driver's-side mirror.

CHAPTER TWENTY-EIGHT

Axeviathon could have followed the SUV on foot—his species was capable of moving that rapidly. He could have also followed the driver from the air, releasing his wheat-colored wings, a perfect match to his dirty-blond hair. While none of the Dragyr could shift into fully formed dragons, they all had use of both wings and scales, and if all that was too much or too complicated—following Amber while trying to remain invisible—he could've leaped blocks at a time if he needed to.

But Axe was a bit more practical than that, and he had no internal need to manufacture high drama. So he pulled an effortless vanishing act, hiding his molecular structure from human peepers, and climbed onto the roof of the vehicle. He tried to time it perfectly, settle his weight on the SUV just as Amber was settling into the backseat; and while the driver jerked, ducked, glanced upward, and frowned, the human male could not make sense of the strange sensation.

Mortals were so out of touch with their intuition.

Even when it screamed, "Something's going on here!"

If they didn't see it, hear it—touch, taste, or smell it—they were highly unlikely to act on it.

One less problem for Axe to solve, one less mind to manipulate...

He rolled onto his back, crossed his legs at the ankle, and linked both hands behind his head.

Ten minutes...

Fifteen?

Probably no more than twenty...

And Amber would arrive at the field for her rendezvous with Tony.

Whatever, Axe grumbled inwardly. Didn't matter if Tony thought he had a date with Amber—truth was, Axe had a date with Tony, and Tony had a date with death.

* * *

Amber still could not believe her luck.

Nothing...

Absolutely nothing of any consequence had happened.

Amber had walked out of the concert, immediately identified the correct car by the glaring orange ribbon wrapped around the mirror, and climbed in the backseat with zero interference. And the drive across town had been equally uneventful. In fact, as the SUV now slowed to a crawl and pulled to the curb, alongside a barren field and a dry canal, the timing was virtually perfect:

Twelve o'clock midnight on the dot!

"Thank you," Amber said softly, bending forward to remove her leather boots. While she didn't relish the thought of padding through the dry brush and wild sod in her stockings, she knew she couldn't run in such high, spiked heels, and they would just sink into the uneven turf anyway.

The young, bright-eyed driver turned around and glanced at Amber with suspicion. "You want me to drop you off here?"

"Yep."

"You sure? There's nothing around but a dark, empty field. That can't be safe for a woman on her own."

Amber forced an insincere smile. "It's fine. I know this area— I grew up on the other side of that field. Trust me, there's no one around this time of night."

The driver peered through the passenger window and surveyed the field in earnest. "You sure? Seems kind of creepy to me."

Amber reached into her purse, withdrew ten twenty-dollar bills, and handed them to the driver. "Here. The ride itself was already paid for on my card, but this is something extra for you."

The driver smiled, took the cash, and tucked it inside his wallet. "Thanks, but I really didn't do that much."

Amber nodded. "You got me here safely and without any drama—that was all I asked and more than I could hope for." She sighed as she reached for the handle on the backseat door.

Safely and without any drama...

That still remained to be seen.

She stared through the window, out into the darkness, and tried to calm her nerves.

Amber was *this close* to freedom...

This close to hooking up with Tony and finally getting away from Axe.

So why did the whole arrangement feel ass-backward?

Why did she feel as if she was about to make the biggest mistake of her life?

Amber had no intentions of staying with Tony, not anymore, not after everything that had gone down with that monster named Trader, and all she had learned about Zeik and Grunge. The trio still held the power of life and death over Amber; they still had the ability to turn her over to the police and have her arrested for the convenience store robbery. They still had all kinds of influence over judges and courts and legal proceedings—and now that Amber knew what Zeik and Grunge really were, that was the understatement of the century—but they no longer had any influence over Amber. Her perspective had changed, and her desire to live free, or die trying, had finally surpassed her fear. Even being locked up in a jail cell would be better than the way she had existed for so long...

Climbing out of the SUV, she thanked the driver one last time and stared across the field.

She couldn't see Tony—at least not yet—but she knew he was out there, somewhere: waiting, hiding, biding his time in the darkness, ready to reclaim his most prized possession, the girl who had been too weak to fight him. The girl who had walked out of a convenience store, ten years earlier, and given the sick, twisted bastard her entire life.

She laughed softly beneath her breath.

Karma could be a bitch, and the irony wasn't lost on Amber:

Someone bigger, *badder*, and far more determined than Tony had also claimed Amber as his own and taken her back, away from her captors. Tony had lost Amber the same way he had gotten her, and as absurd as it sounded, that *someone* was a dragyri male named Axeviathon. And in his own blunt, possessive, hard-ass way, he had given Amber the one thing Tony had managed to keep from her all those years—her self-respect.

Amber Carpenter no longer felt worthless.

No, her circumstances hadn't really changed—Zeik, Tony, and Grunge could still cause her harm, and even Axe wouldn't let her go that easily. But knowing she had value, that her life might just be worth living, had given her everything she needed to fight for her freedom.

Nothing and *everything* had changed for Amber.

CHAPTER TWENTY-NINE

THE PANTHEON

Ghostaniaz Dragos paced restlessly along the winding, vertical edge of the aqua-blue infinity pool on his private ocean-side balcony, outside the Diamond Lair. The male felt twitchy.

He felt irritable, bitter, and completely amped up.

He knew he should've been feeling something softer, prettier, like compassion or empathy, maybe even remorse for the way he had brutalized another dragyri mercenary. After all, that shit he had done to Axe—ripping the male apart like some random, worthless carrion—crushing his bones and rending his flesh? A reasonable being would have felt something other than *twitchy*, right?

But Ghost was anything but reasonable.

Anything but normal...

And he was tired of the whole damn creep-show, playing his part for Lord Dragos' amusement.

Ghost was ready to get off the ride.

And if that meant finally ending his pointless, miserable existence—pulling the plug, once and for all—then so be it.

The question wasn't *if*, but *how*.

Perhaps he could provoke his demented daddy into doing it for him by saying something—doing something—so vile and disrespectful that the dragon lord would snap. Or perhaps he could take a solo trip through the portal, head earthside without any backup, and see what kind of trouble he could get into. Humans could also be provoked to great violence with the right incentive, but damnit, just how would that work?

A hail of bullets wouldn't do anything to a dragyri male but tickle him.

Hell, even a well-tossed grenade would bounce off Ghost's scales, and releasing the thick, hardened armor would be instinctive, the moment the missile was tossed in his direction.

Perhaps a cannon or a B-52 Bomber would do the trick, but for that, he'd have to visit a war zone. And where was Ghost going to find a B-52 Bomber, conveniently flying through the air, scanning the ground for a strange and dangerous supernatural creature to strike with its entire payload? He would have a better chance of finding Michael Myers or Jason Voorhees, fictional characters from human horror flicks.

Perhaps he could take a stroll through a field littered with land mines, do his damnedest to hold back his scales and set off so many explosions in a row that something finally hit a vital organ. But then again, so what? Unless the damn things blew his head off and ripped his amulet from around his neck, his immortal heart would keep right on ticking until Lord Dragos could sew him back up. Hell, Ghost was the antithesis of Humpty Dumpty —the dragon gods could always put him back together again!

But that didn't mean he couldn't do his best to get into trouble.

Do his best to incite his father.

That didn't mean Lord Dragos could never be provoked to kill his own Genesis Son.

Yeah, Ghost was going to head earthside and see what he could see.

Who knew?

Maybe he'd commit a crime so abhorrent the humans would lock him up—and he'd let them. Fast-forward to execution—*now, wouldn't that be a hoot?*—Ghost could watch the Homo sapiens watching him with surprise when their lethal injection didn't do jack shit or the electric chair shorted out. *Did humans still even use that contraption?* He could wait until they chopped him up into itty-bitty pieces and accidentally got that amulet off.

Whatever.

He'd figure it out when he got there.

Reaching for his amulet, he thumbed the flawless diamond and opened the portal. If nothing else, he could work off some nervous energy, piss off his dad, and provoke the kind of beating that would make the punishment Ghost had given Axe look like child's play.

If nothing else, Ghost deserved that much...

CHAPTER THIRTY

EARTHSIDE

Trader Vice sank into the shadows behind a dead, rotting cottonwood tree rooted along the bank of a dry canal. The night air was balmy—calm, warm, and still—and Amber Carpenter was traversing the field, heading in Trader, Tony, Zeik, and Grunge's direction like a little lamb winding her way to the slaughter.

She had no earthly idea what was waiting for her beneath the pale, leaden moonlight.

But that wasn't the shit that got Trader excited.

No, the pagan sin-eater was almost aroused by the scent wafting to his keen, flared nostrils: the scent of a powerful dragyri male following the human girl like a lovesick bitch. Trader had to suppress the urge to laugh out loud. So, the son of a hyena thought he could just render his body invisible and take out the human without a single glitch. He had no idea he was walking into an ambush, that *he* was the guest of honor.

Zeik, Grunge, you pickin' up on this shit? Trader called to his demon companions telepathically.

If a grin could be heard through a telepathic transmission,

then Zeik Craven was grinning from ear to ear. *Yeah, I can smell that crap*, he grunted.

Twenty paces behind his girl, Grunge cut in.

Trader shook his head as he turned his attention to Antonio Rossi—the poor, pitiful Italian was waving his arms, jumping up and down from inside the bottom of the dry creek bed, trying to get Amber's attention. *Did he really think his demon cohorts gave a flying fig about his love life or his plan to retrieve his girl?*

This shit was going off like clockwork...

Amber saw Tony waving and made an instant course-correction, picking up her speed and heading in the human's direction, even as Zeik and Grunge rose from beneath the earth, about ten feet east of the riverbed, like specters arising from a shallow grave, and made their presence known.

Amber skidded to a halt.

And the dragyri male flashed into view, dropping his invisible camo with a quickness.

So, it *was* Axeviathon Saphyrius, after all, and the male was radiating all kinds of angry, protective, no-nonsense power: sapphire, citrine, and *emerald*?

What the hell?

Trader grew instantly serious; it would take all three demons to bring Axe down, and the goal was not to behead him, but to get his huge, hulking ass back to Lord Drakkar—to usher the male to the underworld as a trophy!

Zeik moved first. He covered the meadow in two seconds flat, hurdled the riverbed, and dove at Axe, wielding his powerful fists like a battering ram, one lightning-fast blow after another, aimed at the dragyri's face.

Axe blocked that shit like he had second sight *and* tunnel vision, knocking each punch away with ease before landing a blow of his own—a wicked, powerful uppercut—right to the center of the demon's rib cage. The splintering bones crackled and popped, and Grunge dove into the fray. He summersaulted over the two tangling males and landed on Axe's back, anchoring one arm around the dragyri's throat.

"Amber, help me out!" Tony was extending his hand to the girl, trying to crawl out of the riverbed—that human piece of trash was going to try to make a break for it.

Try to take the girl and run...

"There's nowhere you can hide," Trader growled, slinking from behind the cottonwood. "We get Axe; you get your girl. You try any other foul, duplicitous shit, and your bitch-ass is dead. *Comprende?*"

Tony's glassy green eyes grew wide.

Yeah, he got it...

Tony motioned for Amber to step back and retrieved a loaded Luger P08 from the back of his belt, also revealing a leather sheath containing two lethal stilettos, and took several retreating steps in the bottom of the ravine, even as he nodded his head. "Just get him down here," he murmured, mustering new courage and referring to Axe.

Axeviathon released a menacing set of jagged fangs and sank them into Grunge's arm. He bit down hard, snarled like a rabid beast, and wrenched his head from side to side, tearing a hunk of flesh from the demon's arm.

Grunge grunted, but he did not let go.

Axe dropped into a squat, tucked his head forward, and flipped the sin-eater over his back. And then he fell downward, bent his right leg, and slammed his knee into Grunge's face.

The sin-eater's nose exploded.

But Zeik was now back on his feet.

One hand braced against his shattered rib cage, the other fisting the hilt of a dagger, Zeik leaned over Axe and stabbed him in the neck, sinking the blade to the hilt about three inches forward of the trapezius and two inches above the clavicle—right before the neck met the shoulder.

Axeviathon growled in pain...and fury.

And that's when Amber screamed—so the female was finally starting to get the picture.

"Amber, run!" Axe shouted, wrenching the blood-soaked blade from his neck, twirling it through his dexterous fingers, and thrusting it upward into Zeik's exposed groin. He nailed Zeik's right gonad like he was playing Pin the Tail on the Donkey, and the otherwise invincible pagan hit the deck.

Meanwhile, Grunge spit out a mouthful of blood and saliva, grasped Axe by both ankles, and tugged. The dragyri fell onto his back, and Grunge tried to drag him, snake him forward, pull him closer to Tony and the ditch.

Axe wrenched one leg free and stomped Grunge in the face, dragging a spiked spur across the demon's eyes. And then the dragyri got well and truly pissed. His skin hardened, calcifying into leathery scales, and he threw back his head and roared. The meadow shook, the ground began to undulate, and several dead branches on the cottonwood tree snapped and fell to the ground.

And then a sweltering, glowing red flame erupted from the dragyri's throat, streamed forward in an arc, and scorched the earth in front of the sapphire dragyri's feet, engulfing both Zeik and Grunge in the fire.

The demons were smart enough to get the hell out of Dodge —they both pulled a vanishing act at once, reappearing on the other side of the ravine, next to Trader, where they could heal their injuries and swiftly regroup.

Shiiiiit...

Trader had had enough of the nonsense.

Any minute now, the entire Sapphire Lair was going to appear in the field, and the element of surprise would be lost—the ambush would be over. And that meant, between Requiem Pyre and Lord Drakkar, Trader would be nothing more than a memory, the ghost of a demon whose soulless black heart had been ripped out by his king or Drak's sorcerer.

Hell.

No.

Trader wasn't going out like that.

He moved so quickly his lunge was a blur; snatched Amber by her dark-gold hair; and dragged her back to the edge of the ravine, to the outer and upper bank of the dry riverbed. "Axeviathon," he snarled. "Watch me kill this bitch!" He ran the tip of his tongue along the length of her jugular, held his left arm in the air for added drama and effect, and released the demonic turquoise-and-black tiger snake.

The serpent struck Amber posthaste, sinking its fangs deep into her neck, but Trader hesitated to release the fast-acting, lethal venom...just yet. Amber was far too useful as a pawn and a lure. The way Trader saw it, the dragyri couldn't risk bathing both Trader *and* Amber in scorching flames—the male would have to get *up close and personal* to save his dragyra—and that was exactly where Trader wanted him.

The realization must've hit the dragyri because Axe jack-knifed off the ground, landed on his heavy feet, and dove through the air like a rocket, at Trader.

The wily demon was ready.

He withdrew the snakebite, shuffled to the side, and spewed a torrent of acid into the air.

As Axe's head jerked back and his talons sliced forward, Trader spun around with the speed of a preternatural turbine and elbowed the dragyri in the chest. Axe's large, hulking body jerked upon impact, changed course in midair, and flew into the ravine.

And just like a good, dutiful human, Tony unloaded the Luger P08.

But Trader wasn't about to stop there!

He understood his true mission, and he understood it well.

Bracing both palms on his knees, he began to heave...and retch...and heave...

And retch...

Until the once-dry riverbed filled to the brim with Requiem Pyre's viscous, granular, iniquitous quicksand and Axeviathon Saphyrius sank like the lost *Titanic*, deep into the paralyzing concoction, all the way up to his neck.

CHAPTER THIRTY-ONE

Amber watched in stupefied horror as the grisly scene played out in front of her.

She had tried to run—she really had—but she hadn't gotten more than fifty yards when that giant of a demon, Trader, had snatched her by the hair, dragged her back to the edge of the riverbed, and released a freakin' blue-and-black snake that had bitten her in the neck.

Those fangs had felt like two rusty nails—worse than that really, the sting of a dozen scorpions at once—but for some strange reason, it hadn't released any venom. At least Amber didn't think it had, because in that case she would already be dead.

And *oh, gods, oh gods, oh gods*, Zeik had stabbed Axe in the neck; Tony had shot him multiple times; and now the immortal dragyri was practically drowning in front of all of them, stuck in some bizarre, thick, unnatural substance—Axeviathon couldn't move or fight!

What was it Trader had said?

"We get Axe; you get your girl..."

The whole damn thing had been a setup all along!

Amber had followed Tony; Axe had followed Amber; and Zeik and Grunge had been waiting from the start—everyone had known, but her.

Amber's stomach heaved, and she felt light-headed.

Yet, as much as every instinct in her body told her to run—get away from the riverbed and at least try to hide—she couldn't look away from the morbid scene in front of her.

It was all happening so fast.

Too fast...

Axe's features were strained—he was trying to move, but for some unknown reason, he was virtually powerless. He couldn't even spit fire from his throat, and unlike that night in Amber's living room...her and Tony's master bedroom...the Sapphire Lair was not showing up.

Amber gulped, and her heart began to beat a cacophony in her chest, threatening to rupture the cavity. Trader was sliding down the bank of the riverbed, swimming through the supernatural quicksand—*why wasn't it paralyzing him, too?*—and slowly making his way toward Axe, even as Tony had retrieved a stiletto, waded out into the center of the channel, and creeped like a slinking predator, coming up behind Axe.

Oh, gods!

Oh, no...

What the hell...what the hell...

What the hell!

Tony looked positively possessed, his crystal-green eyes growing dark with shadows—with desperation—as he brought the dagger forward, swung his arm around Axe's neck, and drew the blade crosswise, against Axe's throat.

Amber screamed!

And so did Trader...

"Rossi! What the fuck! *We need him alive.* Back off, Tony—let us take it from here!"

Tony wasn't listening.

It was as if he were deaf.

He began to saw the stiletto back and forth, carving Axe's neck with the blade, and Amber's knees gave out beneath her: *Mother of Mercy, he was beheading Axe right in front of her.*

Her mouth fell open, and something slipped out of it, something akin to a keening wail. With every slice of the sharp, silver stiletto, Amber felt like a piece of her heart was being sliced in two...as if Tony were carving them both to ribbons.

Her body began to tremble uncontrollably, and then it struck her—

The stiletto!

The stilettos...

Tony had been hiding a Luger P08 in his belt, along with *two* concealed stilettos in a leather sheath, and when he had reached out to Amber for aid—*Amber, help me out!*—she had reached toward Tony with her right hand extended and slipped the second stiletto out of the sheath with her left, tossing it behind her, onto the ground.

How the hell had she forgotten that?

Axeviathon groaned in pain, even as Tony kept slicing at his throat, and all of a sudden, the moonlight brightened, the air around the field grew eerily still, and Trader, Zeik, and Grunge's angry protests dimmed until they were practically muted.

Time stood still.

Amber glanced behind her shoulder...

She could run now. She could truly get away. All three supernatural males were hyper-focused on Axe, and no one would notice her escape.

Needless to say, Axe would never come after her—the male would be dead and gone.

Amber could finally be free.

Free!

Not owned or claimed by anyone.

And then she heard a harsh, desperate, singular voice rising up from the riverbed, out of the quicksand: "Amber girl, run...get out of here while you can."

Axeviathon...

And he sounded utterly desperate and resigned.

Amber's eyes filled with tears, and her heart filled with shame.

This son of a sapphire dragon was going to die for her.

She scrambled to her hands and knees and started searching the ground in earnest, dragging her fingernails through the dirt, and swiping her palms over the wild grass, again...and again...and again.

Where was it!

Where is it!

She pounded the dirt with her fist...

Where the fuck is that stiletto!

* * *

Axeviathon Saphyrius did his level best to ignore the indescribable pain, to keep from crying out in agony or dying with shame. Nine or ten more swipes with that stiletto, and Tony was going to strike Axe's bone—and then there would be little left, but time and anguish, until a blasted human male removed Axe's amulet.

It seemed too surreal to be true.

After two and a quarter centuries of living...

And Amber, Axe's beautiful, strong dragyra, she was standing on the bank of the riverbed, watching Axe die.

Shit, this nightmare just got worse and worse...

Axe couldn't move a muscle, not even a twitch, and he

couldn't call out to his lair mates—it was as if even his neurons were firing through sludge.

At first, when the demons had initially revealed their presence and Grunge had struck so fast, Axe hadn't had time to think about anything other than defending himself and protecting Amber—and then trying to get that freakin' snake off her throat. Reaching out to Zane, Jace, Levi, or Nakai had been the last thing on the dragyri's mind. And that momentary hesitation—that split-second decision—was about to cost him his life.

"Amber girl, run...get out of here while you can." He tried to croak out the sound through a raw, dissected throat, but all Amber had done was stare ahead, blankly, and then crawl around on the ground. She was digging in the dirt, swiping at the dried, prickly wild grass, and pounding her fists in frustration—*what the hell was his sweet angel doing?*

And then just like that, Amber jumped to her feet, turned around, and ran.

Good!

Finally.

Axe let out a breath he didn't even know he was holding.

At least if his dragyra got away—

What...

What the hell...

What was she doing now?

She careened to a stop, about ten yards out, turned around to face the riverbed, and narrowed her stunning amber eyes into machine-like focus. Both gleaming pupils were like mechanical lasers, fixed unerringly on Axe and Tony.

And then she started running forward, pumping her arms for speed, her long, amber hair flapping behind her as she came faster and faster...and faster. Her left heel hit the edge of the bank, and she pushed off her foot like an Olympic sprinter trying to clear an impossibly high hurdle, springing into the air. Axe's gaze flashed molten as he watched his dragyra fly to the middle of the ravine, land on top of the human behind him, and drive a fisted stiletto downward, deep into Tony's skull. She was grunting...screaming...driving it home, and all the air left Axe's body.

Oh, Gods of the Pantheon, what had Amber done?

The quicksand, the viscous substance, it was some sort of hexed booby trap, conjured to capture one's enemies. She would either be caught, or she would drown—but she could never free Axe from the snare.

He tried once more to marshal his strength, to pull his powerful arms out of the concoction, but nothing.

Nothing!

He was still as good as dead.

And now, so was his dragyra.

As Tony's knife-hand stopped moving and his arms fell away, Axe felt the moment his dragyra realized she was trapped along with Axeviathon—

And then he felt something else.

Something faint.

A stirring, like a *tap-tap-tap* in his brain.

Someone reaching out telepathically—someone almost checking in—someone trying to check up on Axe without being noticed, and the imprint felt like...it felt like...

Ghost!

Axe shut his eyes, slowed his heartbeat, and called upon the power of all three ancient lairs: citrine, sapphire, and emerald. He concentrated as hard as he could on reaching out, seizing the connection, just making a momentary link with Ghostaniaz Dragos. Axe didn't know if there was a time limit on the quicksand, but in short spurts and starts, he began to gain milliseconds —dull, flashing instances when he felt like the power in the substance might be fading...lifting—and he had to ride one of those transient waves right now!

Ghost! he shouted telepathically, straining his temples in the process. *Ghost! Lock in on my position, brother; I am well and truly fucked.* He tried to add something else—his position, the need for the entire Sapphire Lair, what was awaiting the dragyri in the field—but the wave and the opportunity had passed.

And then, like a warrior-angel descending from the heavens, surrounded in jet-black and phantom-blue wings, Ghostaniaz Dragos dropped out of the sky and began to spiral downward toward Axe and Amber. As the male plunged like a comet into the quicksand, he hooked both Axe and Amber by the cavities beneath their armpits, shoved them upward, and tossed them effortlessly into the air and onto the bank, even as he spiraled... descended...and sank deeper into the pit...into the quicksand, a newly trapped enemy.

Axe rolled around on the bank, trying to get the blasted substance off his body.

When that didn't happen fast enough, he bathed his own torso in silver flames, fanning and waving as much fire as possible over his pulverized neck, and then he leaped to his feet and called out for backup, summoning the sapphire, diamond, and emerald lairs: sapphire, because they were Axe's brothers; diamond, because they had a stake in Ghost's well-being; emerald, because they had promised to follow up if needed; and all three, because it was only a matter of time before the meadow filled up with demons.

In the meantime, Axeviathon was prepared to defend Ghostaniaz to the death.

No one was going to sever the fearsome male's head.

But then...

They didn't have to.

Trader Vice had Ghost by both arms, and the pagan demon was smiling like a crazed, deranged warlock. Before Axe could react—or the lairs could appear—an enormous pair of disembodied hands, with long, spindly, skeletal fingers, reached out from the bottom of the pit, snaked around Ghost's heaving body, and pulled the male underneath the quicksand.

The viscous substance disappeared, and so did Trader and Ghost, leaving only Tony's limp, lifeless body sprawled at the bottom of the ravine.

Axe blinked three times, and Zeik and Grunge shimmered into view.

Briefly...

"Your buddy's in the underworld," Zeik snarled.

"Sorry, but you can't follow us home," Grunge snorted.

And just like that, the demons were gone, and the meadow was silent.

CHAPTER THIRTY-TWO

SAPPHIRE LAIR ~ 2:00 AM

T he air in the Pantheon was thick with smoke.

The trees shook, the ground undulated, and the rivers ran scarlet with blood—even the clouds wept crimson tears as flames filled the dragon skies as far as the eyes could see.

And Lord Dragos, the first and diamond lord of the sacred Dragons Pantheon, soared through the dark, beleaguered heavens —over and over again—thundering his pain, roaring his rage, and bellowing his grief from on high. No one could comfort, console, or appease the diamond deity, not even the remaining six dragon lords. His mortal enemy had captured his Genesis Son, and the dragon was beside himself with mourning.

Axe ran his hand through his recently washed, damp hair, disheveling the locks as usual, even as they fell into a perfect, haphazard shape. Once again, Zane had come to his rescue, at least in terms of healing the last of his wounds: knitting that ruined throat back together and seeing to it that Axe was back to one hundred percent.

Nakai had tended to Amber's injuries, even as Jordan had tended to Amber.

The moment the couple had arrived through the portal, Nakai had healed the abrasions on Amber's feet, the puncture wounds in her neck, and several strained or bruised muscles, before Jordan had whisked her away to her and Zane's private quarters.

Yeah, that didn't sit so well with Axe.

Another male bathing his dragyra in intimate fire...

One of his lair mates examining her body, checking for injuries, open wounds, and *who knows what* other trauma, but there it was—what was done was done.

Yet having another dragyra—another female, whom Amber trusted, to presumably help Amber clean up, give her a chance to debrief, offer her an *all safe and clear* zone, so to speak, where she could get whatever she needed off her chest—had been a blessing to both Axe and the Sapphire Lair. And knowing Jordan, the dragyra would have likely gone to great lengths to clear the air around Amber's deception...her attempt to escape...and she would've provided Amber with a much-needed opportunity to process what had happened with Ghost.

What had happened with Ghost...

Axe bit his bottom lip and shuddered all the way down to his bones.

The grief-show going on outside with Lord Dragos was one thing—the guilt, regret, and shock pinging around in Axe's head was another. Axe had seen it all go down, firsthand. He had called out to Ghost for assistance, and he had watched as the male descended into that pit of quicksand, never to be seen again. *Unbelievable, really!* That solitary, *broken*, black-hearted male—the son of Lord Dragos who didn't give a shit about anything or anybody— had sacrificed everything to save Axeviathon and Amber.

And damn it all to hell, if Axe hadn't walked right into that ambush...

If Axe hadn't gone after Amber's human lover, maybe Ghost would still be around.

Axe gritted his teeth and shook his head: Vengeance was part and parcel of being a Dragyr male—no self-respecting son of a dragon would've let Antonio Rossi's insult stand. Not one. And truth be told, Axe wasn't an idiot—he had considered the possibility of a trap, that Tony might not show up alone. But *hell's bells*, he had been a thousand percent confident that he could handle whatever came up. After all, he hadn't gone earthside to battle a handful of demons; he had gone to that field—he had followed Amber—in order to kill one weak, defenseless human and to bring his dragyra home.

In and out, quick as lightning.

Strike.

Retreat.

Open a freakin' portal.

How hard could that be?

But Axe hadn't accounted for that blasted quicksand, some sort of magical stew concocted by the dark lord of the underworld himself.

But he should have!

And that was the point.

The back-and-forth insults had been between the Seven and Lord Drakkar from the beginning, from the moment Axe had left that missive in the bank, and any mercenary worth his salt would've added that factor into the equation, would have expected Lord Drakkar to strike back.

"Stop it, Axe," he murmured beneath his breath. "You can't turn back the hands of time. And even if you had exercised more caution—brought the whole damn Sapphire Lair with you as backup—there would likely be *five* Dragyr trapped in the under-world now, as opposed to only one."

No one had ever seen that malicious quicksand.

No one had even conceived of such a thing.

Zane's words echoed in Axe's memory: "Brother...dragyri... don't let that shit eat you up. Ghost was already playing with fire when he went through the portal alone; the male was looking for trouble, and he found it. He didn't have to dive into that pit—he could've reached out to the Diamond Lair. But more important, and as hard as it is to hear, you still have a dragyra to tend to. You've got four more days, Axeviathon. *Three* dragon sunsets before you take your mate to the temple, and the two of you have had very little time to bond. Go get your mate. Go *claim* your mate. Make that woman your own, once and for all. She put everything on the line for you, my brother. Show her that you're ready to see this through."

Axe blinked away his anguish and swallowed his regret.

He took a slow, deep breath before opening the master bath-room door and reentering his suite. By now, Amber would be waiting for him in his sitting room—she would be alone in his apartment—and Zane was right: Nothing else in this world of dragons, pagans, and fearsome lords mattered.

Not tonight.

The door to the en suite bathroom opened and shut behind Axe, and the male strolled out in his bare feet, wearing nothing but a pair of faded blue jeans.

Amber gulped.

His dirty-blond hair was damp, yet perfectly mussed as usual; his fathomless sapphire eyes were shadowed, yet filled with some deep, dark purpose; and his thick upper lip was parted, ever so slightly, like there were a dozen words on the tip of his tongue just waiting to spill out.

The dragyri strolled across the suite with determination, and Amber took a hesitant step back toward the ambient fireplace, suddenly self-conscious about her thin, silk pajama bottoms and the matching spaghetti-strap tank top. She suddenly wished she had worn a bra, even if it had looked ridiculous. "Axe," she murmured softly, "are you okay?"

His already shadowed gaze darkened.

Amber took another, more generous step back.

"No," he growled, reaching forward and encircling her waist. "No more cat-and-mouse, Amber girl. What you did tonight... that choice you made in the meadow...I'm ruined, sweet angel—I don't want to be apart from you any longer."

Amber gasped. She arched her back to look up at him, and what she found was guileless, open, and raw. Axeviathon was standing on the edge of reason and regret, desire and shame, hunger and repentance...lust and being lost. And Amber was his anchor, his way back home.

She didn't know if she could carry such a heavy burden.

And she certainly wasn't ready to match his intensity.

He was right—she had made an irreversible choice in that meadow, the choice to save Axe and give up her freedom, but she hadn't thought it through. She had just reacted.

"That's just it, dragyra," he rasped, nuzzling the hollow of her throat. "Too much thinking. No more thinking. The truth between us; it's just instinct." He dragged his teeth along the same sensual path and tightened his arm around her.

Amber's head fell back as she lost her balance, and she pressed her palm against his bare, silken chest in an attempt to regain her equilibrium. His heart was beating like a heavy bass drum.

He covered her hand with his and squeezed it.

And then he brought it to his mouth, kissed her palm, then the base of her fingers, trailing his way up until he drew the tips of her fingers into his mouth and bit down, ever so lightly.

Amber shivered as a course of electricity shot through her, but her dominant emotion was still fear, not arousal.

Sensing her emotion, he spun her around, wrapped his arms around her waist, and pressed his chest against her back. And then the wild, untamed male began to devour her neck...her shoulders...the top of her back: nipping, kissing, tasting her skin...

Sucking, biting, caressing with his lips.

Amber shuddered, let out a moan, and his left hand snaked into her hair, fisting a handful to hold her steady beneath him.

She gasped, and his right hand slid up, along her rib cage, tested the weight beneath each of her breasts, then caressed her passionately through the silken tank top.

His thumb brushed over her nipple—back and forth, lighter and lighter—until the peak grew hard beneath his touch. He tugged on it gently and groaned in her ear, before turning his attention to the other breast...the other peak...until he was kneading her flesh beneath the silk covering.

Amber's knees grew weak beneath her, and she reached up to cover his hand with hers.

He groaned, and then he purred like a satisfied lion, sliding his palm back down to her stomach.

Tension, heat, and desire began to flood her core, and she tightened her stomach muscles and clenched her thighs in a futile attempt to control the sensations.

Restrain them.

Put some much-needed distance between her brain and her awakening desire.

Axe sensed her weakness—her indecision—like a predator might sense hesitation in its prey.

He stood up straight, spun her back around, and tunneled both hands into her hair.

And then he tilted her head backward and virtually devoured her mouth.

There was *nothing* the male didn't kiss, taste, or explore...

He drew each of Amber's lips into the warm, moist cavern of his own hungry, seeking mouth, one at a time, tracing the soft, pliable flesh with his tongue, nipping at the skin with his teeth, and then he kissed her with wild abandon, only to pull back and repeat...

And repeat.

His examined the contours of her tongue, of her teeth...the corners of her mouth...using the tip of his tongue—then his fingers—to trace every hollow, angle, and curve, then he devoured her mouth, yet again.

On and on...and on.

Growing ever more passionate, ever more predatory, ever more sexual in nature.

At last, Amber couldn't take it anymore. She wrapped her arms around his neck and kissed him back with fevered abandon. She had never tasted anything like him: smoke, fire, and primitive hunger.

Pure, raw, uninhibited masculinity.

Passion. Love. Primal desire.

And unrestrained lust...

He dropped to his knees, fisted the globes of her ass, and buried his mouth between her legs, doing unthinkable—impossible—things through the barrier of Amber's silk pajamas.

She fisted her hands in his hair, let her head roll back, and whimpered.

He ripped the pajama bottoms along the seam, tugged on her panties, and slid two fingers inside her quivering body.

"Axe!" She hadn't seen that coming.

Oh, gods, oh gods, oh gods...

He was delving, teasing, tasting...exploring...taking turns with his mouth and his hand, and all the while, he was massaging her ass—raking his fingers along her skin—like he knew just where to stop short before drawing blood or scoring her flesh.

The sensations were overwhelming.

All-consuming.

He raked at her ribs, then her stomach; he clawed the inside of her thighs—never hard enough to hurt her, but never gentle enough to console her.

He kept her on the edge of arousal and fear.

And then he filled her core with his tongue, stabbing deep, and Amber's body fractured; it trembled and came apart from an orgasm that lasted and lingered...and tortured.

Axe rose to his feet in one lithe motion, lifting Amber off the ground with one arm. He carried her to the master bedroom and laid her, stomach first, across the edge of his bed. He dropped to his knees behind her, spread her thighs apart with his hands, and rotated his thumbs in teasing, yet purposeful circles, stretching and opening her core. And then he freed his arousal from his unzipped jeans, sliding the denim down his hips, and pressed the large, blunt head of his sex against her while pressing down on her lower back.

Holy shit, he was pinning her in place...

Amber dug her fingernails into the mattress, trying to gain purchase through the duvet—she arched her back and let her head fall forward, bracing herself for the full sensation...

Axeviathon did not disappoint.

He thrust inside her like a wild beast, stretching her core impossibly, and then he began to rock back and forth, plunging deeper and deeper, until he, at last, began to thrust in earnest.

Amber cried out.

She bit down on her bottom lip and grunted—she couldn't help it.

Axe was taking her body, consuming her soul, like he was starving, and he would never get enough. He leaned forward, slid his hands up along her back, and anchored a fist in her hair, and then he wrapped his other arm around her stomach, drew her, hard, against his pelvis, and took everything Amber could—or couldn't—give.

There was nothing left of the careful, tempered suitor he had shown her that first night in the Pantheon. There was only fire, sweat, heat, and lust: a wild dragyri animal and its mate.

Claiming.

Worshiping.

Conquering...

And when he threw back his head and shouted his release, a second orgasm rocked Amber's tender, sensitive body, and she screamed along with Axeviathon.

CHAPTER THIRTY-THREE

Ghostaniaz Dragos was summarily fucked.

And he had to admit, when he had contemplated going earthside to incite his father—when he had considered all the ways he could provoke his ultimate death—*this* had not been one of them.

Those giant hands had dragged him beneath the quicksand, and then he had felt like he was falling, tumbling...plummeting downward as time stood still. The next thing he knew he was being dragged across an ancient wooden platform—a drawbridge encased in fog, overlaying a moat—and lining the archaic bridge were rows and rows of curious, hissing, snarling pagans: demons lined up along the right, a row of beasts who looked like men and feasted on human sins, and shades along the left, a column of skeletal soul-eaters whose ghoulish mouths fell open in monstrous contortions as if they were starving to eat Ghost whole. All were dressed in ceremonial robes with an all-too-familiar emblem on their breasts: a witch's pentacle etched into the pommel of a sword; a reversed numerical seven inscribed in gold below the crossguard; and the tail of the *seven* was outlined in permanent blood, extending along the length of the blade.

The sky above him was neither light, nor midnight blue, but a thick, murky haze that permeated the oppressive sky. If the Pantheon was saturated in brilliant, vivid colors; lyrical, living sounds; and everything grew to perfection, then this place—this abomination—was its polar opposite: a dark, inky replica of a thousand shades of gray and black; a subtle, but grating, disharmonious drone; and dead grass, dead tree limbs, dead vegetation as far as the eye could glimpse.

The drawbridge led to an enormous gothic castle, and the disembodied hands proceeded to drag Ghost across a mammoth foyer to one of two parallel doors, each set about fifty feet apart. The door on the left swung open, as if on its own, revealing a large, rectangular, torchlit throne room. Ghost turned his head to the right, drawn by the popping, crackling sound of a roaring fire —it almost sounded like demonic laughter—and he realized that flanking the two arched entries to the Great Hall, the bestial throne room, was a massive, towering fireplace made of pure obsidian stone.

He cast his glance forward, and *oh shit, oh shit, oh shit!*

A garish red velvet throne, smack-dab in the middle of the hall, and the blood-red cathedra was occupied by a glaring, smirking, demonic king: Lord Drakkar Hades, Father of the Pagan Realm, Ruler of the underworld...sire of the Pagan Horde. Ghost's stomach muscles clenched as he studied the entourage surrounding the evil deity.

Perched behind the malevolent ruler were nine males, a mixture of demons and shadow-walkers, and their robes were literally dipped in blood. This had to be Lord Drakkar's congress —but why only nine?

To the king's left stood some sort of dignitary, and the words *Killian Kross* practically echoed through the hall. It was as if the demonic fire were cackling the name. Ghost shivered and shifted his gaze to the king's right. The space beside him was empty—

Oh, wait...

Not anymore.

The disembodied hands that had dragged Ghostaniaz out of the field, out of that dry riverbed, and underneath the quicksand —the prickly, bony digits that had dug into his flesh—were now clasped together, almost in glee, as another demon, with steely, deep-blue eyes and long, dark hair plated in shell-and-bone braids, took his rightful place beside his king. The male was wearing the tenth blood-drenched robe.

The fire cackled again: *Requiem Pyre, chief sorcerer to Lord Drakkar and esteemed member of congress.*

That shit was so damn freaky!

Ghost swept his own phantom-blue eyes back to the VIP named Killian Kross, concentrated for a moment, and waited as the fire danced, sparked, and crackled: *Chief counselor to the Chosen One.*

Shiiiiiiit.

Ghost rolled his head on his shoulders, stretched his back, and popped his neck two times, grateful to be free of those creepy claws, Requiem Pyre's fingers. He watched as a row of human servants—*no, slaves*—filed in with their heads bowed low and kneeled in front of the throne at Lord Drakkar's feet, their prostrated bodies facing out toward the hall opposite Ghost: four stunning men and three breathtaking mortal women. All seven were naked, except for some animal-skin loincloth, and their perfect bodies were slathered in oil.

Ghost looked away—*this shit was just too damn vile*—and tried to stare at a shadow on the dais instead. First and foremost, he wasn't much for pomp and circumstance, and beyond that fact, he figured he was only a few heartbeats away from having his amulet removed...for good...being sent back to the Pantheon via some sort of messenger or delivered to one of the Seven's earthside businesses.

Whatever...

Just get the show on the road...

One thing was certain, he wasn't taking a single step forward. Now that Requiem was no longer dragging him, Ghost figured he would just stay put.

As if reading his thoughts, the king extended his long, ghoulish, spindly arm and crooked his fingers forward, his long, sharp, pointed nails gleaming pitch-black in the firelight. "Come forth," he bellowed, and Ghost nearly spewed his dinner.

Yet and still, the dragyri didn't budge an inch.

That long, gnarled arm grew longer, snaked forward from the dais, and crossed the throne room like an eel, all five fingers wrapping around Ghost's neck. "I said, *come forth,*" the king snarled as he lifted all six feet, five inches of Ghost's heavy, muscular body into the air, drew him to the edge of the dais, and dropped him on the floor. He leaned forward in his seat, scooted to the edge of the red velvet throne, and added: "Boy, I can see you have a rebellious nature in you, and that's all well and good—I appreciate a hard-ass, cocky bastard more than a sniveling, whimpering bitch. But alas, you do not quite understand where you are. You are not yet clear on *who I am.*" He spoke the last three words with hate-filled emphasis. "So, let me make it clear for you."

Once again making use of that extended arm, Lord Drakkar snatched Ghost's legs out from underneath him, then pressed his stomach to the cold stone floor. Without pause or preamble, he dug his claws into the nape of Ghost's neck, tunneled all five fingers beneath Ghost's skin, and wrapped his bony fist around Ghost's cervical vertebrae. With a violent tug, the king wrenched his fist backward, extracted the entire spinal column from Ghost's jerking back, and tossed it on the floor in front of him.

"Leave your spine at the door when you enter my throne room!" he thundered.

Ghostaniaz had lived for a thousand years, but that one excruciating second had slowed down...lingered...and *punished* longer than his entire wretched lifetime. In the space of one agonizing heartbeat—as Lord Drakkar had removed his spine— Ghost had shouted in agony, pissed on the floor, and prayed to Lord Dragos for death, even knowing that his dark, distant father couldn't hear him.

Now, as he lay paralyzed before the dark lord of the under- world, his mouth hanging open in a pool of vomit and drool, he was more grateful than he could find words to express that he could no longer feel...anything. But blasted demons and cursed shades—*would his damnable existence never end!*—he still remained dragyri, and his diamond amulet still hung around his neck.

Ghostaniaz Dragos was not dead yet.

"Sorcerer..." He heard Lord Drakkar snarl the word, and ten seconds later the demon, Requiem Pyre, was kneeling in front of Ghost.

He picked up Ghost's spine, straightened it out, and shoved it back inside the dragyri's back.

Ghost jackknifed off the floor as his nerves came back online, writhing like a serpent in his own piss and blood, and then Requiem Pyre proceeded to massage the vertebrae back into place and heal the entry wound with thick black smoke.

Silence.

Adjustment.

The pain abated.

Ghost moaned in relief and nuzzled the cold, inviting floor with his nose.

"You will need all your stamina for what is to come," Lord Drakkar said coolly. "Feed and replenish your strength." With that, he booted one of the beautiful human women kneeling before him in the back, sending her flying off the dais and sprawled out in front of Ghost.

The woman screamed like a banshee.

She shot to her knees and tried to crawl away, her terror-stricken features wet with falling tears, but a hand—no, the head of a tiger snake—caught her by the shoulder, clamped down with its fangs, and dragged her even closer to Ghost.

Ghost blanched.

He couldn't do it.

He wouldn't do it—just kill him already—shit!

And then he felt the snake-handed pagan plant his foot on Ghost's back. "My king." The demon spoke eloquently to the monster on the throne. "I know that I promised you Axeviathon Saphyrius." He lowered his voice in both reverence and self-abasement. "And I know that I gave my vow to render unto you the same as payment for the loss of your beloved shades." He took a slow, deep breath. "Milord, we could not capture Axe. The situation was...well, *complicated*, but I have brought you Ghostaniaz Dragos instead, a firstborn hatchling of Lord Dragos, the diamond serpent, a Genesis Son of the darkest dragon god, and I would beg for your mercy...plead for your clemency. Accept this dragyri male instead and erase my debt, if it pleases you. You have my left hand, this gift, and my eternal fealty."

The throne room grew unnervingly quiet, and then at last, Lord Drakkar spoke up: "Make him feed from the woman, and all will be forgiven."

"Noooo!" the piteous female screamed, even as the snake withdrew its fangs from her shoulder, struck Ghost in the back of his skull, and began to maneuver his head like an object in the iron arm of a crane.

The snake opened its jaw, and Ghost's jaw followed suit...

The serpent lowered Ghost's mouth downward, until it caressed the female's neck.

And then, as if acting of their own accord, Ghost Dragos' fangs punched out of his mouth, his eyes heated with molten fire, and the tiger snake did the rest: Together, they found the poor woman's jugular, sank their fangs deep, and feasted as one entity.

Without conscious thought or reason, Ghost let out a bestial moan, extracted the female's blood, heat, and essence, and drew it hungrily into his starving body. He replenished his depleted organs, nourished his strained muscles, and recharged his weary bones. And all the while, he knew—deep in his gut—that his goose was well and truly cooked. Whatever Lord Drakkar wanted from Ghostaniaz, from his newfound prisoner and dragyri slave, it wasn't going to be as simple as death.

As the keening, suffering human female expired beneath him, Ghost saw her death as *mercy*—at least she was free.

Ghost would've given anything to trade places with his prey.

CHAPTER THIRTY-FOUR

FOUR DAYS LATER ~ THE PANTHEON

Amber wandered through the outer foyer inside the Temple of Seven.

She had already cleansed her hands in the sacred fountain, felt the dragon lords pull on her essence, and now she was studying the intricate threads and elaborate weaving in the ornamental rug that lay beneath it.

The entire event felt surreal.

All of it.

From the gorgeous, timeless gown she was wearing—an A-line wedding dress with a plunging V-neck, elaborate lattice sequined lace, an open back, and a sweeping train pinned up in a delicate bustle—to the priceless matching platform pumps, adorned with hundreds of sapphires and diamonds coating the heels and decorating the satin bow and the toe. Her hair was swept up in a waterfall braid that circled the crown of her head, even as loose, curled tresses hung down to frame her face, and pieces of the back and sides were pinned up in elegant curls, all the combs and pins also festooned with precious jewels.

Odd how the entire ensemble would soon be bathed in fire.

"Amber girl, you all right?" Axe's deep, masculine voice almost made her jump. "A penny for your thoughts?"

She frowned and ran one finger along the edge of the ornate ivory fountain.

A penny for her thoughts...

If only...

If only a penny were enough; if only there were adequate words to express what she was feeling; if only it were half that easy—just tell Axe what you're thinking, feeling, experiencing, and he'll wave his magic hands and make it better.

Wave his magic hands...

Despite her mounting trepidation, she managed a faint smile. The male definitely had magic hands—the last three nights had made that clear. And it wasn't just the wild, erotic lovemaking—Axe was also capable of great gentleness and attentiveness. He used those strong, beautiful hands to comfort, caress, and arouse, depending on the situation. He had been wild, yes, but he had also been tender; he had shown Amber several surprising sides of him: laughter and playfulness beneath the Sapphire Lair's magnificent waterfall; gentle but expert ministrations while massaging tension out of her neck; and soft, reassuring touches, whether hooking his pinky finger around hers or placing a loving, tender hand on the small of her back.

Axe was constantly aware of Amber.

And he had taken the time, concerted a lot of effort, to learn more about her past and her experiences. When he could—as he could—he had also shared much of his past and his life with her as well.

The male was an open book.

But that wasn't what had sealed the deal or brought her to such a fateful decision.

That had happened on Monday morning, two days after she and Axe had first made love.

Axeviathon had taken her to the Sapphire Lair's library and sat her down in front of a wide, high-definition computer monitor, before manipulating one of those sapphire spheres to activate the Wi-Fi—Amber now understood just how that worked, how the globes provided access to human technology and signals, the fact that the pagans had manipulated the same, early on, in order to allow Tony to text her...that Axe had known all along that she was texting the human back. She sighed, not meaning to get sidetracked in her thinking, wanting to remember—and focus—on that monumental day in the library when Axe had opened a file full of vibrant pictures, all of a petite, eleven-and-a-half-year-old girl with long, beautiful, straight blonde hair: a girl treading water in a backyard swimming pool, a girl playing croquet with her family on the lawn, a girl smiling broadly as she ate hot dogs and chips at a picnic table in a park near her home.

A girl named Tina Wilcox—that was her new last name— who had been adopted by a kind and loving family six months after Amber had disappeared from their shared, neglectful foster home. Apparently, Nakai had done the research at Axe's request, but the Sapphire Lair had not stopped there: They had purchased a $50,000 college fund for the girl and placed it inside a $200,000 trust, all the paperwork delivered to the family's certified public accountant with a simple note that read: *For Tina from Amber ~ live your best life.*

Tucked away in that stately, sophisticated library on the other side of a remote, mythical portal, while sequestered inside the Pantheon of Dragons, Amber had stared at the monitor for an hour...and wept.

How had Axe known?

How could he have understood...

That a little girl's eyes and her pitiful teardrops had haunted Amber for the last ten years.

That Amber had always been filled with remorse and regret, wondering what had become of Tina.

Now she knew.

That, and something else: that as far-fetched, unbelievable, and impossible as it seemed, Amber had finally come home. She had finally found a real and loving family in an unreal and wild world, with a dangerous, yet dreamy man.

A dangerous, yet dreamy male...

A dragyri, born to a dragon's pantheon.

And she wasn't about to give that up.

"Where'd you go, Amber? You still with me?" Axe's alluring voice again.

Yes, she was still with him—she would always be with him—she was just trying to work this out in her head and her heart. She was trying to gather her courage as well as her resolve, so just this once, she could prop him up, be the one who offered support.

Axeviathon had explained the conversion ceremony in detail —minute by minute, second by second—and while it was terrifying at best, Amber trusted the dragyri implicitly. She knew he would shield and protect her—she knew it in her gut—and while she may endure three seconds of unspeakable agony, *three seconds* was very little to pay for a lifetime of kindness and security. As impossible as it seemed, her greatest fear was not the fire or the seven dragon lords—not even Lord Dragos in his feral state —but somehow letting Axe down. Amber was most afraid that she would not be worthy of the gift—and the warrior—she had been given.

"I'm here," she said, stepping away from the fountain and turning to face Axe squarely. "I'm here, and I'm ready."

He studied her dark amber gaze carefully. "You sure? I know this has to be—"

"Shh," she whispered, placing two perfectly manicured fingers against his thick, sculpted lips. "The fewer words, the better," she told him. "I don't want to draw this out. Axe, can we just go in there in silence, walk up to the platform, and get it over with? All I want is to have this behind me...behind us...all I want is to start fresh with the future, and for that, we have to do this thing." She chuckled softly and added, "Before I lose my nerve."

Axe cupped her cheeks in two gentle hands, bent forward, and pressed a kiss to her forehead, the tip of her nose, and then her lips. "You are such a miracle to me, Ambrosia Carpenter. I can't really comprehend that this moment is happening—that *you* are happening—that any of this is real."

She smiled faintly. "Well, if it's a dream, I don't want to wake up." The words were too intimate, the sentiment too vulnerable, and she cast her gaze to the floor.

Axe lifted her chin with the pads of his fingers. "Look at me, sweet angel."

She blinked two times and stared into his magnificent sapphire eyes, hardly believing that just nine days earlier—eight, if she counted the fact that it concluded after midnight—she had been in this very temple with Lord Saphyrius: blind, petrified, and naked in the Oracle Pool. And Axeviathon Saphyrius had been a virtual stranger.

No more...

She only hoped that in time, he would come to love her.

"Hold up," he said, reaching for her hand. "You're projecting your thoughts again."

She grimaced, closed her eyes, and lowered her head —*damnit, she hated when that happened.* If nothing else, it was so darn embarrassing. "Forget I said that," she whispered. "Forget I *thought* that."

Axe drew her close and wrapped his strong arms around her, pressing another chaste kiss to the crown of her head. "Oh, sweet angel—you slay me, you really do. You think I would ignore—*or forget*—a thought like that? I would've said something earlier—it's been on the tip of my tongue a dozen times—but you are kind of skittish when it comes to emotions, and I was trying to ease you into our life. Amber girl..." He caressed both her shoulders then gently pushed her several inches back so he could look into her eyes. "Don't ever, *ever* doubt it. More than all the stars in the dragon's night sky; more than all the flames in the dragon sea; more than all the years that have come and gone since the dragon lords emerged from the cosmic explosion, I love you, Amber girl. I have waited a lifetime to find you, and I love you from the depths of my soul."

Amber shuffled back, stunned by Axe's confession.

She studied his eyes, his brows, his expression, looking for signs of dishonesty—he couldn't possibly feel so strongly so soon, but there it was, etched into his features: The male meant every word...

She gulped as the realization overwhelmed her, and then she glanced toward the doors to the inner sanctuary. "I love you, too, Axeviathon. Let's do this damn thing and get it over with."

Just when Axe thought nothing could surprise him about this amazing and wondrous woman—not even the fact that he had never been forced to tell her he would lose his life if she didn't go through with the conversion; she had agreed to it all on her own— her courage and her words laid him bare: "I love you, too, Axeviathon. Let's do this damn thing and get it over with."

Out of respect for his dragyra—Amber's need to embrace the silence, to focus all her energy on just getting through the conversion and rebirth—and because Axeviathon was also terrified all the way down to his soul (he knew full well what was about to happen), Axe led Amber through the inner sanctuary without uttering a single word.

To Amber's credit, she didn't react to the near-blinding light refracted from the shimmering glass floors, nor did she glance up at the high, coffered ceiling, with its resplendent layers of gilded jewels. She didn't turn to regard the Oracle Pool, with its pearlescent living waters. She simply kept her dark amber eyes focused straight ahead as the couple made their way to the platform.

She was steady as a cucumber as they climbed all seven steps and faced the seven ornamental thrones. When the floors began to vibrate and the walls began to teeter—when the seven ancient dragons took their respective cathedrals—Amber's arms coated with goose bumps, and she shivered from her head to her toes. Yet and still, the brave, determined female didn't turn on her heel and try to bolt. *In for a penny, in for a pound* would've been the understatement of the century; Amber had an unyielding resolve and the courage of a majestic lioness. She had truly given her heart—and her future—to Axe, and he was humbled by her stunning and brave devotion.

He sidled up behind her and grasped her by the waist, trying to impart both warmth and courage with his touch. Hell, she was doing better than he was. And then Axe's dragyra noticed the two fireproof loops anchored to the platform floor, and for the first time, she listed to the side, almost losing her balance.

"I've got you, Amber girl," Axe rasped in her ear, tightening his grasp around her midriff and holding her steady.

She nodded, straightened her spine, and raised her chin. It wasn't precisely courage, but it was a valiant attempt at faking it. The temperature in the sanctuary began to rise as dry, radiant heat intensified all around them, and Amber's breaths became short and shallow.

"Breathe, Amber girl. In and out. You're halfway there already."

She took several slow, deep breaths and leaned back against him. He nuzzled his chin in her hair. And then, one by one, each magnificent dragon lord rose from his corresponding throne, starting with an angry, bereaved, half-feral Lord Dragos, rising from the center diamond cathedra. "Look at us!" he thundered, his terrifying baritone ricocheting off the sanctuary walls.

Axe blanched, and Amber shivered.

From what Axe had been taught about the ancient ritual—from all the lore and stories his Dragyr brothers and cousins had shared with him over the centuries—the proper refrain should have been, *You may regard our eyes*; still, he figured Lord Dragos was doing the best he could. "Just look at Lord Saphyrius," Axe whispered in Amber's ear, feeling her muscles tense beneath his palms and her legs begin to tremble.

As was customary, the dragon lords were in amalgamated form—spectral prisms of light reflecting the colors of their dominant gemstones—while their enormous serpents, their primordial dragons, flanked them as silhouettes. The moment Axe and Amber looked up, both souls locking their eyes on Lord Saphyrius, all seven camouflaged beasts traversed to the fore, overshadowing their human-like personas. They assumed their scales, revealed their sharp, pointed ears, and gnashed their massive, jagged teeth, all the while emitting thick, inky wisps of smoke from their extended, bestial snouts.

"You strong enough to kneel?" Axe murmured to Amber.

She shook her head rapidly from side to side. "I think I'm about to throw up."

Axe splayed his fingers over his dragyra's quaking belly and commanded the muscles to relax. Then he placed both palms atop Amber's shoulders and gently pressed downward, forcing her insubstantial weight to the floor. Her knees gave out, and he caught her by both hips, pressing his chest against her back to force her forward. "Give me your left hand." She placed it in his, and he stretched her arm, up and outward, before wrapping her fingers around the first of the two handholds. "The other one," he murmured.

She took a deep breath and froze. "Axe, I can't—"

"Shh. Yes, you can. You're doing beautifully. Give me your right hand, Amber girl."

Her head fell forward as she struggled for breath—she was nearly hyperventilating—and Axe didn't waste any time. He took her right hand, extended her arm, and curled her fingers around the remaining handhold. "Whatever you do, don't let go. Everything else, I will take from here."

She shivered against him, and her stomach lurched—but she didn't faint or vomit.

Lord Saphyrius whipped his long sapphire tail in front of him, curling it around the sapphire throne, and then he cleared his throat—it sounded like the tremolo of a freight train—and narrowed his piercing, almond-shaped eyes on Axe. "Son of my lair, we will hear your invocation."

Amber was weeping now, warm, moist, crystalline tears, streaming from her eyes in rivers.

The female had surpassed fear and entered the realm of panic...

Desperation.

Hell, she was both petrified and despondent.

But there was nothing to be done about it now. The most Axe could do was push forward, get this over with, take his dragyra to, through, and beyond the terror and meet her on the other side.

He wrapped his arms around her, released his satiny, wheat-colored wings, and enfolded her body beneath him, tightening both annexes into an airtight cocoon. "I love you, Amber girl," he whispered, and then he turned his full, undivided attention on his seven dragon masters:

. . .

"Great dragon lords, from the world beyond;
    fathers of mystery, keepers of time;
    I bring to you this mortal soul.
    Born of fire, bathed in light;
    to guard by day and watch by night;
    to live, and love, and breathe as one,
    the *fated* of a dragon's son—
    be gentle with her soul.
    Through sacred smoke and healing fire;
    a flesh-and-blood, renewing pyre;
    I give my life, with one desire—
    reanimate her soul.
    Great dragon lords of the sacred stones;
    from the Temple of Seven, from your honored thrones;
    renew my dragyra and bless the Sapphire Lair."

A distant drone.

The tremor of an earthquake.

The deep, throaty purr of a thousand lions...

The cacophony of sound rose to a thunderous crescendo, and then a wall of flames struck the platform, and Axe's breath whooshed out of his body.

Great lords of creation, the heat was indescribable, and the agony was beyond withstanding—nothing Ghost had done in this very hall could even come close by comparison...

Axe threw back his head and shouted in torment.

He bucked and writhed and keened in savage misery as the flames grew stronger, hotter, more intense, and his flesh began to melt.

The sound he was making was neither human, nor bestial, but some sort of primordial wail as his bones began to disintegrate, and his wings succumbed to cremation. Yet and still, he protected Amber, hovered over her body, and held on.

He couldn't think.

He couldn't reason.

He couldn't even remember his name, but he just knew, somewhere deep inside—by instinct—that he couldn't let those flames cut through his liquefying wings.

Sixty seconds, hell!

It felt more like sixty eons.

As his wings finally melted away, and he dropped his head over Amber's, trying to shield what he could with all he had left...

His dragyra suddenly jackknifed and began to writhe beneath him, her unholy bellow wrenching through the din of flame and smoke and torture.

Oh, gods, his beautiful Amber was burning.

And then she collapsed beneath him, the flame of her mortal candle finally going out.

Axeviathon wanted to pray for death, just one second of reprieve while he joined her, but there was no merciful amnesty for the son of a dragon—the torture was incessant, unrelenting, and vicious.

And then the blazing orange-and-red flames cooled to silver and blue, and Axe took his first deep breath.

His Amber girl began to emerge from the darkness—from the stillness—from the nothingness of her mortal death, and her heart began to beat anew.

Stronger.

Faster.

Alive with power.

Even as Axe's skin regenerated, his wings knit back together, and his bones grew hard and strong.

Quiet.

Serenity.

The sanctuary grew tranquil, and Axe rocked back onto his heels, reached for his dragyra, and gently spun her around. "Amber...*Amber*...look at me, baby. Are you okay? How do you feel?"

Her waterfall braid had come loose, several tightly curled tresses had collapsed, and those random hanging sections of dark-gold locks had fallen into her eyes. She peered up at him through dark, sultry lashes and blurted, *"What the actual fuck!?"* She swept her hair out of her eyes and added, "Was all that really necessary?"

Falling in love with his dragyra all over again, Axeviathon chuckled. "Well said, sweet angel."

She ran her hands up and down his arms. *"Blessed Mother of Mercy*. I think the real question is are *you* okay?"

He smiled and shook his head. "I think I'm beginning to hate this damn temple," he groused, "but yes, my beautiful dragyra, I'm right as rain. Everything's copacetic."

She glanced down at her lap—then his—and patted both of his legs. "I think we made it; I think we did it!" Her voice was filled with both wonder and relief. And then her eyes grew wide as saucers as she slowly raised her left hand and gawked at the glorious ring nestled securely around her fourth finger, a flawless, dazzling sapphire set inside an antique band, which was shaped in the form of a dragon and surrounded by six additional stones: a diamond, an emerald, an amethyst, an onyx, a citrine, and a brilliant topaz. "Oh!" she exclaimed, her voice revealing her excitement. "I was hoping I would get one of these! After seeing Jordan's..." Her voice trailed off. "This has got to be worth—like a *gazillion* dollars! How will I ever wear it in public?" Her laughter was infused with wry humor as she nuzzled Axe's neck. "I'm just kidding, Axeviathon—I couldn't care less about the value of this ring, although it's truly breathtaking. All that matters to me now is you."

Momentarily at a loss for words, he corrected the use of his consecrated name. "*Axe,*" he said, feigning indignance. "And yeah, my sweet angel, we did it." He enfolded her in his arms and held her close to his heart. "I do love you, Amber, always and forever."

She pressed several soft kisses along the bend of his neck and shoulder, and he felt her mood grow solemn. "Please don't ever lie to me, Axe." Her voice was barely audible.

"Never," he promised. "You have my word."

"And don't ever betray me," she added.

He sighed. "I only wish to love you...serve you...make you unbelievably happy."

She chuckled softly. "Axe, I do believe you, and I'm trusting you with everything, almost afraid to hope..." As her last words lingered, she briefly shut her eyes and shivered. "Don't ever hurt me, Axe. Promise?"

He held his dragyra tighter and listened to the steady thrum of her heart. "Oh, Amber girl, I can't make that promise, at least not when it comes to your feelings, to your perceptions—I'm not a very refined dragyri. Hell, some might say I'm a coarse, ill-bred bastard. Half the time, I don't even know which way is up, at least when it comes to dealing with a female. But I'll never hurt you on purpose, and I'll do my best to learn. You're safe with me, Amber —that I can promise. I hope it's enough."

She drew back, lumbered onto her knees, and cupped his angular jaw in her hands. And then she kissed him until his head was spinning, his groin was aching, and he no longer gave two shits about the seven dragon lords...

"Welcome to the Pantheon of Dragons," he breathed into her open mouth. "Can we *please* go back to the lair?"

EPILOGUE

FOUR WEEKS LATER ~ THE PAGAN UNDERWORLD

October 31st...
Halloween...
It had always been one of Bethany Reid's favorite holidays.

Even at the age of twenty-nine, she kept with the yearly tradition of meeting up with a handful of her best girlfriends from both high school and college—*their friendships had lasted that long!*—dressing up in elaborate costumes as they tried to outdo each other, and frequenting the scariest haunted house they could find. Afterward, they would go out for drinks, tell scary stories, and end up at one or another's living room, watching classic horror flicks until they crashed on the couch or the floor.

At this point in her life, and even though she was now a well-paid, successful administrative assistant to a smart, if not demanding, finance company CEO, she just couldn't let go of the custom...or the nostalgia. It wasn't so much about the costumes or the holiday—she had pretty much grown out of her love for being scared witless and having to sleep with the lights on for a week—but the easy, unrestrained comradery and banter, the chance to reconnect with lifelong friends and solidify those bonds. As the only child of a gorgeous African-American mother and an upwardly mobile German-and-English father, Bethany considered her girlfriends her family, the sisters she'd never had.

But tonight had been different...

Heaven help her, had it been different.

This Halloween had been a true, waking nightmare, and Bethany was still too terrified, confused, and disoriented to wake up.

She didn't want to wake up, lest she find that the skeletal man with the long, wispy white hair was real: the dark malevolent presence that had emerged from the fog in the haunted house, wrapped its long, spindly arms around Beth, and dragged her into the shadows, separating her from her friends. The man who had stabbed her in the arm with a syringe before she even knew what was happening, injecting her swiftly with some sort of tranquilizer.

At first, she had thought it was part of the act, someone from the crew who ran the haunted house, and since she and her friends prided themselves on not screaming, never showing fear, she had giggled nervously and glanced around in the darkness, waiting to see what would happen next.

The syringe had answered that question.

Next was going to be too late.

Next, she had felt like she was falling...spinning...traveling at some ungodly speed through time and space.

Next, she was being carried into some garish fortress, like a gothic castle from a vampire novel, and dragged to the base of a nightmarish red velvet throne.

Next, she was staring into a pair of impossible, glassy eyes—diamond irises framing phantom-blue pupils—and the powerful, muscle-bound creature who owned them was glaring back at Beth like she had stolen his firstborn son.

* * *

Ghostaniaz Dragos watched as Wraith Sylvester, one of Lord Drakkar's loyal shadow-walkers, a soul-eater, dragged a stunning human woman with thick, wavy, dark-brown hair and terrified yet exotic dark-brown eyes, the pupils rimmed in gold, to the base of the pagan king's throne and presented her to the ruler of the underworld.

Lord Drakkar appraised the woman from head to toe and then gently inclined his head in a nod, which meant the female was acceptable—he would receive her as a replacement for the beautiful human slave Ghost had drained to the point of exsanguination...expiration...*death*—just four weeks earlier.

It hadn't been Ghost's choice, or his fault, feeding on the human slave like that—

Trader Vice had left Ghost no choice.

He, too, had been captured...taken...exploited by the Pagan Horde, ensnared in an earthside trap, a creek bed filled with hexed, paralyzing quicksand, and snatched away to the underworld one month prior. And Trader had used that abominable hand, the one that was missing a palm, a thumb, and all four fingers, the one that had been replaced with the head of a turquoise-and-black tiger snake, instead, to force Ghost to feed, to evoke his dragyri instincts.

What was done was done.

Ghost didn't have the time or the pleasure to entertain regrets.

His every breath was now about survival: finding a way to withstand and eventually escape this gods-forsaken realm.

True: The night he had been captured, he had been feeling reckless, suicidal—he had left the Pantheon and traveled through the portal, alone and by his own accord, amped up and looking for trouble. But he had gotten a helluva lot more than he had bargained for. He had never intended to end up as Lord Drakkar Hades' favorite pet, a tool to be used and tortured for the dark lord's amusement, a way for the pagan king to strike back at the Seven, his ancient co-creators who had chosen another life.

Ghost's top lip twitched, and he restrained a feral snarl.

Since he had arrived in the underworld, he'd had every bone in his powerful body broken. He'd had several organs ripped from his torso, only to be returned, restored, and regenerated. And the demons had likely split his skull open a half-dozen times—Ghost had quit counting.

What he had quickly learned was that eternity was going to be a very long time if he didn't get his shit together, formulate a plan, and do something—anything—to stop the incessant torment.

Ghost was a *hard-ass* by nature—tainted, broken, way beyond cynical—and there wasn't much he couldn't endure.

But this shit?

Nah, this was way beyond the pale.

And the way Ghost figured it, he had to have something of value, something he could barter, something he could offer Lord Drakkar in exchange for a *cease-fire* on all the beatings. The bludgeonings. Ghostaniaz Dragos was a Dragyr male, an embryonic hatchling from the first of the dragon lords, the Genesis Son of the diamond dragon, Lord Dragos, first of the sacred Dragons Pantheon—in a sense, he was Lord Drakkar's nephew, just a thousand years removed...

But whatever.

Point was: The Pagan Horde was powerful—both demons and shades had wicked supernatural powers—but a dragyri male was stronger...faster...superior. And that gave Ghost an advantage. It made him both a scourge and a celebrity in the underworld. Furthermore, he had a sacred amulet hanging around his thick, corded neck, and at least when earthside, he could use that amulet to open a portal, gain access to the Pantheon, a place

Drakkar and his minions couldn't travel. Ghost had knowledge about the Dragons Pantheon, the lairs, and the Temple of Seven, and if he could sell the fact that he hated his lineage—that he despised his dragon daddy, which wasn't that large of a stretch—he might be able to win Lord Drakkar's favor.

The enemy of my enemy is my friend...

Maybe Ghost could convince his uncle Drak that they weren't entirely on opposite sides of the cosmic spectrum, that Ghost might have more value as a spy or an informant than a punching bag or a flesh-and-blood play toy.

Slowly, but surely, the plan was working, although Ghost had almost lost track of all his lies. In truth, he might be coerced to screw with Lord Dragos, but he would never betray his diamond lair brothers; nor would he expose the Pantheon to a full-on demon attack. So basically, he was walking an extremely dangerous line: giving the pagans just enough information to be credible, but never enough to be lethal.

And now—this night—Lord Drakkar had summoned Ghost to the throne room to ask him something about the various regions in the Pantheon: the grasslands or rolling hills; the mountain regions and the Garden of Grace; the white sandy beaches with an ocean of fire; the dry desert in the east; and the tropical flatlands, also known as the plains. He had wanted to know the precise positions of all seven lairs so Killian Kross, his chief counselor, could add them to the topographical map the shadowwalker was creating.

And that's when Ghost had seen the girl.

The beautiful human woman, first carried into the dark throne room, then set on her feet and dragged before Lord Drakkar.

That's when Ghost had rolled his shoulders, popped his neck, and waited for the stupid, inane scene to unfold with cold indifference—Drak's human slaves, his personal or abhorrent proclivities, were none of Ghost's concern, and he was never going to get out of that damnable place if he let minor underworld politics distract him.

But that was also when Ghost had seen the quick *flash*...

Less than a second, really, maybe a heartbeat or two at the most.

That was when the stunning, half-drugged woman's darkbrown eyes had flashed as diamonds, their color shifting from umber to crystal-and-phantom blue. And that's when Ghost's diamond amulet had heated to a searing spark and burned an indentation in his chest.

He had quickly covered the gemstone with his hand, appraising Lord Drakkar and his nearby minions to see if anyone else had noticed—it didn't look like they had—and then he had stared the woman down like he had been alone on a desert island for a century, and this was his first, astounding contact with other sentient life.

Hell's fire and brimstone...

Literally.

The shit had just hit the fan!

Ghostaniaz Dragos was standing in the Pagan Underworld, of all places, the prisoner of an ancient, savage, demonic king, and he was staring at his *fated*...his dragyra...and the woman was Lord Drakkar's newest slave. As if that wasn't horrific and unthinkable enough, Ghost only had ten days to somehow get this lady out of the underworld and into the Temple of Seven.

COMING NEXT TO THE PANTHEON OF DRAGONS SERIES
GHOSTANIAZ – SON OF DRAGONS

JOIN THE AUTHOR'S MAILING LIST

A SNEAK PEEK FROM BLOOD DESTINY

(BOOK #1 – BLOOD CURSE SERIES)

Jocelyn lifted the canteen from the weighty, navy blue backpack and took a long drink of water. She checked her compass once again, glancing furtively at the sky to determine the position of the sun. She was making great time. There was plenty of daylight left, more than enough to reach the cave before sunset. Placing the canteen back in the pack, she adjusted the weight evenly on her shoulders, her mind continuing to analyze information as she headed deeper into the forest.

Jocelyn knew that she didn't have permission to move on the tip her informant had given her. She wasn't supposed to be there. And if anything went wrong, she was on her own. But she also knew that it couldn't wait. *Human trafficking. Ritualistic killings.* The entire case was so bizarre.

As an agent of ICE, a highly specialized department within Homeland Security, Jocelyn Levi had been investigating one particularly shocking human-trafficking ring for months. Unlike more typical rings that forced young women into sexual slavery or sold children into forced labor, these victims were being taken for much darker purposes—to be used as sacrifices in ritualistic killings.

But by whom?

Jocelyn shook her head, carelessly tucking a handful of thick brown hair behind her ear. Over the last two months, her unit had discovered three freshly discarded bodies, each one showing signs of the same hideous brutality. The sight of the mutilated corpses had been abominable, but they were close to finding the head of the ring, or at least finding the man who was selling the women. Still, they had no idea who was doing the actual killings: what kind of cult could be behind such gruesome acts of evil. They had never managed to uncover an actual crime scene.

Jocelyn sighed, hoping that today would be a major break-through. If the information her source had given her about the cave was correct, then she was about to make a huge discovery.

Her informant had assured her that she was not walking into a danger zone, that the site he had told her about was no longer being used by the ring. As always, they changed locations frequently, moving around to avoid detection by the authorities. Unfortunately, this meant that there would be no fresh forensic evidence, but the information Jocelyn hoped to uncover was of a different kind anyway.

Jocelyn slowed her pace as a series of tall, reddish rock forma-tions appeared in the distance, strangely shimmering into view like a desert mirage on a hot day. An eerie chill swept through her body, raising the hair on her arms, and a deep sense of foreboding settled into her stomach. She shivered and stared ahead. There was something about the peculiar canyons that shook her to her very core.

Although most people would have turned back, most people would not have been there in the first place.

Jocelyn was not most people.

Solving difficult crimes was her life. Stopping the *really,*

really bad guys. And she was very good at it. She had always had a sixth sense, an uncanny ability to stay one step ahead of the criminal mind. It wasn't like she was psychic or anything. She just had a way of *feeling* things. Walking into a crime scene and *knowing*. As if the very essence of the place whispered secrets to her of the people who had been there.

Now, after months of dead ends, she finally had a reliable lead; and she had no intention of letting the information go to waste.

Jocelyn drew in a deep breath of crisp mountain air, her lungs working overtime to adjust to the altitude of the Eastern Rocky Mountains. The beautiful, expansive territory ran along the Front Range of North America, full of hidden canyons, dense forests, and towering, majestic peaks; under different circumstances, it might have been an idyllic place to vacation. Her sense of dread grew stronger with every step she took, so powerful that it almost felt as if there were an invisible hand holding her back, something warning her away. She shook her head in an effort to clear her mind as she pushed forward against the invisible barrier.

She had come way too far to turn back now.

The faces of the victims, their broken and tortured bodies, continued to replay in her mind like a gruesome, private slideshow, reminding her of just how much was at stake.

Picking up the pace, Jocelyn headed deeper into the canyon.

ALSO BY TESSA DAWN

(NIGHTWALKER SERIES)

Daywalker ∼ The Beginning

(A New Adult Short Story)

JOIN THE AUTHOR'S MAILING LIST

If you would like to receive a direct email notification each time
Tessa releases a new book, please join the author's mailing
list at...

www.tessadawn.com

ABOUT THE AUTHOR

Tessa Dawn grew up in Colorado, where she developed a deep affinity for the Rocky Mountains. After graduating with a degree in psychology, she worked for several years in criminal justice and mental health before returning to get her master's degree in nonprofit management.

Tessa began writing as a child and composed her first full-length novel at the age of eleven. By the time she graduated high school, she had a banker's box full of short stories and novels. Since then, she has published works as diverse as poetry, greeting cards, workbooks for kids with autism, and academic curricula. Her Dark Fantasy/Gothic Romance novels represent her long-desired return to her creative-writing roots and her passionate flair for storytelling.

Tessa currently splits her time between the Colorado suburbs and mountains with her husband, two children, and "one very crazy cat." She hopes to one day move to the country, where she can own horses and what she considers "the most beautiful creature ever created"—a German shepherd.

Writing is her bliss.

CPSIA information can be obtained
at www.ICGtesting.com
Printed in the USA
BVHW030240291020
592113BV00014B/49

9 781937 223380